The Battlefield Abductions

R. B. Gibbons

Kwitch Books

THE BATTLEFIELD ABDUCTIONS
First Edition

ISBN-13: 978-0-9949572-0-7

CHAPTER ONE

Of the eighteen students who vanished, only two reappeared—one broken physically and one broken mentally. The adults had mundane explanations, of course, but by now, most of the students at Battlefield High believed something strange was happening every twenty-second day of May.

Erica was one of the first to become suspicious. For a year, she'd been turning the evidence over in her mind, and she was certain the explanations were part of a cover-up. But that didn't get her any closer to determining what was really going on or make it any easier for her to cope at school today.

On her way to chemistry, Erica turned the corner to see her friend Renee reach into her locker to grab a textbook from a mound of school supplies. The whole pile tipped, spilling over the floor. Renee groaned, her dark blonde head shaking in frustration. She squatted and began shoving everything back in while dodging the feet of the uninterested students in the hallway.

"Need some help, Ren?" Erica said. She knelt beside her sixteen-year-old friend and began stacking the textbooks.

Giving a wan smile, Renee glanced up from where she had been retrieving a tiny, pink teddy bear. "Thanks." She sighed, her narrow face drooping. "It's been like this all day. Distracted, I guess."

"Yeah," Erica said. "I've been thinking about it too."

The first time, the school said that the six students had gone on a foreign exchange. The next year, the excuses were a car accident and a pair eloping. Then last year, it was several families moving away and

1

a student being treated for a medical condition in Boise.

It was almost plausible. All the adults still claimed it was simply a series of coincidences. But there were too many unanswered questions. If students went on a foreign exchange, why didn't they tell anyone beforehand, and why didn't they return? Plus, where were the exchange students from the other country? Why would four kids who weren't even friends be driving around at night together? And why was it the same day each year? It didn't make sense.

Erica finished stacking the books and passed them to her friend. Tossing them on top of the precarious pile in the locker, Renee slammed the door shut before it could topple again. She turned the lock, spun around, and strode down the hallway.

Renee was tiny, barely approaching five feet tall, but walked quickly. And to Erica, it seemed as though the more stressed Renee became, the faster she moved. Despite the advantage of an extra eight inches in height, Erica had to scurry to catch up.

"You know, I think it might be different this year," Renee said. At Erica's dubious look, she added, "Everyone's ready this time."

"Hardly. The adults still don't give a damn."

"But they have to be watching. You can't just ignore something like Alex and Jen."

"Yeah." Erica shivered. "I don't know who got it worse."

"Alex. Definitely Alex," Renee murmured. She had seen the photos.

"Maybe." Erica shook her head. "In any case, if anyone really cared, the cops would be crawling all over here today. But nobody's doing anything. It's like they're deliberately ignoring us. We're lambs waiting for the slaughter."

Renee's face grew hard. "I'm no lamb. If anyone tries anything with me..." Covertly, she reached into her pocket. She pulled her hand out a few inches, revealing the brown handle of a folding hunting knife. After half a second, she slipped it back.

Erica's eyes widened, and she lowered her voice. "If a teacher sees that, you'll get suspended."

"The least of my worries."

"Do you even know what to do with that?"

"It's a knife. How hard could it be? Eyes. Neck. Gut." Renee's eyes narrowed. "I know one thing... if I need it, I won't hesitate."

Walking around with a huge knife seemed insane, but was

anything really insane today? At least Renee was doing something. Perhaps she should be doing the same.

Pushing her curly, brown hair back from her face, Erica took a deep breath. "I just hope you don't get caught."

"I won't." Renee stopped in front of her classroom door. She turned to Erica, the weapon seemingly forgotten. "Walk home with me after school?"

"Sure." Erica gave Renee a brief hug before heading across the hall to her chemistry class. "See you later."

The class was starting soon, but only about half the students were present. That wasn't unusual today. But to Erica, the only thing worse than coming to school and talking about the disappearances all day was staying home and thinking about them. At least here, there were distractions.

Erica slid into her customary chair beside Ian, Renee's seventeen-year-old brother. He looked unworried, his dark brown hair somehow artfully yet carelessly arranged. His plain black T-shirt and well-fitted blue jeans gave him a look of dressed-down formality. She couldn't help wondering whether he had a hidden weapon too.

"Hi, Ian," Erica said.

"Oh, hi. Ready for another exciting day with the Mad Podiatrist?" Ian said. The teacher had earned the nickname based on a combination of his fondness for destroying lab equipment and his near-religious devotion to Tevas with bulky, orthotic inserts. Erica had once seen him wade through eight inches of snow in those sandals.

"Yeah," Erica said, "though I'm thinking that for once, Mr. Ambrose blowing up test tubes in the name of science could be the least interesting thing that happens today."

"I don't know. He tries to make each demo more exciting than the last, and it's hard to beat lighting your lab coat on fire like he did yesterday. It's the fastest I've ever seen someone get undressed."

"Oh, and have you seen a lot of people get undressed?" Erica asked with mock severity and an arched eyebrow.

"Some," Ian said with a broad smile. "But not as many as I'm planning to."

A few years back, that square-jawed grin and those warm brown eyes would have set Erica's heart racing. She'd had a huge crush on him in seventh grade, but she'd gotten over it when she realized Ian just saw her as his younger sister's friend.

And frankly, Erica was relieved. Messing around with your best friend's brother was not cool. Luckily, Renee had recognized the crush for what it was—a product of Erica's active imagination, too many bad preteen novels, and her admittedly good-looking older brother. She didn't hold it against Erica.

A buzzer announced the beginning of class, and the chemistry teacher began to lecture. "Continuing with our exploration of the periodic table, today we will cover the alkaline earth metals…."

As Mr. Ambrose droned on, the dark thoughts running through Erica's head returned. The most puzzling thing about the disappearances was that the adults' reactions were so subdued. Some chain-smoking mother was accused of killing her baby and it was on the nightly news for months. You'd think that with three years of suspicious disappearances and deaths, someone would do something to stop it from happening again. Or at least investigate. If she could connect the dots, surely some of the adults could as well. But it was May 22 again and nothing had changed.

Erica's reverie was interrupted by the muted sounds of sobbing coming from somewhere behind her. She looked back. Katie, a girl Erica barely knew, had cradled her face in her arms on the desk. Her shoulders were shaking.

It took half a minute for Mr. Ambrose to notice. "Katie, is something wrong?"

Katie raised her tear-stained face. "No." The whole class was staring at her. "Well, you know."

"No, I don't," he said. "What's the matter?"

"It's just… What if something happens today?"

The teacher sighed. He lowered his notes and leaned forward, placing his hands flat on the table in front of him. "This paranoid speculation is ending now. The police have been notified. It's their job to take care of these things, not ours."

"But how do you—?"

"Katie, we will not get into a prolonged discussion about your irrational fears. That will just scare everyone and accomplish nothing. The police will do their job and we will do ours. We're not here to speculate. We're here to learn chemistry. So either stop being disruptive or leave."

He stared at Katie. She shifted uncomfortably, looking away.

Finally, still sniffling, she packed up her books and fled.

Erica swallowed. The teacher had given the standard line they'd been giving for months, as if he were reading from a script. It was all so inadequate. She glanced to her right. Ian was obviously taking the date in stride. She envied his calm demeanor. He looked as composed today as he had every other day this week.

"Now, back to chemistry." Mr. Ambrose pulled a Bunsen burner out from under his table with a flourish and lit it. "Time for the demonstration. Hopefully, it won't be as enlightening as the one yesterday." He chuckled as he donned some heavy gloves. With a pair of tongs, he snagged a silvery-white ribbon of metal from a container.

"Based on its electrons, what do you think will happen when I put this piece of magnesium into the flame?" he asked while polishing the ribbon with a piece of sandpaper. He looked around at the students sitting quietly in their seats. With the whole class studiously avoiding eye contact, Mr. Ambrose gestured to the left side. "Cam, how about you give it a shot?"

Erica had known Cam for years, but not because of his success in answering questions in class.

The scrawny boy with the greasy, black hair and poorly fitted clothes blinked a few times, swallowing. He stared at a chart on the wall, as if the answer might be written there, and then, without looking at the teacher, said, "Well, it's metal, so it should turn red hot." His Adam's apple bobbing, he took a quick glance at Mr. Ambrose and added, "Um… and melt." His hands were trembling.

Erica knew the answer was wrong, and she wasn't even paying attention. Ian's slight grin at her conveyed his opinion of Cam's response.

Vincent, a tall, muscular boy who had never been accused of having an excess of empathy, took the opportunity to offer some constructive feedback. "Cam, you really think after three weeks of lighting things on fire and blowing stuff up that he will be melting some metal? I don't know whether it will explode or burn, but whatever happens—it's going to be at least six times brighter than you."

The class laughed, perhaps harder than the joke deserved. Cam turned a deep shade of red and stared at his textbook on the table.

"That's quite true!" Mr. Ambrose excitedly began. Abruptly, however, he became more formal. "I mean, Vincent, please come see me after class." Vince grimaced.

Erica had little sympathy for Vince. Cam had been one of Vince's primary targets for as long as she could remember and not just verbally. In the second grade, Cam tried to go down a slide while Vince was coming up. That encounter resulted in a broken arm for Cam. Then, two days later, while attempting to prove to his friends that the plaster was harder than rock, Vince shattered the cast as well. Vincent seemed to deserve the punishments he received and then some.

The teacher continued, "But what I mean to say is you'll find that this reaction is amazingly bright. Erica, please turn off the lights."

She did and returned to her table. Still using the tongs, Mr. Ambrose poked the end of the magnesium ribbon into the flame. After about a second, it flared. A brilliant white light lit the room. The class gasped.

"Vince wasn't kidding," someone muttered from a few rows back.

"Although, it's more like sixty times, not six," pitched in someone else. Cam slumped deeper in his chair.

Mr. Ambrose chose not to hear the comments. "Now, magnesium fires are amazing. They're really hot—over five thousand degrees Fahrenheit. And water won't put them out. Magnesium reacts with water, producing hydrogen, which also burns."

The teacher produced a spray bottle to squirt the ribbon. Each time he did, it flared up even more. As the class made appreciative sounds, Erica glanced over at Ian.

He smiled at her. "Pretty cool," he whispered. Erica nodded.

The rest of the hour passed uneventfully. The whole class was distracted, and the Mad Podiatrist seemed to recognize the vacant looks in everyone's eyes. He was far less energetic than usual, and, perhaps discouraged by his failure with Cam, he didn't bother asking his usual questions.

Erica was glad when the buzzer finally sounded. As she gathered up her books, she turned to Ian and asked with a drop of irony, "So, got any plans tonight?"

Ian shrugged. "Not really. I was planning to go over to a friend's house, but my mom wants me to stay home."

Erica's eyes widened. That wasn't sarcasm from Ian. "Wow, you're serious, aren't you? You'd really go out tonight."

The two of them walked toward the door. "Yeah, well, as far as I can tell, it didn't make any difference where people were every other time. Why not just go on living life?" Ian said.

"You've got to be safer at home. It's obviously easier for someone to mess with you on the street than at home."

"Yeah, could be. I don't know," Ian replied in a flat tone.

Erica's words came gushing out, getting louder and louder. "How can you be so calm about it? Especially after Alex and Jen. That could be you tonight. Or me. Or one of your friends!"

"Yes, I guess so."

Erica missed the coolness in Ian's voice and the terseness of his answers. "Come on, Ian, even if you don't care about yourself, surely you have to be worried about your friends? How can you not care about them?"

Ian stopped walking, his body rigid. He put his hand on Erica's shoulder, pivoting her to face him. His eyes were stony. "You know about Morrison?"

Erica nodded, her eyes wide. Morrison had committed suicide about six months ago.

"Morrison was my best friend since before we were even in school. And now you're asking about what I'll do if something happens to a friend? Something already happened to a friend—my best friend. How much worse can it get? I'll survive whatever happens. Whether it's to me or another one of my friends, I'll survive." Ian didn't raise his voice at all, but anger underpinned his words.

Erica bit her lip, glancing toward the door. She scratched her left calf with the other foot before looking back at Ian.

Ian stared at her for a few seconds and strode out of the room.

#

Usually, the dinner table at Erica's house was a comfortable oasis. Even in the most hectic times, Erica's parents used the meal as an opportunity to have an open conversation about the news of the day.

Today was different. The topics her parents discussed seemed more inane than usual. Erica's mother, Lois, talked about how one of her patients, upon finding out that his cancer was in remission, had made Lois a tiered cake with one level for each stage of treatment. Erica's dad, Philip, talked about the legal ramifications of attempting to raise chickens in your backyard in an urban area.

Neither said a single word about the date or the disappearances.

Finally, Erica could take it no more. When there was a break in conversation, she edged in. "Do you guys have any thoughts at all about the topic of the day?"

"And what topic would that be, honey?" Lois innocently asked.

"The disappearances, of course. It's May 22. At school, everyone was so obsessed with it that nobody even talked about Mr. Ambrose's accident yesterday."

Erica's dad glanced at his wife, shifting in his chair. "Oh, yes, Mr. Ambrose. How is he doing? You said before that he seemed fine."

"Yeah, he's great. But aren't you guys worried about something strange happening?" Erica looked at her mom and dad in turn.

Lois shook her head, dabbing at the corner of her mouth with a napkin. "I've heard your theory, but I still think you're jumping to conclusions. It's a coincidence. And even if it's not, the police have been informed and have said that everything is under control. I trust them."

"I don't. This has been going on for three years. And in that whole time, the cops have done nothing but eat donuts," Erica said.

In a firm voice, Philip said, "I thought we taught you to respect the police. It's a hard job, and our local police force is among the best in the state."

Erica snorted. "Well, maybe they should show it then. They're either completely incompetent or they're involved in some way."

Her mother said, "I'm sure they're doing their best, honey. Why, just last year, I treated Officer Jameson for that stomach—"

"Yes, I remember," Erica interrupted. "But do you think something will happen tonight?"

"I think we're going to finish our dinner. And then you'll go to your room and do your homework. That's what I think will happen tonight," her dad said.

"Why don't you want to talk about it?" Erica demanded. As she stared at her mother, she tossed her fork down beside her plate in frustration. "Ignoring it won't make it go away."

Lois gave a slight smile. "It's just that we don't have anything to say about your wild conspiracy theories, darling. We never have."

Erica shook her head. Usually, her parents were able to listen, but sometimes, they seemed to have no clue about the things that mattered to her. It was like they were being deliberately stupid.

She shoved her chair away from the table. "I'm done. I'm going upstairs."

"Okay, dear. Maybe we can talk more after you've finished your homework," her mother said.

"Yeah," Erica said, but her tone said otherwise.

#

Erica was in the middle of an algebra problem when she heard the doorbell ring.

"Erica, someone's here to see you," her mother called up the stairs.

She wasn't expecting anyone. No one had texted. Was this how it started? Her pulse racing, Erica descended.

When she turned the corner at the bottom of the stairs to enter the living room, she knew instantly that the moment the whole school had been dreading was happening. Happening to *her*.

About six feet away from her mother stood four tall strangers, three men and a woman. They were dressed in identical, high-collared, black military uniforms, leaving almost no skin exposed except for their faces. Though she didn't see any weapons, each had on a headset and a black work belt with various pouches and tools. Their eyes narrowed as they saw Erica. They stepped toward her.

Erica instantly reacted. She spun around and raced back up the stairs.

Two soldiers pursued. Three-quarters of the way up, one grabbed her leg. Erica fell to her hands and knees, kicking her foot back with all her strength. She heard a grunt as her heel connected with something solid.

Erica tried to keep going, but the delay had cost her. The second soldier grabbed her leg, his arms encircling her waist. He restrained her for a few seconds until the other solider, his nose dripping blood, was able to help him.

"No!" Erica shouted, but her struggles were futile. Together, they carried her down the stairs to where the other soldiers waited. Erica's mom remained motionless in the corner.

"Mom?" Erica screamed. "Help me!"

But Lois looked on calmly, with the slightest of smiles, and she did nothing.

The female soldier grabbed Erica's shoulder, and, before she could react, plunged a syringe into her neck. The room went dark.

CHAPTER TWO

Erica struggled out of unconsciousness, trying but unable to focus her mind. The room seemed to spin around her in a white blur. She felt certain she was missing something important and shook her head, trying to pull her thoughts together enough to pin down what it was. Was she late for school? Was it someone's birthday?

Erica struggled to sit up, but her arms seemed belong to someone else. She lay there, fighting against the wooziness.

Finally, the foggy whiteness resolved itself into panels on a luminous ceiling. The air smelled stale and dry, like on an airplane. She could feel her hands again. Erica turned her head sideways on the pillow and saw another mattress on the floor beside her. Someone was lying there on top of the white sheets.

The scene in her house flooded back to her. She began to tremble. The soldiers. The sharp pain of the needle in her neck. And her mother?

Erica put her hand to her neck where the needle had entered. She didn't feel any blood.

She pushed away the sheet that covered her. Her shirt and jeans from last night had been replaced by a form-fitting blue T-shirt and black yoga pants. Her feet were bare. She shuddered when she thought about someone dressing her.

Erica eased herself into a sitting position, her gaze flitting from side to side, trying to take in everything at once.

The room was white concrete, about twice the size of a classroom. In the center of one wall was a dull metal door. It had no markings and no doorknob, but a keypad was beside it. A second exit was on the opposite side of the room—a doorway blocked off by a limp, white curtain.

The third wall held a glowing digital display that could have been torn from a clock radio. It gazed down on her like a malevolent red eye. The number seventy-five was easily readable, even from Erica's mattress forty feet away. The final wall was almost bare, with only the faint outline of a square.

The most noticeable feature to Erica was the five other beds—really no more than mattresses, sheets, and pillows—and the people sleeping on them. She recognized them all.

Both Renee and Ian lay beside each other on the farthest pair of beds. The middle row had two of the other students from her chemistry class, Cam and Vincent. A pretty, pale-skinned girl with long, straight black hair slept on the mattress beside Erica. She didn't know her, but she had seen her in the halls at school, always perfectly groomed.

Six of them. Just like all the other times. Almost involuntarily, Erica's eyes darted toward the door once more. She could feel her pulse pounding in her ears. Every instinct told her to run, to escape before something terrible happened.

But Renee and Ian were there.

Pushing down the rising panic, Erica stood up and tried to walk to Renee. That was a mistake. The room spun once more, and she dropped to the ground, bruising her knee on the concrete.

Erica glanced once more at the door.

No. One task at a time. The only thing she needed to do now was to get to her friend. Fearful of falling again, she put her head down and crawled to Renee's mattress.

Renee's eyes were closed, but her chest was rising and falling. Not dead, at least.

"Renee, wake up," she said, shaking Renee's shoulder slightly, but she didn't even stir. Erica jostled the girl in a much more vigorous way. "Renee, come on," she loudly said. "Wake up!"

Renee didn't react at all, but Ian moved his head, so Erica switched her attention to him. When she grabbed his arm roughly, he pulled away, mumbling. She persisted and, within a few minutes, Ian opened his eyes, staring right at her.

It took a few seconds before his eyes seemed to focus. "Erica?

What are you doing in my room? Did you sleep over last night?" he asked. He shook his head, blinked a few times, reddened slightly, and added, "I mean, with Renee?"

"Ian, just lie still for a minute. You've been drugged, and we're not in your room."

Ian sat up suddenly, and then he fell back on the bed.

Erica's lips twisted in a slight smile. "Or you could do the opposite of what I suggest. Whatever works for you." The mild, sarcastic rebuke was almost instinctive, a carry-over from their classroom conversations. The comment seemed take the edge off the panic, as if her body had decided that, if Erica was still joking with Ian, the situation couldn't be that dire.

"Oh man." Ian groaned. "I'm totally dizzy. What's going on?"

Erica looked at the door and then back to Ian. She swallowed. "We were abducted. Soldiers came to my house. I tried to run away, but they were too fast. They grabbed me. I struggled, but I couldn't do anything." Just thinking about it made her tremble. "They stabbed me with a needle, and I woke up here."

The soldiers. They'd restrained her. Drugged her. Changed her clothes. *Could they still be in the room?* Erica flinched, her gaze jumping to the curtain. They might be hiding there, waiting to leap out.

No, the curtain wasn't even moving. It must be her imagination.

"Soldiers?" Ian said, his brow furrowed. "I don't remember any soldiers."

Erica forced her eyes back to his face. "Really? What happened to you last night?"

"Nothing. I stayed home. Surfed the web, did some painting, some homework, and went to bed. And then woke up here." Ian tried once more to push himself up. With her help, he was able to rise into a sitting position. His clothes were similar to the ones she was wearing.

"Have you looked around yet?" Ian asked.

How could he be so calm? Still, his composure somehow helped her stabilize the quiver in her voice. "Nope. I wanted to check on you guys first."

Ian's eyes finally focused on the back of Renee's head. His face turned ashen. "Oh no. Not Renee." He reached over and began to shake his sister.

Erica said, "Yeah. Renee, Cam, Vincent, and some other girl from school."

Ian glanced in the direction of the sleeping girl. "Denise." He turned his attention back to his sister. "She won't wake up," he said, his voice quiet and rough.

"Don't worry. I'm sure she's fine," Erica gently said, "She's breathing. She's tiny, so maybe the drug is taking longer to wear off."

"But you're not that much bigger than she is."

"I was grabbed before you. About nine." Focusing on the facts instead of the horror of their situation seemed to help. Gradually, her pulse slowed.

"Oh." Color was returning to Ian's face. "How are the others?"

Erica tentatively walked around, examining each bed's occupant. "Everyone's breathing."

"I don't see what we can do to help them, so let's check out the door," he said.

He staggered to his feet. Erica, who by this time was feeling almost normal, grabbed Ian's arm to steady him. Together, they made it across the room with no mishaps.

Without a handle or hinges, it wasn't even clear to Erica how the door would open. She pushed on it, trying to slide it. It didn't budge. "Locked," she said.

"But of course," Ian replied. "Because you'd have to be a particularly stupid breed of criminal to abduct someone and then leave the door wide open for their escape."

Ian's familiar—if somewhat strained—banter was somehow reassuring to Erica. "I wouldn't give our captors too much credit." She gestured to her right. "They've installed the keypad to open the door on the wrong side of the wall."

Ian smiled. "Good point." He typed in a random series of buttons. After six digits, it beeped three times and flashed INVALID ACCESS CODE across its tiny LCD screen.

"I guess that one's wrong," he said. "Only about a billion combinations to go." He shrugged, turning away. "Let's look behind the curtain."

Erica's heart began to thud once more. There was nobody behind the curtain. She was sure of it. Nobody was waiting there to leap out and attack them when they pulled the cloth aside. It was all just her imagination. Wasn't it?

They walked to the other side of the room. Ian's steps were

steadier, but Erica maintained her grip on his arm anyway.

Ian paused in front of the curtain, took a deep breath, and looked at her. "Ready?"

Erica crouched down slightly, knees bent. She nodded.

He cautiously shifted the curtain to the side, revealing a starkly functional bathroom with a toilet, shower, and sink.

Erica exhaled, her fists relaxing. "I was wondering how I'd deal with such issues," she murmured.

Ian nodded. "The shower's a nice touch."

Erica stepped inside, pressed a button on the wall, and the shower turned on. A second touch turned it off. "I'm not so sure. On one hand, I'm a big fan of not stinking. On the other hand, it seems to imply that we'll be here long enough for hygiene to matter." She grimaced.

"An interesting point. Before today, I wouldn't have thought that something could be both considerate and menacing. I stand corrected."

Behind them, they heard the creak of a mattress spring. They looked out to see Vincent sitting up, shaking his head. They walked over to him.

"Hi, Vince. Welcome to your new home away from home," Ian said, the hint of an ironic smile on his lips. "It has everything you'd want in a home, except, you know, windows and an exit."

Vince was not in a joking mood. "What are you talking about, Ian?" he growled. He reached up to grab a fistful of his shirt. "Where am I?"

Ian easily slipped himself free. Vince was strong, but clearly still somewhat under the influence of the drug. "Calm down, man. I don't know any more than you about where we are." He adjusted his shirt, ignoring Vince's angry stare.

The discussion roused Cam from his sleep. He glanced around the stark white room and at the two teenage boys. "Oh man. Why am I dreaming of Vince?" he mournfully groaned.

Ian's grin was sardonic. "Don't worry. You're not dreaming."

"Someone had better tell me what's going on, or you're going to seriously regret it," Vince blustered, glaring first at Ian, then at Cam, and then back to Ian. He didn't even glance at Erica.

Cam cringed, and Ian's demeanor became more serious as he explained the situation. Cam folded in on himself, starting to shake.

Vince scowled at him. "Stop wimping out, Cam. There's no time for that. Ever." Cam nodded, but he still continued to twitch. Vince rolled his eyes. "What's that seventy-five over there? And that square on the wall?"

Erica said, "We haven't checked those out yet."

"Well, let's do it." Vince stood up quickly and nearly fell. Erica put her hand on his shoulder to steady him, but he looked at her flatly, shaking it off. He strode to toward the wall with the digital display, stumbled to the right, and tumbled to the ground. He glared up at Ian.

"Not judging, not judging," Ian said innocently, offering a hand to help him rise. Vincent ignored it. He stood up and managed to make his way to the wall though he was staggering like a drunk.

The glowing red display was set flush with the wall and covered by something that looked like glass. It didn't have any buttons, nor did they see any other way to interact with it. Ian rapped on the screen with his knuckles. The glass seemed solid.

Out of ideas, they moved to the opposite side of the room to investigate the square on the wall. It turned out to be the edges of a panel.

For about minute, Vince and Ian used various strategies to try to pry it open with their too-short fingernails. Finally, Erica gave the panel a firm push, and it sprang open. Erica sighed as the door revealed nothing but an empty cupboard about a foot and a half deep. "Well, I guess we could store stuff there," she dubiously said.

Vincent snorted. He went to investigate the door, while Erica, Ian, and Cam returned to the mattresses. In the span of five minutes, Vincent progressed from calmly typing random numbers on the number pad, to pushing vigorously on the door, to pounding on it with his fist, and finally to hitting it with his shoulder using a running start. Nothing he did seemed to have any effect. Eventually, he gave up and went to explore the bathroom.

By this time, the remaining two girls were stirring. Renee woke up first. Instantly, Ian was at her side.

"Hey, Ian, what's up? This isn't my room," Renee asked, frowning and squinting as she looked around.

"Bad news, Ren. It looks like it was our turn this year," Ian said. Renee's brown eyes grew wide as Ian told her what they had learned. Her initial confusion transformed quickly to horror. Tears began to flow.

"This can't be. Why is this happening to me? To us?" Renee asked, turning toward Erica and searching her face as if her friend had some answer that had eluded everyone else.

Erica put an arm around Renee's shoulders. "We don't know. But at least we're all together. We can take care of each other."

At that point, Vincent, having heard the weeping, returned from the bathroom. He looked at her, contempt plastered across his features, and gruffly said, "Don't you know the expression, 'crying just makes everything worse'? It doesn't make the problem go away, but your weakness makes it even harder to solve."

Renee hid her face in her hands, her shoulders shaking.

Erica's mouth thinned. "I'm not sure that's a useful comment right now."

Vince looked at her for a second and nodded. "I guess the rule doesn't really apply to girls."

Sighing, Erica turned back to Renee. She wrapped both arms around her friend.

Ian said, "Don't worry about it, Ren. We're in a lousy situation, but we'll get through it."

At that point, Denise woke up. Her eyes darted around, surveying the room. She looked perplexed, but calm, as if she had just bumped into the others in the mall on a Saturday afternoon.

"Renee, Vincent, Cam, Ian." Denise looked at each of them in turn. "And you're Erica, right?" After Erica nodded, Denise continued, "So, what's up?"

Denise listened patiently, her brown eyes focused on Ian as he explained what they had discovered so far. She asked the occasional question, but her oval face didn't convey a hint of fear. Denise's poise seemed to help Renee regain her composure.

When Denise and Renee were more confident on their feet, they did a more thorough examination of their prison, searching individually and in small groups for any means of escape. Renee was the most energetic, running from the door to the bathroom and back again. In contrast, Denise was limping.

"Did they hurt you?" Erica asked in a low voice as she and Denise examined the sink in the bathroom. At Denise's confused expression, Erica added, "Your leg."

Denise shook her head. "No, it's an old injury. Back when I was ten, I tore my ACL playing soccer. My mom thought it was a bruise, so it took about a month before I went to the doctor. By then, it had partially healed in some weird way, and it was too late to fix completely."

Perhaps in response to Erica's appalled expression, she continued, "It's not a big deal. I can still run, just not as fast as before." She shrugged, stared at the sink for a few seconds, and then shook her head. "This is a waste of time. There's nothing in here." She flung aside the curtain, leaving the room with Erica in her wake.

In the main room, Ian had lifted Renee up on his shoulders so she could examine the ceiling panels. Up close, the panels weren't as translucent as they appeared. Each had thousands of tiny, transparent circles that were letting the light through from above and a spattering of bigger holes, some of which seemed to go right through the panel and some that just looked like dark dots.

But however much the panels looked like glass, they were unbreakable and immovable no matter what Renee did. Vince, doubting Renee's strength, had Cam and Ian hoist him up to give it a try, but he succeeded only in tweaking his wrist. The glass covering the digital display on the wall seemed equally impervious.

Finally, Erica had had enough. She put her back to the wall, exhaled, and slowly slid down until she was sitting on the floor. Her face wan, she said, "I think we're stuck. There's no way out."

Ian frowned, rubbing his forehead. "Looks that way." To Erica, he seemed more somber now than when he had first woken up, as if it had taken the fruitless search for him to realize just how bad their situation was.

Renee shook her head. Her cheeks were flushed and her eyes fierce. "You're giving up too soon. There's so much stuff in the bathroom. We must be missing something there." She darted off behind the curtain, but nobody else followed her.

Cam had been looking at his feet. Hesitatingly, he raised his hand.

Erica looked at him in confusion for a second before asking, "Yes, Cam? Do you have something to say?"

"Um, yeah. Can we try pushing the numbers on that panel? The right code might open the door."

Erica did some quick math in her head, her face set in a dejected frown. "I think there's something like one hundred thousand seconds in a day. Six numbers makes a million combinations. That means if you did one a second, it would take about ten days to try them all. If you could even remember what you had already tried."

Cam grinned, clearly happy that Erica seemed to agree with him. He went over to the keypad and earnestly started pressing numbers.

Erica continued, "You're going to be much slower than one a second. You'll also need to sleep. It could be two months if you don't get lucky. And the right combination might not even open the door." She looked from Cam to the others with a perplexed "why is he even bothering?" expression.

"Just leave him," Vince said smugly, as if he knew Cam better than the rest of them ever would. "It'll give him something to do." Erica shrugged.

Ian turned his back on Cam, and sat near Erica, scratching his chin with his thumb. "We're stuck, but our captors will have to come in here eventually, if only to give us food. What should we do then?"

Vincent smiled in anticipation as he sat opposite Ian. "Take them down, obviously. With three of us, we should be able to do some serious damage to the first person who comes through that door."

Erica frowned. "I saw at least four soldiers. And they may have had guns."

"I'm not afraid of guns," Vincent scoffed, his eyes scornful.

"I am," Ian said. "I don't want to get shot."

"Besides," Erica added, "so what if we beat up one guy? There might be ten others behind him."

Vince sneered at her. "At least we'll go down fighting. It's better than just sitting there."

"Sure. He gets a bruise that fades away in a few days. We get dead, which is slightly more permanent," Erica said, oozing sarcasm. She looked at Denise. "What do you think?"

Denise shook her head, her brow furrowed. "If they wanted us dead, wouldn't they have killed us already?"

"I guess," Erica said. "So you think we should fight?"

"I don't know. Both of you are making great points. Maybe we should talk to them and see if we can figure out what they want, but fight if it seems necessary."

Ian nodded. "How about we talk, but if it looks bad, someone signals and we all attack at once?"

"Yeah, that might work," Vincent grudgingly said. "If I cough, everyone counts to three, and then attacks."

"I don't think you should make the decision," Erica said firmly, looking Vince in the eye despite his threatening glare. "Denise is right. There's a chance talking might work, and you seem way too hung up on fighting." She hated confronting him, but it needed to be said. She gripped her pants tightly so Vince wouldn't see her hands tremble.

"And you five girls…" Vincent sneered, making it clear that he was including Ian and Cam in his count, "seem hung up on having a nice afternoon tea with the maniacs who kidnapped us. I'm willing to do what it takes to escape."

"Enough with the playground insults!" Ian exclaimed, his face reddening.

"Calm down," Denise said. She shot a hard look at Ian before putting her hand lightly on Vince's forearm. "Let's fight with the kidnappers, not each other. And Vince is the best person to do it."

"Why's that?" Erica asked, her eyes narrowed in suspicion.

"Look at these arms. Vince is super strong. And he's been in the most fights, too. With that experience, he's the one most likely to identify the best opportunity to take out our captors. And if talking fails, we'll need every advantage he can give us." Denise's voice was guileless and bright, as if she were discussing what outfit to wear to a party rather than a decision that could lead to their deaths.

Erica didn't really buy her logic, but Vincent looked obstinate. With Denise on his side, it seemed unlikely that he'd agree to anything else. She exchanged dark glances with Ian and then dismissively waved her hands. "Fine. We'll do it your way. Hopefully, we won't need to—"

A muffled thud, like a heavy door closing, interrupted Erica.

Ian's eyes narrowed, the muscles around his jaw tightening. He looked toward the door. "They're coming."

CHAPTER THREE

Cam backed away from the exit as Vincent and Denise advanced to stand on either side of him. After glancing at Vince with a bemused expression, he turned back to the door.

Ian and Erica cautiously inched forward to stand behind them. Renee soon joined them from the bathroom. Though the room was warm, Erica was shivering. They were all silent as they waited.

After a minute, Cam raised his hand.

"What is it, Cam?" Erica whispered in exasperation.

"I don't think that noise came from outside the door."

"What?" Ian said.

"That noise. I was facing the door, and it came from somewhere behind me."

"It wasn't the bathroom," Renee said.

Erica thought for a second and then walked over to the panel on the wall. She opened it, glanced inside, and looked back at Ian. "Well, so much for your theory that our captors will come down to give us food." She pulled out a tray. On it was a jug of milk, two plastic spoons, and two paper bowls filled with cereal.

Everyone gathered around Erica. Cam examined the inside of the cabinet more closely, discovering a thin crack around the top of it. Rapping his knuckles on it, he raised his hand.

"Cam, you don't need to put up your hand whenever you want to speak," Erica said, her tone harsher than she intended.

Cam blushed and mumbled, "Yeah." He pivoted one foot back and forth. "The top of this isn't solid. I think it's a food elevator."

"Like a dumbwaiter?" Renee asked.

Cam glanced at Renee with a slight frown and looked back at the floor. "No, there wasn't a waiter or a waitress. The food came on a little elevator."

"Oh, are those food elevators called dumbwaiters?" Denise asked, although Erica was sure Denise knew the answer already. "That's kind of a strange name. Way to figure it out, Cam." He smiled and quickly looked away.

Erica stared at the cereal, her mouth set in a grimace. "That doesn't seem like that much food for six of us."

"Maybe they could only fit one tray, and if we wait, they'll send another," Denise said.

Vince's lips twisted into a smirk. "Or just have Cam wait. Then it will be a dumb waiter waiting for a dumbwaiter."

Erica glared at him. "Really, Vince? You think that being a jerk to Cam is the right thing to do, right now when we're all locked in here together? I know you've been doing it for years, but come on."

Vince turned to face Erica, inched forward, rolled back his shoulders, and stared flatly at her with a touch of contempt in his expression.

Erica began to look away, but then she jerked her chin back. She pointedly stared at him.

Cam shifted on his feet, looking at the floor. He was shaking.

After a few seconds, Denise cheerfully said, "I'm sure Vince didn't mean it that way. He was just trying to lighten the mood." She slapped Vince on the back.

Vince nodded. "Yeah. Just a joke. You'll have more fun if you don't take everything so seriously, Erica."

Nobody challenged the explanation. They waited in uncomfortable silence for a few minutes. Finally, Ian sighed. "I guess that's all we're getting. Should we eat it? It could be poisoned."

"We may as well," Erica said. "If they wanted us dead, there are simpler ways to do it than abducting us and poisoning the food."

"Maybe it's laced with something else. Not a deadly poison, but something to give us hallucinations, or make us sick, or some drug," Ian said.

"Someone could eat some. Then, we can wait and see if there are any side effects," Renee suggested.

"That's a great idea. Does anyone want to volunteer?" Denise asked, looking from face to face.

Nobody did, so they selected someone randomly by playing rock-paper-scissors. Vincent lost.

Everyone stared at his face as he ate. After the first spoonful, he seemed normal, but on the second, his cheek twitched. He handed the bowl cautiously to Ian and then dropped the spoon. His eyes bulged. Clutching at his throat, he fell to the floor.

"Heimlich! Does anyone know the Heimlich?" Denise shrieked. She knelt beside Vincent, trying to cushion his twitching body.

"That's for choking, not poison," Erica said. She dropped to the floor and then stopped with her arms outstretched, unsure of how to help.

"We have to do something!" Denise shouted.

But it was already too late. Vince went still, his eyes closed.

Nobody moved or said anything for a few seconds, stunned by the suddenness of the death. Erica buried her face in Ian's chest. Denise bowed her head. Her lip trembled and her eyes filled with tears. Cam just gazed expressionlessly at the body.

"Hey. Wait a minute," Renee said, peering at Vince, her brow furrowed. "His chest is moving. He's still breathing."

Vince opened his eyes, smirking. "Ha, got you guys!"

"What?" Ian shouted, a smile curving his lips.

Denise slapped Vincent on the chest as he sat up. "I can't believe you did that to us! That's so mean!" Her voice sounded upset, but she was grinning.

"Well, everyone was staring at me like I was a lab rat. I had to do something." Vince shrugged. "The cereal's fine. It tastes normal."

"That might not mean anything. Maybe the drug doesn't affect the flavor," Erica said.

Denise smiled at Erica. "Smart thinking." She turned to Vince "Let's wait to see if you have any reaction."

Vincent nodded and began gulping down the rest of the bowl.

"Hey, wait," Renee exclaimed after a second, bending down toward Vince and reaching out a hand. "We don't have much. Don't eat it all."

Vince didn't look up. "I won't." He continued shoveling the food into his mouth.

Renee looked at the others, concern etched on her face. "Stop!" She grabbed the bowl with both hands, but Vince didn't release it. As she tried to pull it away, milk sloshed over the side.

"Stop, Vince!" Ian said. He bent down beside Renee, arms outstretched to grab the bowl, but paused, clearly unsure of how to take the bowl without spilling it everywhere.

But Vince stopped on his own. Other than the milk, the bowl was empty. "It's all gone!" Ian stared accusingly at him. "You said you wouldn't eat it all."

"I didn't. There's the other bowl," Vince said belligerently. "I had to make sure I ate enough to get a big enough dose of any drugs."

Ian's stared at him in astonishment, but before he could reply, Denise put her hand on his shoulder, gently pulling him back.

"I agree with Vince," she said. "It's the only way to be certain."

"What?" Ian said. He shook his head, looking from Denise to Vince and finally back to the bowl. Sighing in frustration, he turned to Vince. "Fine. But you don't get any of the rest." He flopped down beside him. "While we wait for Vince to die again," Ian's tone implied that he was no longer sure that would be such a bad thing, "let's talk about what we know about these abductions. There might be a clue from them that will help us figure out how to get out of here."

Denise nodded, and then she and the others sat down. "As far as I know, there were only two people who turned up again after they disappeared—Alex and Jen. When they vanished, everyone just said they moved away. Alex's remains turned up a week and a half later, but the police claimed that he had returned to get some stuff, went for a midnight stroll, and got killed by a cougar."

"You saw the pictures of Alex, didn't you, Ren?" Erica said.

Renee grimaced as she looked down. "Yes," she said. "The guy who found him took photos and texted them to me. I think he was trying to impress me or something." She shook her head. "All I remember was blood. Blood everywhere."

"Did it look like a cougar attack?" Vincent asked.

"I don't know. I have no idea what a cougar attack looks like. And I barely glanced at the pictures. As soon as I recognized Alex, I puked. My mom came over to help. When she realized what I was looking at, she deleted all the photos. And I'm glad. I still have nightmares about it." Renee's face was pale, and her eyes were squeezed shut.

Erica put her arm around her friend. "It doesn't matter. If you didn't notice anything, that's fine." She had to move the conversation along. "Did anyone know Jen? Before, I mean."

Everyone shook their heads.

Denise said in a low voice, "I remember hearing that three weeks after she 'moved away', she was found walking down the street at two in the morning. Physically, she was fine, but her head was messed up. She couldn't even speak." Though Denise's voice was steady, her face was pale.

Cam half raised his hand, jerked it back down to his side, blushed, and said, "I heard she can't feed herself, and they put her in an old folks' home."

Although she already knew the story, Erica cringed. "That's horrible. Imagine being eighteen. You're supposed to be having the best time of your life. But instead, you're locked up with a bunch of old people, unable to say or do anything about it."

Ian nodded in a somber way. "It would be terrible. The only bright side, if you'd call it that, is it sounds like she doesn't even know where she is."

"I wonder why her parents aren't taking care of her?" Denise said.

"They probably can't handle it. Seeing the empty shell of their daughter, every day…." Renee said, swallowing.

They were silent for a few seconds. They had made little progress toward escaping, but had made a lot of progress toward frightening themselves.

"You know, I think our parents may be involved in this," Erica haltingly said. She had been stewing over it since she woke up, but she wasn't sure how the others would react to her fears.

Renee stood up. "No. Absolutely not. There's no way." She began to pace behind the others.

"I think they must be. First, there are Jen's parents. Maybe they couldn't handle taking care of her. But from what I heard, they never even tried." Both Cam and Denise nodded.

"And, in some cases, not only the kids disappeared, but a few families too," Erica continued, her voice growing louder as she watched Renee stride back and forth. "Nobody believes that they moved away. Was the whole family abducted? If that's the case, why isn't anyone from our families here?"

"Maybe our parents are somewhere else," Cam said.

"Yes. A different room. It's strange that *we're* together, not that they're not here with us." Renee said pointedly.

"I suppose," Erica conceded. "But there's also the way I was grabbed. At dinner, my parents didn't want to talk about anything. Like they were hiding something. And when the soldiers attacked me, my mom just stood in the corner. She didn't fight them or even look surprised. If anything, she seemed… I don't know. Content."

Renee shook her head. "I have a different theory. Yesterday, you were worrying all day about being abducted. So when you fell asleep, you dreamed about the soldiers. But you were actually grabbed in your sleep just like us. It makes sense. Why would they do something different with you?"

Erica rolled her eyes. "I have no idea. I do know the conversation during dinner was strange though. Did anyone else have that?" She scanned each of their faces.

"No, our parents were perfectly normal," Renee quickly said, looking toward her brother. Ian nodded.

"My dad was snoring on the couch when I got home. I didn't wake him," Vince said, shrugging. "That's not unusual."

Denise shook her head. "My mom had an evening shift."

All eyes turned to Cam. He swallowed deeply, clasping his knees against his chest. "I don't remember anything."

Renee stopped pacing and looked pointedly at Erica. "You're looking for an explanation where there isn't one. I'm not at all convinced."

Erica was getting angry, whether at Renee for doubting her or her parents for betraying her, she didn't know. She swung to face her friend. "No, I'm not," she emphatically said. "My parents were acting weird last night."

Renee opened her arms wide. "It was May 22. Everyone—"

"Okay, stop!" Denise said, holding up her hands. She looked up at Renee and then over to Erica. "I didn't see anything that made me think my mom was involved. But Erica has good reasons to believe her parents were. Let's agree that we don't know enough to figure it out. It's not like we can do anything about it, either way. Besides, I'm hungry." She glanced toward Vincent with a smile. "How do you feel?"

Erica was mad, but still cool enough to recognize the sense in Denise's words. She took a deep breath, tore her gaze away from Renee, and looked at Vince.

"I feel amazingly spry for a guy who just died. But still hungry."

Ian gave him a dirty look. "Yeah." He turned to the others. "Shall we eat?"

Everyone nodded. The remaining five gathered around the second bowl, passing the second spoon around the circle. They carefully measured every bite, making sure that nobody got more than their fair share. Even so, it didn't take long to finish.

Afterward, Ian went to the door and fiddled with the keypad. Because she didn't feel like talking to Renee and had nothing better to do, Erica joined him.

Ian poked at the lock listlessly, a pensive expression on his face.

"What is it?" Erica murmured.

"I was just thinking," he said. "This could get uncomfortable. There wasn't even close to enough food to feed us all."

"Maybe there will be more next time," Erica said in a low voice.

"Do you think so?"

She shook her head. "No."

#

Ian, Erica, Denise, and Vince showered and then sat on the mattresses to talk. Erica, having never met Denise, was impressed by how well she was handling the situation, almost cheerfully. She complimented Erica's hair, saying it looked great even without being combed, and pointed out the way Vince's shirt accentuated his muscular shoulders.

Meanwhile, Cam and Renee continued to try to escape. Cam returned to the keypad and began typing in random numbers. Denise went over to him to suggest that he try the numbers in order to avoid repeating combinations. But, after looking at the six digits dubiously, Cam replied that he didn't think he could count high enough. She didn't try to dissuade him, and he seemed content to press buttons for hours, confident that if this combination weren't right, then surely, the next one would be.

Renee, on the other hand, darted from idea to idea. She tried to lever the door open with the edge of the plastic tray from breakfast. Flipped over the mattresses to see if anything was beneath. Ran the paper plates down the crack in the door to trip the lock. Pounded the digital display with her palm.

She examined the dumbwaiter for over an hour. She was the youngest and petite for her age. The food must have entered the cabinet through the door at the top. If they could open it, perhaps she would be able to inch her way up the shaft to an exit.

But the dumbwaiter seemed to have been designed to make this kind of escape attempt impossible. Either someone needed to open the door from outside or it would open automatically whenever the cabinet door closed.

When Renee reported her two theories about how the door might work to the others, Vince suggested they shove her in the tiny cabinet and squeeze it shut. If an inner door opened, she'd be able to climb out. Renee had suffered similar indignities with lockers and quietly refused. After a few minutes of sizing her up, Vince gave up trying to convince her. Erica was certain that even Renee couldn't fit into such a small space and suspected Vince had concluded that too.

Eventually, Renee exhausted all the obvious escape possibilities and began pacing back and forth across the room like a caged lion, muttering to herself.

Erica sympathized. They'd only been awake for a few hours and, though the room was large, she felt slightly claustrophobic. The air seemed stagnant, as if it had already circulated through their lungs twenty times. It made her jittery.

She glanced over at the remains of breakfast. Her mind kept returning to the food. Or rather, the lack of food. If they didn't get larger portions, they were in serious trouble. It wasn't enough to sustain them all. Other than Vince "testing" the entire bowl, they'd divided up the cereal evenly, but how long would that cooperation last, once they became ravenous? And how cooperative would Vince be anyway? He was clearly willing to try to grab more than his fair share when the opportunity presented itself. Perhaps she, Renee, and Ian would need to band together to make sure they got enough.

A thud heralding the arrival of their lunch interrupted her thoughts. This time, the tray held two hamburgers and fries covered with aluminum foil. Erica wasn't a fan of fast food, but today, the greasy smell seemed impossibly tempting. Unfortunately, as she expected, there wasn't enough to feed two people, let alone six. Nevertheless, led by Ian, they meticulously divided up the meal into equal portions and drank water from the sink in the bathroom to wash it down. It barely took the edge off her appetite.

As Denise began tidying up by tossing the plates and foil toward the area they had christened "garbage corner," Erica saw a flash of blue on one of the plates. Her eyes narrowed. "Wait a second, Denise. Pass me that plate."

Frowning slightly, Denise did. "Why? What's wrong?"

Erica flipped the plate over to reveal some cursive writing. She held it up for the others. "Look."

The handwriting was almost indecipherable, as if the writer had more pressing concerns than the legibility of the message. Everyone gathered around where Erica sat on a mattress, trying to work out what it said.

Ian figured it out first.

Watch out. One of you is not as they appear.

CHAPTER FOUR

"What does that mean?" Denise asked with a frown.

"It seems obvious to me," Vincent said, his tone ringing out with an obvious 'duh' sound. "One of us is a plant. A spy. What else could it mean?"

Everyone looked at each other, trying to determine if anyone looked guilty or was acting strange.

After a few seconds, Denise broke the silence, her voice light. "Come on, this is silly. First, if they added a spy into our group, why would they tell us? And second, there's nobody here we don't already know. We were all in the same school, right? And third, why would they bother using a spy? Just use cameras."

Erica's eyes narrowed. "Why are you trying to persuade us there's no spy? That itself is suspicious. And it's not like I knew you well before."

"No, but Renee did. We were in the same classes every year." Denise looked around. "In fact, all of us were born in Battlefield and have been in the same schools for our whole lives. You can't fake that."

"No, unless you're an identical twin," Vince said.

"Oh wow, that's totally it." Cam said, sounding as if he actually believed it. "That happens all the time on TV."

"Yes. But that's TV," Denise said in a kind tone.

Vince and Cam both looked unconvinced. Denise shrugged and looked at Renee. "Ask me a question about anything we both know. I'll give you the right answer."

Renee nodded. "What caused Jason Eller to run out of the classroom in second grade?"

"He was so nervous about giving the book report presentation in front of everyone that he peed his pants."

"What's was the last thing you bought with your money from waitressing?"

"I bought a novel when I started a year ago. My mom said it was a waste, so she tore it up. Now the money I make goes toward household expenses."

Renee nodded. "Yeah, you're Denise."

Ian sighed. "May as well do everyone." He turned to his sister. "What's the deal with that one ugly horse?"

Renee giggled. "We were in Canada on summer vacation, and we drove by this field with all these brown horses. And I said, 'That's one ugly horse.' But it wasn't a horse. It was a moose. So you pointed at the horses and said, 'No, those are ten beautiful moose.'"

Erica decided to jump in. "What meal did you eat at my house that caused you to throw up?"

Renee grimaced. "Some sort of noodles with bean sprouts on them. I hate sprouts, but thought I should be polite and eat them since I was at your place. Turns out that I'm allergic to them." Erica and Ian nodded.

One by one, everyone answered questions about their lives. Interrogating Cam and Vincent took longer, since the others didn't know them quite as well, but eventually, they were satisfied they were all who they appeared to be.

"So if there is a spy, then it's someone we've known for years, who has decided to work with our kidnappers," Ian said, his eyes narrow as he looked from face to face.

"Why would one of us do that?" Renee asked, sounding confused.

"Could be anything. Money. Blackmail. Threats against them, their friends, or their families," Ian said.

Erica nodded. "But why tell us, and why not use cameras instead?"

"Maybe there are secret spy cameras," Cam mumbled.

They peered around the room as if they had somehow missed cameras on the walls.

A few seconds later, Vince looked up. "I bet they're in the ceiling. They make really small cameras these days, probably small enough to fit in those darker holes."

"Of course! That's got to be it," Denise exclaimed. She looked at Vince with admiration. "That's so smart, Vince. I never would have thought of that."

They spent a half hour examining the panels covering the lights, first from the ground, then from each other's shoulders. Some of the panels' circles were darker than others, but there was no way to be sure they were cameras.

Denise suggested covering each of the darkened circles with fragments of the paper plates, glued with saliva. It seemed to work for a few minutes, but eventually, the paper would fall to the floor. It seemed impossible to cover them all, so they gave up and returned to the mattresses.

"Even if we can't be sure, I think those must be cameras," Vincent said.

"I agree," Ian replied. "But in that case, why have a spy? And why tell us?" He rubbed his forehead as he looked at Vince.

"The note is pretty messy. Maybe the writer was in a rush. Maybe one of our abductors is trying to help us, but doesn't want the others to know," Erica said.

"Wouldn't the other kidnappers figure it out when they saw us reading it?" Denise asked.

"Maybe there aren't any cameras," Renee said.

"No," Ian said firmly, a touch of frustration entering his tone. "We're going in circles. They must have some way of watching what we're doing."

"But then why the message?" Denise asked again, her brow furrowed.

Everyone thought about it for a few seconds.

"It doesn't make any sense," Erica murmured. "There must be some other reason for the note." Suddenly, her eyes widened. "We're rats."

Cam looked confused at the sharp left turn the conversation had taken. "Um, what?"

Ian blinked and his jaw dropped. "Like test subjects," he replied. "They're running some sort of experiment on us."

"A psychological test. That's brilliant, Erica," Denise said. "They gave us the message to see how we'll react."

"Yeah, like seeing what we'll do locked in a room without enough food?" Renee said. She had leaped to her feet to start pacing. "Can they make us turn on each other using a simple message on a paper plate?"

Erica's mind was racing, trying to put all the pieces together at the same time. "Does that explain Alex and Jen?"

"Maybe someone thought Alex was the spy and beat him up. And Jen was driven insane by the experiments?" Denise tentatively said.

Renee shook her head. "Alex was cut up, not beat up. And I doubt you could have a complete mental breakdown just from people playing mind games."

"Maybe the message and the food is just the start," Vince said. His face was grim.

It was not a reassuring idea. Everyone went quiet.

Ian snapped out of it first. "Regardless, this is our best theory so far to explain what's going on. It's unlikely that someone we've known for years is a spy, so let's not get too paranoid. But we should watch each other's backs."

"I agree. If it is an experiment, then the message is probably intended to make us fight. Let's do the opposite. Let's stick together," Denise said, reaching out to grab Vince and Erica's hands.

Everyone seemed to buy into the idea except Vince. The most they got out of him was a muttered, "I'll think about it".

They spent the next few hours talking about the psychological experiment hypothesis, but they didn't come up with any more evidence either way. The theory at least gave Erica the beginning of an explanation for why her parents may have allowed her to be abducted.

Throughout her entire childhood, Erica's parents had taught her to draw conclusions based on evidence. Her mom treated science with almost religious reverence, considering it the highest form of reasoning. If it was for the expansion of scientific knowledge, and if her parents believed that she wouldn't be hurt, and if they couldn't tell her about it because it would ruin the experiment, then maybe, just maybe, that was why they allowed her to be locked up in here.

But that was a lot of "ifs". And even if that explained their reasoning, they still had no right to put her through this horrific experience without her consent. The "anything for science" explanation made her more angry, not less.

Eventually, they heard the now-familiar thud that signaled the arrival of dinner. After only eating what amounted to two small snacks over the course of the day, they were ravenous.

Vince was the first to the panel. He swung it open, releasing a scent that reminded Erica of watching movies at home on a Friday night. Her mouth watered.

"Pizza," Vince said. He closed the panel again and stood in front of it, blocking the others, who were just approaching from the mattresses.

"What's up?" Denise asked with a confused look.

"We're going to divide the food up differently this time. At some point, we will have to fight our way out of here. If I'm weak, there's no way we'll win," Vince said, his left hand casually massaging the back of his right fist.

"What are you saying, Vince?" Ian quietly asked.

"Isn't it obvious? I'll take half the food, and the rest of you can split the rest. That way, I'll remain strong enough to get us out of here when we get the chance. It's a sacrifice, but necessary to ensure the team stays strong."

"You know I'm not going to let you do that," Ian said with deceptive calmness, his eyes narrow.

Vincent solemnly looked at Ian. "I was going to suggest you and me split the food so we're both strong, but you don't want to leave the others to starve, do you? I think that would be wrong."

"Please, Vince," Denise said, gently touching his right arm. "We all need to work together, right?"

Erica agreed. "It's important that we all have our fair share."

Ian nodded. "We're splitting the food evenly," he said, looking at Vince, his expression hard although he hadn't raised his voice. "Don't worry. You'll get as much as everyone else. Bring out the food, and I'll divide it up."

"Why are you letting these girls tell you what to do?" Vince asked. He shook his head, standing even taller. "We're trapped, and someone needs to make the hard decision to keep us strong. If you can't make that decision, I will."

Ian advanced until he was six inches away from Vince. He stared him in the eye. "Move. Now."

"No."

Ian tried to push Vince away from the panel, but Vince shoved him back, hard. Ian staggered, regained his balance, and strode forward, swinging his fists.

But Vincent was ready. He blocked Ian's first blow, and then punched him in the stomach. As Ian gasped for breath, Vince struck Ian's face hard, knocking him to the floor.

Denise stood frozen, her hand over mouth and her eyes wide. Trembling, Cam inched away from Vince to stand behind Renee. Her hands were fists, as if she were about to leap forward to take on Vince herself.

"Stop, Vince!" shouted Erica. She knelt down beside Ian. Blood dripped from a gash on his cheek. Instinctively, she moved her hands toward the wound, not knowing how to help him, but needing to do something. "You're bleeding."

Ian pushed aside Erica's arms and slowly climbed to his feet. He threw another punch toward Vince, but it bounced harmlessly off his shoulder. Vince counter-attacked with a short right jab. Once more, Ian fell to the floor. This time, he seemed dazed.

He struggled to stand. Erica put one arm around his back and held onto his hand, helping him rise. He was bleeding from a cut on his forehead. He wiped at it with his cuff as it threatened to drip into his eye.

"Stay down," Vince advised him. "Every time you come at me, I'll put you on the ground. Just give up and we can eat."

Renee interposed herself between her brother and Vince, putting a hand on each of their chests. "Stop it now, you guys! We're sharing the food in a fair way."

Vince shook his head, looking at her with contempt. "Come on. You saw what I did to your brother. Don't think I won't do the same to you if you make me. I've warned you. It will be your own fault." He knocked aside her arm and shoved her sideways, firmly enough that she would have fallen if Cam hadn't braced her.

Renee regained her balance and then spoke casually, belying the tension in the room. "Yes, you can certainly beat me up. Heck, maybe you can beat all of us up at the same time, though I'm not so sure of that.

"But, if you think about it, you're trapped in a room with us. There's no escape, and eventually, you will have to sleep. And at that point, you'll be defenseless. Any of us can do anything to you then.

"I'm not some fragile flower. I will do what it takes to survive. If you stop me from eating this meal, you're going to have a very, *very* bad night. So the way I see it, you have two choices. You can either do the right thing, step away from the food, and let us all share it. Or you can fight us all right now and hurt us all so badly that we won't be able to take you out later, while you sleep. It's your decision."

She stared coolly at Vince, calm but ready for anything.

Vince's eyes narrowed. He looked from Renee to each of the others, one by one, and swallowed. Erica could almost see the gears turning in his head.

"Fine!" Vincent said. He scowled at Renee and stepped to the side. "I was just trying to make sure that we remained strong enough to escape. We might have to make sacrifices to get out of here, and if you girls are too weak to do that, we'll all have to live with it. And I don't know why you're suddenly talking about cowardly attacks while people are sleeping. Ian and I were just settling a disagreement the way men do."

Renee rolled her eyes, but before she could reply, Denise jumped in. "That's okay." She put her hand on Vince's arm and smiled. "I don't completely agree, but I understand the logic. You wanted to stay strong so you could protect us. And I appreciate the sentiment."

Vincent brusquely nodded. "Exactly. But if we're not going to do that, I'll have to figure something else out."

Renee stepped forward, opened the cabinet, and got the food, while Erica took Ian to the bathroom. Tearing a strip off the bottom of her shirt, she used it to stanch the flow of blood. After a few minutes, she rinsed it out and wiped his face.

"Thanks, Nurse Trestle," Ian murmured.

"That's Doctor Trestle to you."

"Oh, you want to play doctor now?"

Erica blushed. She had to admit to herself that Ian could still get to her sometimes. "That's not what I meant." She quickly changed the subject. "So. Psychological tests, right? How do you think we're doing?"

"What, eight hours into our first day, and only one fistfight? We must be winning." He sheepishly grinned.

When they returned to the main room to eat, the others had assembled on the mattresses. They had already checked the plates for a message and found nothing.

Everyone seemed reserved during the meal. It felt like a whole new low. The abduction was terrible, but the one saving grace was that they were all in it together. They all knew each other from school and could rely on each other. But if the message on the plate had made them begin to doubt each other, the fight had shattered that trust entirely.

Vince had harassed Cam and other kids since elementary school. He'd been in countless fights over the years. Some boys just did that, and Vince was one of those boys. The fights were a natural consequence whenever someone tired of his "jokes." He was aggressive, but, most of the time, he'd back off once he'd shown the other guy who was boss.

This fight felt different though. Part of it was the situation. They were all alone, yet Vince was willing to attack the only people in this place on his side. The other part was the utter disregard for the rest of them. He was so casual in sacrificing them to get enough food for himself.

And yet, he had a point. There wasn't enough food. They either had to find a way out or they would starve.

After dinner, they broke into several groups. Cam went back to the keypad. Erica, Renee, and Ian sat together on one mattress, while Vince went and lay down on another, as far away from the three of them as he could get without actually moving the mattress.

Denise, meanwhile, spent time with everyone. She even stood beside Cam for half an hour punching in codes. She didn't talk about anything deep, but rather how important it was to work together if they wanted to get out. Erica noticed that she spent a particularly long time with Vince, resting her hand on his arm and knee, grinning and laughing. Vince even smiled back.

Eventually, the lights dimmed, although it was still possible to see. They all went to their mattresses and tried to sleep.

Within a few minutes, Erica heard muffled crying. She lifted her head. Cam's shoulders were shaking.

"Shut up," Vince growled. "What would your father say?" He rolled over noisily.

Cam gurgled and went silent.

Nevertheless, it was hours before the last of them fell asleep.

#

Soon after the lights turned on in the morning, the muffled thud that they had begun to associate with food woke them all up. Erica was the first one over to the dumbwaiter.

"How thoughtful of our hosts," she said with a crooked smile. "They've given us a nice change of clothes." Erica pulled out a folded pile of T-shirts, yoga pants, and underwear, identical to what they were already wearing.

"Wow, if we get great clothes like this every day, I know I'm going to regret that I never took yoga," Ian said, walking toward Erica.

"It's never too late to start!" Erica chirped with exaggerated cheerfulness. Then, looking past Ian, she did a double take. "Hey, the display isn't seventy-five anymore. It changed to seventy-seven overnight."

Other than the number, nothing about the display seemed different.

Ian turned to stare at the number. "It's got to mean something. What's changed since yesterday?"

"It's a different day," Denise said. She rubbed her chin. "Though, if it were counting days, it should have only gone up by one. And I don't know why it would've started at seventy-five."

"It could be counting from a certain date," Erica said, scrunching up her face. "Today's May 24th. So what was seventy-seven days ago? Like mid-March?"

Ian shook his head, staring toward the ceiling. "It's not days because it went up by two. The only unit of time that would fit is half days, but that seems silly."

"At least it's not counting down," Erica dryly said. "If it was, I'd be worried about what would happen when it hit zero."

"The difference is two. So what's changed by two?" Denise said. "We've had three meals."

"It's our second set of clothes," Renee said.

"Only one since yesterday," Vince contradicted, his voice implying that Renee should have known better than to suggest something so idiotic.

Finally, Renee threw up her hands and rose. "Nothing's changed by two. I give up. I'm going to have a shower." Picking up her clean clothes, she went into the bathroom.

Ian shrugged. "I can't think of anything either. Maybe it's only meaningful to our captors." He grimaced. "Even if it does mean something, I doubt we'll be able to figure it out until we see how it changes a few more times."

The others nodded their agreement.

After showering, they discussed whether they should put the dirty clothes back in the dumbwaiter to dispose of them, but decided it was possible they'd need them later. So they left them in a heap in a corner near the bathroom.

"Now this place really is starting to feel like home," Ian said.

In a few minutes, cereal arrived for breakfast. As had become their habit, they ate sitting on the mattresses. This time, Vincent didn't attempt to claim more than an equal portion, and Erica pretended it didn't even cross her mind that he might try.

Denise had the spoon first, but before she ate, she raised the bowl above her head to look at the bottom. Once more, a message was messily scrawled in blue ink. They spilled a bit of the cereal as they crowded around her, trying to decipher it. After only a few seconds, they worked it out.

> *There are three ways out. Jen found one. Alex found another.*
> *Find the third.*

CHAPTER FIVE

"Wow," Ian said, with a wry smile. "If the person writing these notes is trying to be helpful, they really aren't very good at it."

"It's more of the same garbage. Just messing with our heads," Denise said, a drop of anger seeping into her tone.

Erica chewed on her lower lip. "Strangely, I find it reassuring. If I have to choose between a bloody death, losing my mind, or door number three, I'll take my chances with the third option."

Denise's brow furrowed. "Maybe the third way is to persuade our captors to let us go."

"Or overpower them when they come in," Vince suggested.

Erica pursed her lips, shaking her head. "Really, it could be anything." Her eyes darkened. "The message is meaningless."

Ian nodded. "But it does imply that there's a way to escape and that Jen and Alex were here."

Erica grimaced in frustration. "We can't even assume that. They could have overheard us discussing Jen and Alex and decided to include them in a message."

Renee rubbed her temples. "Now my brain hurts. I can't figure out whether we should trust the message, ignore it, or assume the opposite of what it says."

Ian shrugged. "I don't think we should do anything differently. Just make sure we're prepared," he looked meaningfully at Vincent, "if someone comes to visit."

Vince nodded and held up a fist. "That works."

"And," Ian said, "spend our free time looking for a way out, because, really, what else is there to do? We'd be doing what the note suggests, but not because of it."

They spent the rest of the morning planning out in detail how they would attack their captors. They wrapped up when lunch arrived. The three sandwiches barely made a dent in their hunger pangs, but once again, they did not discuss dividing up the food in another manner. Apparently, if they were going to starve to death, they'd starve together. *Or at least delay the second confrontation until they were more desperate*, Erica thought.

Afterward, the group looked for the so-called third way of escape. They spent hours tapping on walls, playing with the keypad, poking at the digital display—which now said seventy-eight—and opening and closing the dumbwaiter. Eventually, Ian hit upon the idea of burning something. He theorized that smoke detectors might cause the doors to unlock automatically.

"On the survival shows, they make fire by rubbing sticks together," Cam mumbled.

Vince's lip curled. "We're not in a forest. Do you *see* any sticks here?"

Cam shrank back, shaking his head minutely.

"The curtain," Renee said. Before any of them could move from where they were sitting on the mattresses, she raced over to the bathroom. She jumped up, grabbing the curtain rod.

"Don't break it!" Vince yelled.

Renee hung there for a second before lifting her legs. Erica winced as the rod bowed down in the middle, certain that it was about to snap. Then one of the ends slipped out of its hole.

Renee fell on her behind with the curtain on top of her. "Ouch." She flailed around as the others ran toward her. "I'm fine. I'm not hurt," she said as she got her head clear.

"Why are you always such a spaz? You nearly snapped it. I could have pulled it out easily." Vince glared at Renee, a look Erica thought was completely out of proportion to her transgression.

"I got it, didn't I?" Renee said, standing and rubbing her leg. She twisted her torso, trying peer at the back of her thigh.

Ian unthreaded the curtain rod. Other than the white paint, it appeared to be a simple dowel. "It's wood," he said, turning it over in his hands. "It could work."

After a brief break for dinner, Ian tore one of the dirty shirts into a thin strip of cloth. He wrapped it around the rod so that pulling the cloth back and forth would cause it to spin. Erica stacked some of the discarded paper in an indentation in the sink. After a few adjustments, they were able to align the dowel so it would spin in place on the top plate.

It was much harder than Erica expected, but eventually, Cam was able to generate enough heat to make embers on some small strips of toilet paper. The paper plate beneath it turned black and a flame appeared. Everyone cheered.

Cam tossed the burning plate into the middle of the bathroom. Saving the dowel, they heaped the remaining plates, the cutlery, most of the toilet paper, and even some of the dirty clothes onto the flame until they had a furious blaze.

Ian looked at Renee and smiled. "That's one ugly campfire."

She grinned back. "If only we had marshmallows. Or rather, moosemallows."

Erica giggled. Ian and Renee had been doing variations on their "That's one ugly horse" riff for years.

The bathroom grew hot with noxious. Coughing, they retreated to the main room. Even far away from the fire, the smoke stung their eyes. Surely, there would be enough to set off a detector.

Erica shifted her gaze from the door to the ceiling and back, looking for any sign that the lock was about to open or they had triggered an alarm.

"Just wait," Ian said, staring at the door expectantly. "It'll work."

After about thirty seconds, he walked to the door and tried to push it open, but it wouldn't budge.

A few minutes later, the fire exhausted its fuel. Other than a blackened spot on the floor and the lingering smell of burnt plastic, the fire appeared to have had no effect whatsoever.

"I can't believe you just wasted our whole day like that," Vincent snapped at Ian.

Ian's eyes narrowed, and he sighed. His shoulders slumping, he turned away.

"Hey, the display's up to eighty-one," Denise said. "Did anyone see eighty?"

Renee's brow furrowed. "I'm pretty sure it was seventy-nine when we went into the bathroom to light the fire."

"So it's skipping numbers," Erica said. Her eyes widened. "Or…

wait a minute. Do you find it warm in here? Warmer than it used to be?"

Vince rolled his eyes. "No kidding. We lit a fire."

"Yes," Erica said, as if she were talking to a small child. "But what's room temperature? About seventy-five degrees?"

"And eighty-one is warm," Denise said. Her face lit up. "The number might be the temperature in the room."

"But why bother?" Renee said.

"Maybe they expected us to start a fire?" Denise said.

"Without matches or anything? That seems unlikely," Erica said. Her eyes narrowed. "But if we're lab rats, perhaps it's a test. Like the notes on the plates?"

"What would it be testing? Whether we figure out it's a thermometer?" Denise asked.

"Maybe. I don't know."

When the lights dimmed, the discussion trailed off. They hung the curtain again to restore the privacy of the bathroom, and everyone went to bed. But Erica couldn't sleep. She was famished and kept thinking about what they might have missed. Her mind spun through all the items in the room.

Water, food, trays, paper plates, plastic knives and forks, the foil that had covered the food, clothes, sheets, pillows, mattresses, the curtain and rod, the sink, shower, and toilet. If she stretched, they also had air, blood, and hair.

Was it possible to combine those things to escape? It seemed like hours, but no matter how much she turned it over in her head, she couldn't figure it out. Yet, she couldn't put it out of her mind and sleep either.

There must be a way, and she needed to find it before they suffered the full impact of their slow starvation.

She had been so confident in the afternoon, buoyed by the optimism of a possible way out. And it was crushing when they failed. Almost worse was the expression on Ian's face, the forlorn emptiness of a man shuffling down a corridor on his way to an electric chair.

Tears rolled down Erica's cheeks, and she drew a shuddering breath. She knew the truth. There was no escape. Vince was right. Give them enough food for two and let them fight over it. The strongest would survive, and the others would starve or be killed.

Could she become desperate enough to fight her friends to save herself? Even thinking about it was horrific, but Erica forced herself to consider the question. The answer was simple. Tonight, she'd rather die than hurt Renee and Ian.

The realization that she had just accepted her own death spawned another flood of tears.

Erica felt the mattress shift and opened her eyes. Ian was sitting on the bed beside her. He gently reached out, wiping her tears away.

"Feels pretty hopeless, huh?" he whispered.

Erica nodded. She didn't trust herself to speak.

Ian tenderly took her hand. "It hit me hard too."

They were both silent for a minute until Erica could speak without dissolving. "Do you think there's a way out?"

"I don't know. I thought we found it. I was sure we had it." He paused. "But you know what? I'm not sure why, but I think we'll escape."

Erica looked up at his face. The light was dim, but she'd known Ian for long enough. He wasn't just saying it to comfort her. He truly believed they'd escape.

Somehow, Ian's simple faith seemed to lift a weight from Erica.

Neither of them spoke again that night. They simply stayed there, Erica lying and Ian sitting, comforting each other with their company.

#

"So what do we have here?"

Vince's question woke Erica. She was greeted by Ian's face. During the night, he must have lain down beside her.

"I didn't know that you two were like that," Vince said with arched eyebrow.

By now, his voice had roused everyone. Erica glanced at Renee. The curiosity in her eyes turned to concern as she saw Ian and Erica sharing a bed.

"Erica wanted to talk last night. I guess I fell asleep," Ian said in a matter-of-fact tone.

"Yeah, right," Vince sarcastically said.

"That's all it was. We've been friends for years."

Ian said exactly what Erica would have said had she spoken instead of him. Yet, hearing him say it somehow felt like a punch in the gut.

Denise smiled. "He's telling the truth. She's under the sheets. He isn't." She tugged on Vince's arm. "Let's go see if breakfast is here yet."

Renee stared at them for a second more, frowned, and followed Denise and Vince, trailed by Cam.

Ian looked back at Erica, smiling in reassurance. Suddenly, she felt like a trespasser in her own bed. What had been a comforting distance "alone" with Ian in the dim glow last night seemed unbearably close in the bright lights of the morning. It wasn't that she wanted him to leave. It was just that she was acutely conscious that she didn't know where to look.

The moment lasted for only a few seconds before Ian stood up and strolled over to the others.

Erica lay back for a minute to breathe before getting up to join them.

#

After the failure yesterday, it was hard to be enthusiastic about searching for an escape today. Several half-hearted ideas were proposed, but quickly discarded as unfeasible. The group eventually broke up, with Cam returning to his obsessive number punching, Denise and Vince talking on one mattress, and Erica, Renee, and Ian on another.

Today, the number on the wall said eighty-two, and the air seemed heavy. Erica could almost taste the toxins released by the fire worming their way into her lungs with every breath. Even the walls seemed grayer than when they first arrived. Whether that was a result of the smoke or was simply her imagination, Erica didn't know. She felt lethargic, as if she'd never leave the mattress again. She'd just sit there, talking pleasantly with her friends, until she died of starvation.

Renee, on the other hand, was fidgety, constantly shifting around and shooting looks at Erica. Finally, when Erica excused herself to go to the bathroom, Renee followed.

The second they were behind the curtain, Renee grabbed Erica's arm and spun her around to face her. "So what was last night about?"

"I was crying after everyone else fell asleep. I was quiet, but Ian must have heard me because he came over and sat down. We talked."

"Nothing more than talking?" Renee's eyes were hard.

"No, just talking."

"Erica, I saw your face when Ian said you were only friends."

44

"You *know* how I used to feel about him," Erica said, her tone almost pleading.

"Do you still feel that way?"

"I don't know," Erica murmured, looking down. "I didn't think so. But last night, it felt so hopeless. I felt all alone. Then he came, and… we talked. Now I don't know how I feel."

Renee turned away, disgust splashed across her features. "Come on, we're not kids any more. Your obsession with him has gone from cute to creepy. Even hearing you say stuff like this makes me want to puke."

"I don't mean to react to him. It's this situation. Trapped in here with him. It's messed up. I'm trying," Erica said, clutching at Renee's arm.

"Try harder. If you go any farther, we couldn't be friends anymore. I've told you all these private things about me. I don't want you sharing all my secrets with him. And when he acts like a jerk, who am I supposed to talk to about it? His doting girlfriend?" Renee's angry whisper had grown loud enough that Erica was starting to become concerned someone outside would overhear.

"It doesn't matter. Nothing's going to happen."

"Promise me."

"What?"

"Promise me you won't go any farther with him."

Erica studied the floor. Renee was her best friend. And Ian didn't like her that way anyway. She was giving up a fantasy, nothing real. She looked up. "I promise."

"Good." Renee turned, shoved aside the curtain, and marched out of the bathroom.

Returning to the larger room, Erica's stomach felt the exact way it did when walking into a final exam. It seemed as if everyone's eyes were glued to her even though they really only gave her brief glances.

Ian calmly took in their return. It seemed almost impossible to Erica that he could be so placid when she felt so taut.

The rest of the day inched by. They began to play games and found out quickly that a round of *I Spy*—a game that Erica hadn't played since she was ten—lasted an average of three seconds in an empty, white room.

The game soon degenerated into trying to name something in the room in the most bizarre manner possible. Cam and Vince refused to play, but the others kept at it for hours. Between that, charades, and every word game they had ever played on a long road trip, they passed the time. To Erica, it wasn't fun, but rather an escape, a way to avoid thinking about the white room, the locked door, and the horror of their slow starvation.

After dinner, Erica noticed a bead of sweat dripping down Ian's face, though he had done nothing but sit on the mattress for the last hour. She glanced at the display on the wall.

"Look. It's eighty-five now," she said. "We might have a problem."

Overhearing her from his position on one of the other mattresses, Vince sneered. "It's only ten degrees higher than when we arrived. Deal with it."

"The temperature keeps increasing, and it's already warm in here. How hot will it get?" Erica struggled to keep her rising panic from leaking into her voice. She wasn't sure whether she succeeded.

Ian swallowed. "We can cool off in the shower if we need to."

"That will only help so much. What if it hits 100? 120? 150?"

Denise's face was solemn. "Then we need to escape. Fast."

In the half hour before the lights dimmed, they scrambled around, looking for anything they might have missed. They found nothing.

CHAPTER SIX

By the next morning, the number had ticked up to eighty-eight. It was sweltering.

"Is it speeding up?" Renee asked, her hands twisting nervously together.

"It might be," Ian said. "We need to get out of here." His eyes veered from the bathroom to the steel door on the opposite wall.

"But we've tried everything," Renee cried. She put her hands over her face, defeat written all over her body.

"We have to keep trying," Ian said, squeezing Renee's shoulders with his hands. "Get creative."

They spent the morning attacking the door, lights, and dumbwaiter to no effect. With each of them drinking several bowls of water every hour and spraying water onto their clothes to keep cool, there was a near constant procession to the bathroom. As the temperature continued to rise—hitting ninety—they became frantic.

Burgers arrived for lunch and with them, another message.

Above 95 degrees, people start dying.

Renee gasped and looked at her brother. His face was frozen, eyes wide.

Cam's eyes flicked from side to side, and he took three steps back. Wrapping his arms around his chest, he began to shake.

Erica bit her lip hard enough to break the skin. "Could it be a bluff? Would they really kill us?"

"It's no bluff. They've killed before," Vince growled. He started stuffing one of the two hamburgers into his mouth. Ian frowned, grabbed it from his hand, and apportioned the food. They gulped it down in a few seconds.

"We have to do something. We have to figure it out!" Renee said. Sweat streamed down her face.

"Yes. We just need to be methodical about it," Denise replied. Though she looked calm, Erica saw Denise wipe away a trickle of blood from her lip. Apparently, she wasn't the only one who chewed her lip when stressed.

Ian nodded, his face severe. "Yes. Renee and Cam, you search the dumbwaiter for anything we missed." He looked toward Vincent and Denise. "You two do the door. Erica and I will search the bathroom." He marched toward the curtain, not even glancing back to see if anyone was following his directions.

Erica shrugged and followed him.

She started with the shower, peering down the drain. "We could pry up the grate, but the hole is too small to fit a hand, let alone someone's body." Erica looked back at Ian and sighed. "You know, even if we find a way out, I'm sure they're listening to everything we say. They'll know what we're planning and stop us."

Ian nodded. "Particularly if one of us is a spy." He thought for a few seconds before he motioned for her to get out of the shower. After he turned it on, he paused. "There's something I've wanted to tell you since the other night."

Ian grabbed Erica's hand, tugging her gently toward him until they were almost touching. With their faces so close together, his level gaze and faint, hesitant smile seemed impossibly intimate. He pulled her into a hug so that his lips were nestled beside her ear.

"With the shower on and us whispering, I bet they can't pick us up on microphones," Ian said.

Erica's eyes widened, even as her breath stuttered in her chest from his closeness.

"Do you trust me?" Ian said.

"I do."

"I trust you too. And Renee. I'm not sure about the others, but I'd stake my life that neither one of you is a spy."

"Me too."

He paused and then murmured, "I was thinking about this today. We need to be able to talk without our captors hearing, and whispering in each other's ears is the only way to do it."

Erica nodded, the feel of his silky lips touching her cheek beside her ear making her suppress a shudder.

"So I think we should get affectionate. Nothing too extreme. Just enough to fool the cameras and the others. Enough to give us an excuse to sleep on the same mattress so we can talk at night."

Erica was glad he was so close that he couldn't see her heated cheeks. Her heart was pounding so hard she was sure he could feel it. "But will it even matter? If we don't get out soon…"

"We're not dead yet. And tonight, being able to talk without being overheard might make the difference between life and death."

After her promise to Renee, it seemed like a terrible idea. Could she pull off something like that? Yet, Ian was right. There was no other way ensure that their captors didn't overhear them. Or was that just an excuse to justify doing what she really wanted?

Finally, Erica whispered, "Okay." Inwardly, she cursed the tension that caused the slight quiver in her voice.

"Don't worry. You can trust me. I won't take it too far. We both know that it's a way to get some privacy, nothing more."

"Yes, nothing more," Erica echoed. Her emotions were going haywire, unable to reconcile Ian's words that it didn't mean anything with the intimate hug and lips lightly brushing her ear. Not to mention her promise to Renee.

Ian seemed oblivious to what he was doing to her. "And when one of us gets a chance, we can tell Ren what we're doing. So she doesn't misunderstand."

"Yeah." Erica didn't trust herself to say anything more.

"Good. Now let's show the cameras." He released the hug and leaned back slightly, keeping his eyes on her face. She couldn't meet his gaze.

With a slight smile, Ian lifted her chin and kissed her gently on the lips. It wasn't a long kiss, but it seemed to flood Erica's body with warmth. As he drew back far enough to see her fiery cheeks, Ian's mouth slightly quirked.

"Oops," he said in a normal tone, clearly intended for the microphones. "Got distracted and forgot about the shower." He turned off the water. "I still can't think of any way to use the water to escape."

Erica tried to calm her spinning thoughts and focus once more on the task at hand. "Neither can—"

"I've got it!" Renee's voice rang out. After a brief exchange of glances, Erica and Ian pushed aside the curtain and rushed out.

Elbowing Denise out of her way, Renee studied the number pad. "This is a really common security system, the GZ 8500. It's for turning home security on and off. They must have sold two million of these." She pushed firmly on the top and bottom of the number pad and then on the sides. With a click, the front panel came off in her hands, revealing wiring beneath.

"What? How did you do that, Renee?" Ian asked in astonishment.

Renee showed them the back of the panel. "See, the panel has these hidden latches so they can remove it for maintenance. They don't sell this system anymore because someone figured out how to beat it and posted instructions on the Internet. Pretty soon, every small-time burglar learned how to crack one of these."

"That's not what I was asking," Ian said. "I mean—"

"Just a sec!" She ran across the room to the corner, grabbed the foil that had been covering the hamburgers, and marched back while twisting the foil into two strings. "Watch this."

Detaching one of the wire ends, she used an aluminum string to extend it, attaching it somewhere else. She formed a bridge between two other wires with the second string.

"What are you doing? Don't break it," Erica said, putting her hand on Renee's arm.

"I'm not. We need to enter a code, any code." She typed six digits.

The panel beeped, and the door slid open. The stream of cooler air was like the first gasp of oxygen after surfacing from a deep dive.

Erica let it flow across her face and then shook her head. "What the heck, Renee?"

"Yeah, what's up with that?" Vincent said, crossing his arms over his chest. "It took you four days to 'remember' how to hotwire the lock? How stupid do you think we are?" He looked around at the others. "It's obvious now who's our spy."

"I'm not. I just didn't remember anything about the lock until now," Renee said defensively.

"What do you mean? How did you know how to override it at all?" Ian said, blinking at her. "You've never had any interest in electronics."

"I don't know," she said, sounding confused. "I just remembered how to do it. Maybe I watched a video about it on the Internet a while back and forgot until now. It just occurred to me that I recognized the type of lock on the door and how to crack it."

"Oh, come on!" Vince said, glaring at Renee. "Do you really expect us to believe that? It all makes sense now. You knew I was strong, so you encouraged the others to attack me when we were talking about how to divide up the food. You've just been trying to weaken us and make us fight each other."

"I know it seems strange. But I've been trying to do what's best for us the whole time. In fact—"

"Guys!" Erica said, holding up her hands. She wished she could compare notes with Ian in private to determine if Renee really had some interest in locksmithing, but there were more pressing issues. "Has it occurred to you that we've opened the door, probably triggering an alarm somewhere, and we're standing around, arguing about whether Renee's a spy? How stupid are we? Besides, I'm just about ready to melt."

Denise nodded. "Good point. Let's get moving and worry about this later."

"Fine," Vince said, his tone making it clear it was anything but. He stared at Renee, his eyes narrow. "But I'm watching you."

In response, Renee sneered, pointed two fingers at her eyes in an exaggerated "I'm watching you" mime. Vincent scowled.

Leaving the sweltering room was like plunging into a cool pool on a hot day, though the room beyond was only a small, white stairwell. It was empty other than a keypad opposite the keypad in the original room and a spiral staircase made of dark metal three feet away against the far wall. The air smelled faintly of iron.

Cautiously, the group crept forward and peered up. Fifty feet above, the stairs ascended through a hole in the ceiling.

They climbed the stairs in single file, footsteps echoing in the silence, holding onto the thin, metal rod that acted as a handrail. The rail seemed low to Erica, not enough to be dangerous, but enough to be unsettling as they rose high above the floor. At the top was a room as small as the one below. Unlike the sliding door on the first room, this room's metal door had a handle.

They crowded into the tiny space in front of the closed door. Ian touched the door handle, but instead of opening it, he paused. Putting a finger to his lips, he motioned for them to return downstairs. With some confusion, they did.

"We should have a plan for what to do when we open the door. If it's unlocked, that is," Ian said.

"Aren't we just going to fight whoever's there?" Cam asked in a mousy voice. Vince nodded.

"It depends," Denise said. "It might be a guardroom, but it could just be the kitchen that sends us food. Or even empty."

"Who cares who it is? If someone's there, we need to attack," Vincent said, his whole body tensed up.

"I agree. Normally, I'm not a shoot-first-ask-questions-later kind of girl," Erica said, "but anyone behind that door is involved in this. And if they wanted to talk, they've had four days."

Denise pursed her lips, nodding.

"Ian and me should be in front, followed by Cam and the girls," Vince said, pointing to people as he said their names, his face hard. "Regardless of the number of people, we have to go for it. We only get one chance at this and surprise is the only advantage we have. Go for the weapons first and then use them."

Erica was uncomfortable with the idea of using weapons on unarmed people, regardless of what they did. But, seeing the others nod at Vince's words, she decided now wasn't the time to disagree.

"What if the room's empty?" Cam asked eagerly.

"Then it doesn't matter what we do. Do you never think before speaking?" Vincent said, his voice contemptuous. Cam shrank back.

"No. Cam has a point," Denise interjected, resting her fingertips lightly on Vince's forearm. "There could be those laser alarm things or something else that isn't immediately obvious."

Ian nodded. "So if nobody's in the room, we take some time to look around before entering."

"Sounds like a plan," Erica said. She shook out her arms and legs as if she was preparing to race.

"Yes, let's do it," Vince said, turning to the stairs.

Ian reached out and squeezed Erica's hand. "Good luck." He followed Vince.

Erica hurried after him, her face warm. The others exchanged glances while Renee frowned.

They gathered in the upper room and got into position. Ian held up three fingers to begin a silent countdown.

The image of a cougar in a stark white room flashed through Erica's mind. *Great*, she thought. *I'm about to fight for my life and all I can think about is the way Alex died.* It almost took physical effort to ignore the image and focus her attention on reacting as fast as possible to whoever was behind the door.

Ian's countdown reached zero. Slightly crouched, he swung open the door, ready to race inside.

This room, like their original room, was rectangular, about sixty feet by eighty feet, stark white, and almost empty.

But Erica barely noticed the room. Her eyes were drawn to the cougar in the far corner.

It was massive, the size of a St. Bernard, its paws bigger than a man's hands. Its unblinking yellow eyes locked on them as it opened its mouth, revealing inch and half long fangs. For a few seconds, the cougar was completely motionless except for the tip of its thick, velvety tail that twitched as it stared.

Then, in a single, fluid motion, the cougar rose. Its powerful muscles rippled beneath its yellow-brown fur as it padded silently toward them.

"That's one ugly horse," Ian said faintly.

CHAPTER SEVEN

Ian closed the door firmly and swallowed. "Darn," he said. "We totally forgot to come up with a plan for what to do if there's a cougar in the room."

All the blood had drained from Renee's face, and she was slightly swaying. "Oh no. It's like Alex."

Erica put her arm around Renee's shoulder. "I know. I was just thinking about that."

They heard scratching on the door. The door opened away from them, but Ian still grabbed the handle to make sure the animal didn't somehow bounce the door open.

"I'm suddenly glad these doors are made of steel," Denise said. She was trembling.

"I feel like we've been abducted by super villains," Ian said, his tone unreasonably light. "I mean, what kind of freak uses a cougar to guard his prisoners?"

Erica couldn't help but smile. "It does seem impractical. I wonder how they decide which soldier has to clean up the kitty litter."

"Maybe they're trying to save money. You wouldn't have to pay it like you would guards. Toss in some ground beef and the occasional bit of catnip, and you're done," Ian replied earnestly.

Erica said, "But it's probably—"

"That's enough!" Renee said, glaring first at Ian and then at Erica. "You can joke all you like, but if that thing gets through the door, it will tear us to shreds. And we still haven't found a way out."

"Actually, I saw a door on the other wall," Vince said.

"Which wall?" Denise asked.

"The far side of the room. If we ran, we might make it."

"No way. There's no way," Renee said. Her face had turned white, and she looked like she might faint.

"It might be possible. It's about twenty yards, I'd say," Ian said. His eyes flicked from Denise's knee to her face. "How fast can you run with your leg?"

"Fast enough."

"There's no way," Renee repeated.

"Well, we can always leave you behind," Vince said as if he were suggesting something she should truly consider.

There was a hollow thud from below.

"Huh, dinner's arrived," Ian said. His eyes narrowed as he looked down the stairs.

"We just escaped," Erica said quickly, sensing the direction of his thoughts. "We shouldn't go back even for food. We might get trapped again. We need to move quickly, not dawdle around, wasting the element of surprise. Once we're out of here, we can eat as much as we want."

Ian shook his head. "There's the cougar though. I don't see the harm in going down to get something to eat while we talk about how to get by it. I'm totally starving. I'm not saying stay there for hours. Just long enough to eat and figure out what to do."

"Do you actually think it's safe to leave the cougar alone?" Renee said, her tone making her own opinion clear.

"Well, the door is heavy and opens into the room. It's pretty unlikely that it could turn the knob even if I let go of the handle. And he's not even trying," he said. He released the door handle.

Erica nodded reluctantly. Ian was right. Until they had a way past the cougar, it didn't make sense to ignore the food when they were all so famished. Still, as she followed Ian down the stairs, she couldn't help but feel like a mouse trying to snatch cheese from a trap.

Renee hesitated. But as the others descended, she looked at the door, looked back at the others, and scurried after them.

Opening the door had cooled the room below significantly—the thermometer now read 85. After stuffing some of the dirty clothes in the doorway so the door wouldn't slide closed, they looked in the dumbwaiter.

This time, the meal was two plates of spaghetti and meatballs.

There were only five meatballs, so they divided up the spaghetti first, waiting until they had enough space to chop the meatballs into six portions. It was a messy process, but they were all so hungry that nobody objected.

"I think Vince is right," Ian said as he ate. "We just have to run across the room to the other door."

Renee scowled. "You're not serious about that?" She stood up and began kicking the mattress, occasionally bending down to grab some of her small portion of spaghetti.

"Um, yes," Ian replied as if it were obviously a great idea. "We have to go. We can't just stay here."

"That's insane," she said flatly, holding out her hands. "It's a wild animal, a predator with fangs and claws designed for killing. The cougar can probably run three times as fast as any of us, and when it catches us, it won't pause a second. It will rip out our throats and tear us to pieces."

"I don't think we have a choice," Denise said in a sympathetic voice. "It's the only way out."

"We don't even know if the other door is unlocked." Renee said.

"It has to be," Ian said. "I was joking about the super villain thing, but seriously, who would put a cougar in a room guarding the only exit? This has got to be some kind of test."

"Or a psycho death trap," Renee said, her voice rising and her face darkening. "It's practically straight out of ten different horror movies. Make the kids run for a door. It's locked, and they all get mauled by the cougar. If you had a cougar, would you really leave it in an unlocked room?"

"Erica thinks her mom is involved," Denise said. "Would she put Erica in a situation where she was certain to die?"

Erica blanched. She had forgotten about her mom, or maybe blocked out her involvement. Locking her in a room with some friends for a psychological experiment was one thing. Making her run through a room with a cougar was something entirely different. Her mother had limits to what she'd do for science, didn't she? It was so confusing. She wished she could ask Ian his opinion. He knew her mom.

Renee didn't seem to notice Erica's reaction to the mention of her mother. "I don't know. In any case, we'd be nuts to try."

Thoughtfully, Vince looked at her. "You might be scared of it, but really, the cougar wasn't that big. Like a large dog. If we had to, we could probably kill it in a fight."

"Maybe," Renee said. "I'm a bit surprised that it came toward us. They tend to avoid humans and typically ambush their prey, not attack head-on. Only something like twenty people have died from cougar attacks in the last century. But even if we could beat it, someone's likely to get mauled. And cougars favor attacking children and small women. Like me." Her tone was bitter.

"Well, you are the smallest one," Vince helpfully pointed out. "I'd go for you, too. Or Denise because of her limp. But if you're right, it could be scared of us anyway."

"Unless it's trapped in there without enough food, just like us," Denise said, her eyebrows raised. "It might be starving too."

"That raises an interesting idea," Erica said, poking at one of the meatballs. "Maybe we can use food as a distraction."

"Yes, I can just imagine how pissed off the cougar will be when we throw spaghetti all over it," Renee sarcastically said.

Erica giggled as the image of a disgruntled cougar, its face dripping with spaghetti and tomato sauce, popped into her head. "Maybe not the spaghetti. We're mostly done with that anyway. But we still have the meatballs. We can throw them in a corner and run by while it's eating."

Ian nodded. "I hate to waste our food that way, but it seems like it would be worth it."

Vince said, "Yes, it should work." Cam grunted affirmatively.

"This is a terrible idea," Renee said.

"You can stay here if you want, but we're getting out of here," Vince said.

"Come on, Renee." Erica looked at her friend with pleading eyes. "We need escape and this is the only way."

Renee squeezed her eyes tightly shut and shook her head. "Fine! I'll do it. I can't believe I'm agreeing to this…" She thought for a few seconds. "Using the food as a distraction is the only way it can work. And cougars go for the throat, so let's wrap extra clothes around our necks so we at least have some protection."

They spent a few minutes discussing the details of their plan. When they finished eating, Renee went into the bathroom to wash. Erica, recognizing an opportunity to speak to her alone, followed.

Renee turned on the water while Erica tried to find a good way to start the conversation. After a few seconds, Renee did it for her. She turned to Erica and said bitterly, "So, you and my brother."

Erica squinted, frowning like she was on the verge of tears, and held out her arms. Renee, clearly somewhat confused, hugged her.

Erica babbled in Renee's ear, "Ian and I think our captors are listening to everything we say. And we're still a bit unsure if one of the other guys is a spy. So we're pretending something's going on, so we have an excuse to sleep together, so we can talk privately about what to do."

"What? I totally missed that. Can you say it again, slower?" Renee whispered.

Erica repeated what she had said.

"And by 'sleep together' you mean…"

"I mean sleep. We're just pretending."

"He's just pretending, but are *you* just pretending?" Renee pointedly asked.

The question hit Erica's stomach with a jolt of joy, guilt, and pain. Renee knew her too well. "Oh, Renee. I'm doing my best."

"Yeah, that's what I thought," she sarcastically said. "Did you come up with this, or him?"

"Him."

Renee looked at Erica for a few seconds, shook her head, and grimaced. "This is a terrible idea. But it might work. Just remember your promise, Erica."

"I will."

They broke the hug, finished washing, and returned to the room.

As she walked to where the others were sitting on the mattress, Erica smiled at Ian. She wanted to signal to him that she'd explained everything, but she couldn't come up with a way to do so without revealing more than she should. So hopefully, he'd figure it out from the smile.

Denise was winding a pair of pants around Vince's neck. Erica started to do the same for Renee.

"I think we're ready to go. We've got the perfect plan," Dense said. She smiled broadly, making eye contact with each of them. "Toss the meatballs in the corner and when the cougar goes for them, run for the door. And if it's locked, we return here. But we leave together. If someone gets attacked, we may have to fight."

Vincent nodded. "Time's wasting. We have to go."

Together, they marched up the stairs and got ready, with Vincent in the lead, Denise second, and Ian in the rear.

"Ready?" Vincent whispered, looking back. Everyone nodded. He cracked open the door.

If anything, the cougar seemed bigger than when she saw it the first time. Erica could almost feel its glistening teeth piercing her neck, its claws carving her stomach. Suddenly, this plan seemed like a terrible idea. She wanted to tell Vincent to stop, to wait, but she couldn't form the words.

Vince tossed the meatballs into the far corner. The cougar padded silently over to investigate.

"Now!" Vincent hissed.

He swung open the door and started running as quietly as he could. The others followed. Erica didn't dare to look at the cat, certain that if she did, it would somehow sense it and pursue her.

The cougar devoured the meatballs in two gulps and then flinched as Erica's shoe scuffed the ground. It looked, saw prey in flight, and instinctively turned to pursue.

Vincent reached the exit first, before the cat was halfway to them. Turning the handle, the door swung open toward him.

The others would have made it too, if it weren't for Renee.

She was running as fast as she ever had. Faster than she should. With a gasp, she overbalanced and stumbled to the floor.

Ian ran three steps past Renee before he could stop to try to help his sister regain her feet. As he turned, she climbed to her hands and knees.

The cougar leaped. It landed on Renee's back, forcing her heavily to the ground, and grabbed her neck in its savage jaws.

CHAPTER EIGHT

"Help Renee!" Ian yelled.

Vince glanced back, shouting, "No, it's too late! She's dead. Get out of there!" He bolted through the exit.

Cam stood rooted near the door, looking first at Vince, then at the others. Denise and Erica didn't hesitate. They sprinted back to help.

Ian cursed. Renee's eyes were crazed with fear, her shrieks resounding. The cougar had a firm grip on her neck and was trying to shake her. Its claws had pierced the shirt on her back.

Ian planted his left foot and, his face contorted, did a low roundhouse kick. His foot connected solidly on the side of the cat's head, breaking its grip and knocking it off his sister.

The cougar shook its head, stunned. It ripped at the yoga pants it had torn from around Renee's neck. Erica and Denise helped Renee up before turning back toward the door.

Just as they began to run, images flashed through Erica's mind.

The four of them sprinting. The cougar regaining its feet.
Leaping onto Renee. Her face smashing into the floor. Jaws
tearing at her unguarded neck. Blood spraying.

Renee had said it. Cougars preferred to stalk and ambush their prey, not confront them head-on. It was insane, but there was no time to think of anything else.

Erica grabbed Ian's hand, abruptly stopping. "Ian, help me!" She spun around to face the cat.

Ian glanced at her, momentarily in shock, and then his expression hardened. He pivoted to look back. The cougar had realized that the yoga pants weren't edible. It crept toward them with death in its eyes.

Erica raised herself on her toes, put her arms in the air, and let out the loudest, most aggressive roar she could imagine.

Ian, catching on quickly to what Erica was trying to do, showed his teeth and let out a thundering growl that sounded like it originated in the throat of a demon.

The cougar didn't expect this. Instead of a herd fleeing in panic, it faced two predators, each as big as itself and ready to fight. It skittered backward, unsure.

Ian took an exaggerated step forward, stomping his foot, and the cougar turned around and slunk to the corner. While still maintaining their aggressive stances, Ian and Erica slowly backed away. After a few seconds that lasted an eternity, they exited the room and slammed the door.

As soon as Ian turned, Renee was there, burying her head against his chest. "I thought I was dead. But you came back for me."

"Of course, Ren," Ian said, hugging her tight.

Renee shook as she came to terms with the magnitude of what had nearly happened to her. "You could have died."

Smiling, Ian shrugged. "Well, I just reacted, and the cougar wasn't as big as it seemed at first."

"It was far too big," Renee said, her face white. "So heavy. I never could have gotten it off me."

"How are you feeling?" Erica asked, examining Renee's upper body. "I don't see any blood on your neck."

Renee released her grip on Ian. She swallowed, touching her neck hesitatingly, first on one side, then the other. "I actually feel fine. Its jaws were crushing, but the neck guard blocked its teeth pretty well." She blinked.

"Well, the cougar was on you for only a second or two before Ian knocked it off," Denise said. "Though after watching, my neck has sympathy pains." She slowly turned her head from one side to the other as if to emphasize her statement.

"Your shirt's torn on the back. And so are your pants," Cam said to Renee.

"Its claws. It was right on me."

"Can I lift up the back of your shirt to look at it?" Erica said.

"Yeah, go ahead."

Carefully, Erica rolled it up. The skin on Renee's back was not only unbroken, but seemed completely normal. "Wow, is that even possible? You're so lucky! It looks like it didn't even touch you."

Vince, who was standing behind Denise, suddenly shook his head, frowning. "Denise, is that blood on your shirt?" he said. "Did you get clawed?"

Denise raised her eyebrows. "I don't think so, but I guess it might have swiped me when I was helping Renee. So much was happening in there, and I was so pumped up that maybe I didn't notice." She winced as Vince delicately touched one of the dark spots.

"Turn around, Denise," Erica said. As she had with Renee, she rolled up Denise's shirt. Four bloody scratches on her left shoulder oozed blood. "You have some claw marks. They're bleeding, but they don't look too bad."

Erica unwound the pants from around her own neck to get something to blot up the blood. That was when she happened to glance around the room for the first time. It looked identical to their first room, complete with mattresses.

"What the heck?" she said. "We're back to where we started." She reflexively looked behind her to make sure that the door through which they had arrived was still there. It was.

Vince rolled his eyes, shook his head, and sighed. "Yeah, try to keep up. That was news ten minutes ago."

"Ten minutes ago is when you arrived. For the rest of us, it's been only five minutes," Erica said coldly.

Vince glowered at her. "I had to make sure there was nothing dangerous in here."

"Yes, Erica," Denise said. "Vince made it to the exit first because he was courageous enough to volunteer to be the first into the cougar room. And he held the door open for us until we got to safety." She put her hand on Vince's arm and smiled up at him, her eyes bright. "It was very brave."

Vince blinked several times and then nodded. "Well, someone had to take the risk of going first. I figured it might as well be me."

Erica sighed. "Whatever. We need to take care of these wounds."

"Hurry," Vince said. "We have to go."

"We'll only be a few minutes. Wait for us." She shook her head. "At least I know where the bathroom is." Erica held the pants against the scratches on Denise's shoulder to stop the bleeding, took Renee's hand, and steered both of them behind the curtain.

Gently, Erica pulled Renee's pants halfway down, so she could see the damage to her thigh. Though there was blood on her pants and skin, when Erica rubbed it away, once again, Renee appeared to be uninjured.

"This is strange," she said, her brow furrowed. "As far as I can tell, you're not hurt at all."

Denise said, "My leg stings though." Her lips were a thin line and her face pallid.

Erica's face scrunched in confusion. "Can I look?"

Denise nodded.

Erica carefully rolled down Denise's pants, revealing four parallel claw marks on her right thigh. "How is this possible? Your pants aren't even torn," she said in disbelief.

Suddenly suspicious, Erica said, "Let me see your neck." Denise lifted her hair aside. While the skin was whole, purple bruises had begun to form. "It's bruised. And your wounds are in the same places as the rips in Renee's clothes."

"How can that be?" Denise asked. She looked at Renee with wide eyes. "What have you done to me?" Her tone was sharp.

"I didn't do anything. Or at least, I didn't try to do anything," Renee said in a small voice.

"Yet, somehow I'm hurt," Denise spat back. She took a deep breath and closed her eyes for a few seconds. Shaking her head as if to clear it, she continued in a calmer tone. "I don't mean to accuse you, but you have to admit that it's odd."

Renee mumbled, "Yes, it is." She looked miserable.

Erica shook her head. She needed time to think. "Let's talk about this with the others. Right now, I need to get you cleaned up." The other two girls nodded.

Erica wet a shirt in the sink and did her best to clean Denise's wounds. The claw marks were about an eighth of an inch deep and she had no way to disinfect them, but she knew Denise was lucky.

If Ian hadn't reacted so swiftly, the wounds would have been much worse. Maybe fatal. No thanks to Vince, even if he had convinced himself that abandoning Renee was an act of bravery, not cowardice. And what was Denise doing defending him?

Erica frowned and asked in a low voice, "Denise, what's going on with you and Vince?"

"Nothing," Denise defensively said. Both Renee and Erica turned to face her.

"Nothing?" Erica asked, her eyebrows shooting up. "You're not interested in him?"

"No."

Erica persisted, some of her earlier anger at Vince bleeding into her voice. "Come on. You're constantly touching him, and you take his side in every argument. That defense of his cowardice in the other room was unbelievable. You like him, don't you?"

Denise shifted from foot to foot, pursing her lips. "Not really." When the other girls didn't reply, but just continued to stare at her skeptically, she sighed and shook her head. "You two are both so observant. It's hard to hide anything from you...." She glanced toward the curtain and then back at them. "It's like this. We're trapped in here and have to work together to get out. But you know how Vince is.

"I once saw him fight a kid in Frankle Park. Totally mauled him. Punched him in the nose to knock him down, then sat on his chest and hit him until his face was nothing but red.

"Finally, he stood up to go. But just when I thought it was over, he stomped on the guy's hand. Broke all his fingers. The kid was unconscious, but his arm started twitching. Like a fish does, after you club it, but before it realizes it's dead.

"He's a maniac. We all know it. But here, that might be what we need. We have to make sure he's on our side. Because if he's not fighting them, he'll be fighting us. We can't have that happen. You saw how easily he beat up Ian the other day. If he becomes unhinged, they won't need a cougar to kill us. He'll do it himself.

"Vince needs to feel wanted, and you two aren't helping with that, arguing with him all the time. He needs to believe that we like him and respect him. Or even admire him. That's what I'm doing, and you should do the same." Her gaze was level and unapologetic.

"The way you're headed, he might think more than that," Erica said. She understood Denise's reasoning, but thought the other girl was opening herself up to getting hurt on a whole other level.

"So let him. If it'll help achieve the goal, it's worth it."

"How far will you take it?"

"As far as necessary. Whatever it takes." In response to Erica and Renee's nauseated expressions, Denise added, "Look. We're in a life-or-death situation. We have to do whatever it takes to get out of here." Her eyes, normally so cheery, were somber.

"But what about after we escape? What will you do then?" Erica asked.

Denise shrugged. "Avoid him, I suppose. I'm not going to shed any tears about how he'll feel next week in school. I'm worried about surviving today."

Nodding slightly, Erica turned back to Denise's shoulder. She didn't like the strategy. It was manipulative and cynical. But it might be working. Vince seemed to listen to Denise a bit more than the others, and there hadn't been a fight since the first day. For most people, that might not seem like a big accomplishment. But for Vince, in this situation, it was.

Erica didn't think she could ever be so callous. She was pretending with Ian, but that was different because they both agreed to do so. What Denise was doing was just wrong.

On the other hand, she wasn't the one manipulating Vince. Denise was. And it wasn't as if it was hurting him. If Denise's act kept the peace and gave them all a better chance of escape, Vince himself would benefit. Maybe it was justified.

Erica finished cleaning, tossing the bloodstained clothes into the corner. While Denise could wear the yoga pants that she'd used as a neck protector, the shirt was a problem. Erica stuck her head out from behind the curtain and said, "Ian, give me your shirt."

"Um, what?" he said.

"Denise's shirt is covered in blood."

Ian shrugged. Taking his off, he tossed it to her.

When Denise was ready, they returned to the main room to find the others sitting on the mattresses. Ian looked up as they approached. "How are you doing?" he asked Renee.

"I'm good. Denise is hurt though. She has scratches and bruises in the exact same spots that I should. I'm not even cut, but she's all gashed up." She paced beside the mattresses as she shared the discovery, while Denise gingerly sat down beside Vince and Erica next to Ian.

Ian's brow furrowed in confusion. "Are you sure?"

Denise's lip curled. "Pretty sure."

Vince stared accusingly at Renee and then Ian. "So do you still think that Renee's not a spy? Now that she's injured one of us?"

Renee began to respond, "I don't know how—"

Vince turned on her, instantly furious. He leaped to his feet. "I don't want to hear from you! You've proven yourself a liar, and you've hurt Denise. There's nothing more to say."

Tears formed in Renee's eyes. Her face collapsed in utter despair. Shoulders slumping, she stared at the ground.

Vince rolled his eyes. "Don't give us that sad little puppy dog face. We've had enough of you. It won't work!"

"That's enough, Vince!" Ian shouted, standing up. Erica saw his jaw clench as he struggled to control his anger. "Did Renee scratch Denise's back with her fingernails? Did she choke Denise to make those bruises around her neck? Tell me, how did it happen?"

Vince advanced until his chest was only a foot from Ian's. "I don't know how she did it. I don't need to know! Denise is hurt, and Renee's responsible. We can't give her another chance to do this, or worse."

"Just because Denise got hurt helping Renee while you were fleeing like a frightened rabbit doesn't make it Renee's fault," Ian said, not retreating an inch.

Erica rose, trying to think of what she could possibly do if Vince started swinging.

"It was her fault," Vince replied, his arms shaking. "And don't forget. Renee opened the lock, too."

"Well, that's not good enough for me," Ian said. Finally, he broke away from Vince to stand beside Renee. "She's my sister, and I trust her with my life."

"Good, because that's exactly what you're doing if we don't do something about her now," Vince said. Beads of sweat trickled down his red face.

Erica clasped Renee's hand. "I trust her too. She wouldn't betray us." Renee peered at her hopefully.

"You would say that," Vince replied. "You're just one of those girls who will say anything to keep her boyfriend happy."

Erica eyes widened. It had never occurred to her that someone would accuse her of such a thing. Ian wasn't even her boyfriend. But how could she defend herself without revealing that their relationship was a sham? She put her arm around Ian's waist and weakly stuttered, "No, I'm not."

Vincent rolled his eyes. "Yeah, right." He looked toward Denise, who had risen and was standing just a bit behind him.

Denise frowned. "I don't see how Renee could have done it, honey."

By now, Vince was so sweaty that he looked as if he'd just come in from a rainstorm. He didn't bother looking at Cam, who was sitting on one of the mattresses, hugging his knees and trying to look small. Vince just scowled at Renee, Ian, and Erica.

Finally, he threw his hands up. "I'm going to check for food." He stomped over to the panel on the wall. Pulling it open, he glared inside. After seeing it was empty, he slammed it shut. He stood there for a moment, breathing heavily, and then punched the panel in frustration. Muttering under his breath, he stormed off to the bathroom.

They were silent for about ten seconds. Erica was suddenly keenly aware of her arm around Ian's naked waist. He was warm and solid. Casting about for something to say, she casually asked, "So did you do any exploring?"

Ian said, "We looked around a bit. It's basically the same room, but the door isn't locked this time. There's another spiral staircase outside."

Erica shivered. "How many rooms like this do they have?"

"I don't know, but I doubt this is the last," Ian said grimly. He gestured at the digital display on the wall. "The display says zero, so it's not a thermometer this time. But I don't see any threat."

"Doesn't matter. We're not sticking around." Erica glanced toward the bathroom. "I hope Vince hurries."

Denise nodded, though she winced when she did. The neck wound seemed to be bothering her, but there was nothing else Erica could think of to help her.

The lights began to dim. "Hurry up, Vince! We have to go," Erica said loudly in the direction of the bathroom.

"Yeah, yeah." Vince pushed back the curtain. In the faint light, they could barely see him.

"Having the lights out might be an advantage," Ian said. "Better for sneaking around." He offered a hand to help Cam off the mattress.

When they opened the exit, they realized they had a problem. There was no lighting at all in the stairway. Even with the door open to let in the dim light from the mattress room, the stairway up only appeared to be a slightly blacker bit in the blackness.

"We can't go up there," Renee said. "I can't see anything."

She was right, but if they were going to have any chance of surprising their captors—which Erica was becoming more doubtful of by the moment—they couldn't wait. "There might be light in the room above. I'm going to check it out."

"I'll go with you," Ian said, grabbing her hand.

"No," Erica said. She made her face look confident, but on the inside, her heart was going into overdrive. "It's going to be hard enough climbing that staircase in the pitch dark without worrying about tripping on you. You guys wait here. I'll go alone."

She couldn't make out Ian's expression, but she could hear doubt in his voice. "Are you—?"

"Yes," she said firmly and, arms outstretched, she shuffled into the stairway.

The room was small enough that finding the handrail was easy. It felt rough and unfinished. She slid her foot forward until her shin bumped against the bottom step. Her eyes hadn't adjusted to the darkness at all for some reason. She still couldn't see anything.

Keeping one hand on the rail and one hand on the post at the center of the spiral staircase, Erica raised her foot to the bottom step. The darkness was oppressive, like she was trapped in a crypt, imprisoned behind a heavy stone door.

She closed her eyes, and it seemed to help. It didn't hinder her at all, and at least she could imagine that she was just ascending a brightly lit staircase with her eyes closed.

So much could go wrong. If a stair was missing, she wouldn't know. She'd fall and break her leg. Or what if there was a cougar in the room above, but it was too dark to see? The shudder that rippled through her was so strong it almost made her miss a step.

Erica pushed the thoughts out of her mind, focusing on lifting her feet, one methodical step at a time.

Eventually, she reached for the next step and found nothing. She must be on the landing at the top. When she opened her eyes, it was the same as if they were closed. Why had she said she would to do this? She'd never been in darkness this black before.

Dropping to her hands and knees, she crawled on the landing until she found the door, and then felt her way up to the handle.

Standing, she turned the knob with a shaking hand, her heart in her throat.

CHAPTER NINE

Erica's ears strained to hear anything as she swung the door open a crack, but the hinges were completely silent. She still couldn't see anything. Was the door even open?

She reached forward, fingers questing. Yes, there was a crack of a few inches. Erica's heart fell. There must be no lights in room. No matter how much she strained, she saw nothing but blackness.

But was there an animal there, a cat that could see in the dark, even now staring at her, standing up, creeping silently toward her?

With a shiver, she closed the door and leaned against the wall, her head slumping. They couldn't continue. Anything could be in the next room. Going in there blind would be suicide.

She crawled back to the stairway and descended it backward as she would a ladder. Near the bottom, she could just see the grey rectangle of the open door. After the complete absence of light, it felt like a sunny day.

Erica sighed in relief as she slipped through the doorway. The other clustered around her.

Ian squeezed her hand. "What was up there?"

Erica shook her head. "Another door. I was able to open it, but there are no lights at all. Pitch black."

"If the door's unlocked, we should go," Vince said. "I'm not scared of the dark."

"Neither am I," Erica said, though her heart was still racing. "I'm scared of what's in the dark. I seriously couldn't see a thing. What if there's another wild animal?"

"We can't go in there blind," Denise said. "Not after the last room."

Renee nodded.

Vince stared at Denise in the dim light for a few seconds. "Fine. If you guys are too scared, I won't abandon you. You'd never get out." He turned, walked to the mattresses, and sat.

Denise followed and sat beside him, her knee almost touching his. "Yeah. We have to work as a team. It's pretty clear now that this is some sort of test, and I think it's testing whether we can cooperate to overcome challenges. Let's show them that we'll stick together regardless of what they throw at us." She put her arm around Vince's shoulders, squeezed him, and released him again.

The others sat down on two of the other mattresses.

"I agree that we need to co-operate," Ian said, "but this seems extreme if that's all they're testing."

"More likely it's the opposite," said Vince, his eyes studiously avoiding Denise's. "They limited our food and put a predator in our path. If anything, this place is designed to weed out the weaklings."

Renee scowled at him. "And I suppose the weaklings would be anyone who's short and not as physically strong. You think it's designed to kill women?" Her tone almost dared Vince to say that was what he meant.

Vince stared back at her. "You said it, not me. But I'm not going to pretend it's anything other than what it is, even if the truth does get your panties in a knot." He looked toward Ian as if hoping for confirmation. "It is what it is."

Ian deliberately turned away from Vince. "If that's all they're trying to figure out, then why bother? It's obvious who's the biggest and strongest. They wouldn't go through all this effort."

"What do you think it is, then?" Vince said.

"I don't know, but it's got to be more complicated than that. Maybe they put a drug in the food or in the air, and they're watching our reaction to it."

"A drug? I think I'd realize it if I'd been drugged." Vince rolled his eyes as he looked at Denise. She smiled back at him. "And why would they bother with the cougar and the heat if it was a drug?"

"Perhaps the drug is designed to help people in high-risk situations like combat. To make us smarter or improve our reflexes or something. It could be anything."

"Maybe it's what Denise said," Renee said. "Like, a drug designed to make us cooperate more."

"Or make us more likely to fight each other." In the faint light, Vince's sardonic grin looked demonic.

Ian sighed.

Erica remained quiet. She was still more than a little creeped out at the dark room above and wasn't in the mood for speculation. Privately, she was skeptical of all the theories—none seemed to explain Denise's injuries. Ian's drug hypothesis seemed the most plausible, but the cougar didn't fit well into that theory. It was just too dangerous. It could have killed any one of them—drug or no drug—and what would that prove? Unless the animal was a drug-induced mass hallucination brought on by their earlier discussions about Alex's death. But it had *seemed* real.

Finally, they decided to go to bed. It was a moment that Erica had been anticipating and dreading all day. Just sitting and chatting with shirtless Ian was hard enough. Even in the dim light, her eyes kept trying to wander from his face across his toned body. Once, Renee had caught Erica zoned out in a daydream, staring at Ian's chest, imagining what his skin would feel like touching her own. The look she gave Erica was poison.

They all went to their own mattresses, but Erica couldn't relax. This was the time she was supposed to talk with Ian, but he hadn't come over to her bed as he had earlier. Should she go to him?

It seemed so forward, but it was what they'd agreed. Marshalling her courage, Erica crept over to Ian and slipped down beside him. If anyone noticed, they didn't comment.

Ian embraced her. She shivered at the feeling of his warm, bare skin against her.

"Hi," Ian whispered.

"Hi," Erica murmured. All day she had been yearning for the chance to talk with him privately, and now she didn't know what to say.

"Did you get a chance to explain everything to Renee?" he said.

"Yeah. She's a bit uncomfortable with it. You know, her brother and her best friend. But she gets it. She'll deal."

"She knows we're just friends, right?"

"Um, yes. Of course." She pulled away from Ian and lay on her back beside him for a few seconds, rigid, barely breathing. Only her arm touched his.

Ian rolled onto his side, holding his head on his hand, and gently brushed the back of his other hand across her cheek and along her neck. Involuntarily, Erica reacted. Her whole body relaxed. It was as if all the nervousness, tension, uncertainty, and fear that had accumulated over the past days were dispelled in an instant by Ian's light touch.

Erica turned to face him and daringly ran her hand lightly across his chest. In the dark, she could see his faint smile as he pulled her into an embrace, nuzzling her neck. She felt closer to him than anyone she had ever touched before, as if she was about to melt into his body.

Then, once again, she remembered her promise to Renee and her stomach roiled. Although she could have sworn she didn't move at all, Ian seemed to read her turmoil through the multitude of places where their bodies touched.

"Don't worry," he whispered in her ear. "It's strange, but you're doing great with this act. I know you don't feel that way about me, but there's no way that whoever's watching wouldn't believe you were into me."

Breathlessly, she whispered, "It's so hard to pretend."

"I know." He paused, and then murmured, "I was just thinking. Everyone was so focused on Renee that nobody talked about what you did, facing that cougar. That was the bravest thing I've ever seen."

"I just imagined what would happen if it caught us from behind. I had to do something. Besides, you did it too."

"Only because of you. There was no way I'd leave you there to face it alone."

"I'm glad you did. It might not have worked if it was just me."

"Maybe, maybe not. It's odd the way things worked out." He paused once more and seemed to be thinking. "What do you think happened? With Denise's injuries, I mean."

Erica chewed on her lip. "I have no idea. Don't take this the wrong way, but something's different about Renee. Strange things are happening around her. Things that don't make sense. The injuries. Cracking the lock. Even her knowledge of cougars."

Ian's voice sounded pensive. "Yes, I agree. She was pretty freaked out when they found Alex last year, so maybe she looked up stuff on cougars on the Internet. But the other two things seem impossible."

"I know. For four days, we were trapped in that room. We knocked on all the walls, typed in countless codes, spent a whole day lighting the fire, and she could have had us out in two seconds. It doesn't make sense."

"Yet, I still believe what she said," Ian said, his voice a soft whisper against her cheek. "I trust her."

Erica thought that over for a few seconds. "Yeah, I've known her long enough to know what she sounds like when she's lying. I'm sure she was telling us the truth, even if the others don't think so."

Ian nodded. "I'm a bit worried about them. Vince seemed ready to go postal on us until he calmed down and thought it through. I think he's had it in for her ever since she stopped him from hogging all the pizza. He was giving her all these dirty looks even before she cracked the lock. And everything that's happened since has only made it worse." Ian shook his head. "It's hard to blame him for being suspicious, though. Frankly, if our situations were reversed, I'd probably have the same reaction he does."

"It's scary," Erica said. "He's always had a short fuse, and I feel like, with all the stress, he might crack and do something drastic. Maybe hurt her."

"Well, we'll have to make sure that doesn't happen."

"Yeah," Erica said. "Thank goodness Denise is here. He seems calmer when she's around." She felt that Denise wouldn't want her sharing the things she had said in the bathroom, but Erica wanted Ian's perspective. As a compromise between curiosity and concealment, she asked hesitatingly, "Do you think anything's happening between those two?"

"Between Denise and Vince? That would be strange." His eyes narrowed. "No. They are sitting beside each other a lot. But I think it's because you, Renee, and I already know each other so well that Denise and Vince feel like outsiders. So they hang out together instead of with us."

"Cam doesn't have that problem though. He didn't say much, but when he wasn't typing on that keypad, he was sitting with us."

"Well, what other option did he have? There was no way he'd go sit with Vince."

"Good point."

The conversation stopped for a minute. Finally, Ian whispered,

"Sleep now?"

"Yes, we probably should."

Ian began to move back, but then, he shifted toward her. Tenderly, he kissed her. For a moment, it felt like the entire universe had faded away and nothing existed except the places where her body touched his. When he pulled away, she sighed.

"Goodnight, Erica."

She could scarcely breathe, and now he wanted her to speak? "Goodnight…"

#

Erica woke up pressed into Ian's back. Her arm was draped over his, her hand resting on his bare stomach. Hastily, while still trying to appear casual in case someone was watching, she turned around, but nobody seemed awake enough to notice how she'd been embracing him. When Denise and Vince sat up, they made a few comments about Erica and Ian sharing a mattress, but they didn't seem surprised. The look Renee gave them, on the other hand, seemed a bit cold, but it could have just been Erica's imagination.

Overnight, the number on the display had increased from zero to three. The temperature in the room didn't seem to have changed and they couldn't see anything different about the room, so they ignored it.

"The lights are on. Let's get going," Erica said. She looked at Ian. "Wake up Cam."

When Cam sat up, breakfast arrived. It was eight waffles with syrup, and everyone agreed that they should eat before leaving. On his second bite, Cam cried out and slapped his shin. In response to the others' quizzical looks, he held up the crushed body of a large ant. "This bit me."

They hadn't seen an insect in any of the other pristine white rooms. So they did a perimeter check, trying to determine where it had come from and whether there were other escape routes. In doing so, they found and crushed several more of the insects. Though they didn't have any real evidence, they eventually concluded that they must have come in under the door.

After their search, Denise opened the panel to the dumbwaiter a second time to reveal neatly folded clothes.

"Finally, I can get a shirt," Ian said. "I was getting a bit chilly."

"Erica will miss being able to stare at you half naked," Vince said.

Erica turned pink. "Denise needed a shirt, and it was his or yours. I think I made the right decision."

"You'll never know," Vince replied.

"I pray that's true," Erica said with a drop of revulsion in her tone. "I'm going to get changed, and then we need to go." Still blushing furiously—but certain she should make a hasty retreat while she was still somewhat ahead—she grabbed some clean clothes and headed for the bathroom.

They soon gathered at the top of the spiral staircase. After their experience with the cougar, they decided to be more careful opening the door. This time, Vince would open it enough to peer in. Then, he'd close the door if there was another wild animal or charge forward if they needed to surprise guards waiting in the room.

Vince did a silent countdown before opening the door a crack. After peering in for a couple seconds, he closed it, and turned toward the others.

"What is it, Vince?" Erica whispered.

"Please tell me it wasn't a cougar," Renee said. She was trembling.

His brow furrowed, Vincent shook his head. "No, not a cougar."

Renee exhaled. "Thank goodness."

Vince looked straight at Renee. "A tiger," he grimly said.

Renee's eyes widened and the blood drained from her face. Her knees giving out, she crumpled to the floor.

Denise and Erica went down on their knees, rolling Renee over onto her back.

"Oops," Ian said, wincing. "I guess I should have caught her."

"Oops," Vince said with a slight smile. "I guess I shouldn't have said there was a tiger."

"What!" Erica said. "You're joking?" Her jaw dropped. "How could you?" She attempted to rearrange Renee's jumbled limbs into a more natural position.

Vince tried to hide his smirk. "Well, yes. She seemed so tense. And really, it's kind of funny."

"Maybe she's tense because she got mauled by a cougar, then you accused her—" Erica didn't complete her thought as Renee's eyes fluttered open. "Don't try to move, Ren. Just lie there for a minute or two."

Renee groaned. "A tiger? And I thought a cougar was bad."

"Don't worry. Vince was messing with you. There is no tiger," Ian said.

"What?" Renee said. She shook her head. Relying on Erica for support, she sat up.

"Yeah, I was just joking."

"Good joke," Renee said flatly. Erica could see she was furious. "So what's in there then?"

Vincent shrugged. "It's mostly empty, except for some strange pyramid in the center."

"Like in Egypt?" Cam looked up, his eyes excited. "I love pyramids."

"Other than the fact that it's black, looks like smooth plastic rather than stone blocks, and is way smaller. Yes, it's exactly like the pyramids in Egypt," Vince sarcastically replied.

A wide grin lit Cam's entire face. "Cool! I always wanted to see those. Now I don't need to fly all the way to Europe. Did you see a sphinx?"

"Um. No," Vince replied, clearly too baffled by Cam's reply to make a snarky comment.

"Too bad," Cam mournfully said.

"Let's go look," Ian said. "More likely than not, it's a trap. So be careful."

Vincent cautiously opened the door. On the floor in the center of the room was the pyramid, its top about as high as Erica's shoulders. It was black, so dark it seemed to suck the light from the rest of the room, and had a shiny, metallic cap that drew the eye like the tip of a spear. On the far wall was an exit with a sliding door, similar to the one in the original room.

"You know, I'm not at all curious about the pyramid. Let's just avoid it and get through that door," Erica said.

"Agreed," Ian said. "No need to make trouble."

From his expression, Cam seemed miffed at the suggestion, but he didn't argue. They gave the pyramid a wide berth as they crept over to the door. When they arrived, they realized that, unlike the last sliding door, this one didn't have a keypad. In its place was a tiny, white panel, no more than an inch square.

"Got to try it," Vince said. He tapped the panel and then pushed as hard as he could. Nothing happened. He half-heartedly pushed on the door, but it didn't budge.

Erica sighed.

"I suppose the pyramid it is," Ian said fatalistically. Everyone nodded. Nobody was surprised.

Cautiously, they moved toward the monolith, ready to react the instant anything happened. They were all so tentative that almost a minute passed before they were gathered around it.

Up close, the pyramid didn't look any different—smooth black plastic, capped by a shiny, silver tip. They studied it warily for a few seconds. To Erica, the large, black shape in the midst of all that white seemed both intimidating and ominous, like a pagan monument for a cruel god.

Eventually, Vince said, "So I guess we have to touch it." He looked to Denise and Ian. "Shall I?"

"Yes," Ian said.

"No, wait," Denise rushed out. "Let's stand back and throw something. Not to be paranoid, but it's got to be a trap, right? It could be electrified or something."

"What should I throw?" Vince asked, glancing around the otherwise empty room.

"How about some of the dirty clothes?" Renee suggested.

"Yeah, that would work," Vince said.

Vince and Denise went downstairs, grabbed some shirts, and returned. They all stood back five yards as Vince crumpled a shirt into a ball.

He crouched down slightly, raised his arms, and tossed the shirt as if he were shooting a free throw. It opened up, caught the air, and fell short. "Lighter than I expected," he said as he bent to retrieve it.

"I think you've been neglecting arm day," Ian said. At Erica's quizzical glance, he mimed lifting weights.

For his second try, Vincent rolled up the shirt and tied it in a knot. "This should work better." As he crouched again, images flashed through Erica's mind.

The shirt arcing through the air. Hitting the metal tip. Nozzles poking out. Dark gas shooting in all directions.

As the shirt arced through the air, Erica instinctively took a deep breath and held it. Just as in her vision, the shirt hit the pyramid. The metal tip popped up, revealing eight nozzles. Black gas exploded outwards.

In less than a second, they were enveloped.

CHAPTER TEN

Still holding her breath, Erica raced toward the entrance of the room with the others close on her heels. When they were all out, she slammed the door shut and began to breathe again. Though the air looked clear, it smelled moldy and sour, as if she had opened a container of yogurt that had been in sitting in the sun too long.

"Downstairs, to the other room," Ian commanded. Nobody argued. Trying to race down the spiral staircase was nerve-racking, but they made it without any stumbles. As soon as they were all in the room with the mattresses, Ian closed that door, too, and continued to try to get as far away as possible, sprinting to the other exit.

"We should keep going," Vince said. He flung open the door to the room with the cougar.

"No!" Renee shouted. Through the doorway, Erica saw the cougar rise and start walking toward them.

"If we go together, the cougar can't get all of us. That gas might," Vince said.

"We'll never make it. Close the door!" Renee tugged on his arm, trying to pull the door shut.

It was futile. With contemptuous ease, Vince planted his other hand on Renee's upper chest and pushed. She fell backward, skidding several feet along the floor. The cougar quickened its pace.

Vince looked at the others, but no one stepped forward to enter the room with the cat. His brow furrowed. He looked into the room, his muscles tensing as if he were going to try to make it by himself.

Seconds before the cougar reached them, Vince closed the door. He shook his head. "We should have gone."

"Too late now," Ian said. "It's right there."

"Only because you guys were too slow," Vince said, his tone conveying his frustration. "We have to move faster."

"The bathroom," Denise said, the words tumbling off her tongue. "The curtain might provide some protection." She took two quick steps in that direction and then paused to look back at the others.

Erica shook her head. "That's a waste of time. We need to block the crack under the door."

"No, don't go over there," Denise said, grabbing at Erica's arm. "That's where the gas will be."

"We need stop it from getting in," Erica said.

"I'm not doing it," Vince said.

Erica scowled at him. "We don't have time to argue." While the others hung back, Renee, Ian, and she raced to the clothes and stuffed them into the crack. Erica couldn't tell whether the air near the door smelled normal, or she had become used to its musty scent. She imagined that with each breath, she was inhaling dark specks of pollen that were even now sprouting in her lungs, eating into her chest, choking off her air. She pushed the image aside and worked faster.

"Thanks, guys," Denise said when they returned to the group. "How do you feel? Any pain or dizziness? Anything unusual?"

Everyone shook their heads. It didn't seem right to Erica to share her fears.

Renee looked around at the others and said anxiously, "What do you think the gas was?"

"Can't be nerve gas," Ian said. "In the movies, that takes effect instantly."

Erica's skin felt tight and grimy, as if she was slathered in mud that was slowly hardening. Was she imagining it or was that an effect of the gas? It must just be her imagination. She shivered as she tried to focus on the question. "If it were tear gas or chlorine or something like that, we'd know already."

"It smelled musty, like an old closet." Ian rubbed his forehead. "I guess it might still be a slow-acting poison. I would think we'd notice effects within a few hours though."

"Or a virus," Renee said. She frowned as she paced back and

forth. "We'll only know that when we get sick. We might seem fine now, but all be dead in two days."

Denise sighed and said, "Maybe I'm being optimistic, but couldn't it just be an inert black gas? Only a test. Intended to scare us, but do absolutely nothing?"

"The gas was black," Erica said, gnawing on her lip. "So either they didn't care if we saw it or they *wanted* us to see it. If they were going to poison us, I'm sure they could have found something that's invisible and put it in the ventilation system. Or tossed a canister into the room while we slept."

"Yes," Denise agreed, brightening. "I'm starting to think that this is the most likely explanation. Why go through all the effort of making a pyramid that shoots gas when someone touches it? They want to mess with our heads, so they use this dark gas to make us freak out, but it does nothing."

Vince nodded, but Renee rolled her eyes. "If someone took a dump on your lawn, you'd call it fertilizer, Miss Sunny Sunshine." She shook her head. "The cougar wasn't harmless. They don't care if we get hurt. The question isn't whether the gas will be toxic. It's how toxic it will be."

Denise frowned, and Vincent's brow furrowed dangerously. Denise looked about to say something, but then squawked. She flicked out her foot and stamped on the floor. "Another ant."

"Maybe the gas is for the bugs, not us. They're just trying to eliminate their pest problem," Ian said with a wry smile.

"They're all over the place again," Renee said. "So gross." She raced around the room, squishing them with a paper plate and dropping the corpses in the toilet. Meanwhile, the rest of them pulled the mattresses into a circle far from the door and continued to speculate about what the gas could be. The list ranged from instantly fatal poisons to hallucinogens. As the minutes ticked by, the possibilities shrank as they eliminated substances that would have had a noticeable effect already.

They were in the middle of discussing knockout gas when Erica slapped her neck "Ouch! Stupid ant. It really hurts."

Denise and Cam nodded. A bright red bump was still visible on Denise's foot where she had been bitten earlier.

"The ant came from the ceiling. I saw it land on you," Ian said. He looked up and then twisted his torso around to gaze at the display, which now said eight. "Of course. The first room was heat. This room is ants. They're coming from those holes in the ceiling."

"But what does eight meant?" Cam said.

"Eight ants per second?" Ian said.

"Not that fast," Erica said. "Maybe eight ants per hour. But increasing."

Denise shivered. Her eyes were round. "That's horrible! My foot still aches and my neck hurts too. We need to get out of here before it gets any worse."

"Sure. Cougar or toxic gas? Which would you prefer?" Ian said as if he were a waiter offering a choice between tea and coffee. Denise's face fell.

After a brief discussion, they concluded that, for now, the ants were the least of the three evils. They'd tolerate them for another couple of hours to provide enough time for the gas above to dissipate or symptoms to become apparent.

While Renee continued her ant patrol, the rest of them brainstormed strategies for opening the exit upstairs. They were all convinced there was a way to escape. They simply needed to find it. Thanks to Renee's efforts, none of them was bitten again. But, after talking for about half an hour, Denise began to shiver. Vince wrapped a sheet around her shoulders, and she smiled gratefully at him.

When lunch arrived, the discussion slowed. This time, the meal was a chicken, rice, and vegetable stir fry in two large bowls.

They were sitting on the mattresses, mostly finished eating, when Renee stopped abruptly, a panicked expression on her face. "Oh no. Is anyone else feeling sick?"

Everyone halted, eyes wide. Erica vocalized what they were all thinking. "It must be the gas. But it seemed to come on so suddenly." Her eyes widened. "Or could they have poisoned lunch?"

"I feel fine," Vince said.

"Me too," Ian said, and the other three nodded.

Renee's neck was bulging. "I've got to go." She ran to the bathroom. Through the curtain, they could hear the sound of her vomiting.

"Should we do the same," Erica said, her face pale, "even if we feel okay now? If the food was poisoned…" She stood up to check on Renee.

Ian shook his head. "It's almost certainly the gas, and we can't afford to waste this meal if it's fine." He looked at Cam. "You were sharing with her. How do you feel?"

"I'm hungry," Cam said, looking down regretfully at the chicken and rice.

"But not sick?"

"No. Hungry."

Erica was about to turn toward the bathroom when her eyes drifted over the bowl in Cam's hand. "Wait a minute. It's not poison. Look at what she was eating."

"Yeah, stir fry. So what?" Vince demanded.

"It has bean sprouts," Erica said. "Renee's allergic, remember? She's refused to eat them since that time at my house."

"I guess she was starving and didn't look closely," Denise said.

Renee lurched back into the room and threw herself down onto a mattress beside Erica. "Hey Ren, I've figured it out, and it wasn't the gas," Erica said. She held up the bowl to her friend. "Look what you ate."

Renee sat up and looked. "It's still stir fry," she replied, her face blank. "What's your point?"

"There are bean sprouts. See?"

"Yes. I don't see why that's so strange. Do you think that they're rotten?" Renee poked at one of them. "They seem fine to me."

"Aren't you allergic to them or something?" Erica asked even though she knew the answer.

Renee frowned. "What makes you say that?"

Erica's eyes grew wide.

"Now do you guys realize she's either not Renee or is completely nuts?" Vince said, his tone implying that he knew it all along.

Renee looked puzzled at the sudden shift in the conversation, and then angry. "What are you talking about, Vince? I'm crazy because I don't have an allergy? Why does that make any difference at all?"

Before Vince could reply, Ian gently said, "You've been allergic to bean sprouts your whole life. Vince is surprised you don't remember that."

With raised eyebrows, Renee looked at Erica. She nodded.

"We ought to throw her back to the cougar," Vince said righteously.

Erica didn't think he was serious, but even the suggestion caused

Renee to gasp and leap to her feet. "No!"

"Hold on a minute!" Ian barked. "We're not going to do anything like that. Vince is just messing with you, Ren."

Vincent shrugged. "I wasn't serious, but maybe we should. She wouldn't die. Her pals would save her, and we wouldn't need to worry about her spying on us anymore."

"But it doesn't make sense," Erica said. "We need figure this out. Renee's our friend."

"Yeah, right. Our 'friend'." Vince's hands made air quotes.

"No, listen to me. If she's not Renee, why is she allergic at all?"

Ian nodded. "And if she was pretending to be sick, why would she forget the thing she was pretending?" He shook his head. "Now I'm confusing myself. In any case, it doesn't add up."

"Maybe we should play the twenty questions game again," Denise said, making eye contact with the others. "It's the easiest way for her to prove she is who she says."

Everyone agreed, with Vince as eager to prove Renee's guilt as Renee was to prove her innocence. They asked her questions for half an hour. Everything they could think of that they'd done or seen together was fair game.

Eventually, all of them, even Vince, were convinced that Renee was herself. She seemed to have gaps in her memory, incidents so significant that Erica thought Renee ought to have remembered them. Yet despite those gaps, she correctly answered four out of every five of the questions they asked.

After much discussion, Ian slapped his forehead. "Of course!" he said. "She fell hard when the cougar landed on her. I think I saw her head hit the floor. She must have gotten concussed."

"Don't you mean that Denise should be concussed, then?" Vince sarcastically said.

"Yeah, whatever," Ian said, his voice tight. "I don't know what's going on with Denise, but it explains Renee's memory lapses."

"It does make sense," Denise said. She grimaced. "I remember wincing when I saw her head bounce off the concrete. And there's no other explanation. Don't you agree?" Her wide-eyed glance at Vince, sitting beside her on the mattress, seemed completely guileless.

Vincent frowned. He stared at Denise for a few seconds, turning a bit pink. "I don't really know. It's possible," he said in an uncharacteristic spasm of reasonableness. "In any case, we've waited long enough. Renee's fine. We need to go open that door upstairs."

Everyone nodded. Erica wasn't convinced that Vince had truly put aside his differences with Renee, but at least his anger seemed to have dissipated. They quickly finished off their food and prepared to return upstairs.

The group had settled on three tactics. First, if the pyramid wasn't attached to the floor, they'd use it as a battering ram. If that failed, they'd use a spring from a mattress to pry the panel open to see what was behind it. As a final option, they would try to determine how the gas came out of the pyramid and investigate whether there was a mechanism within the pyramid that would open the door. Throughout their investigations, they would use their discarded clothes as a filter over their mouths to guard against any gas.

When they returned upstairs, the black gas had dissipated and the silver cap on the pyramid had returned to its original position. Erica crept close to the massive object, knelt down, and inspected its base, careful not to touch the pyramid itself. There was a small gap around the bottom.

"The pyramid's not a part of the floor," Erica reported. "Unless it's locked down somehow, we might be able to move it."

"So do we just grab it and not worry about the gas?" Denise asked. This topic had been discussed at length downstairs. Vince was the chief proponent of just doing it, Renee was reluctant to do so because of possible consequences, and the rest of them were somewhere in the middle.

"Just avoid the metal part," Vince said. "That's what set it off last time."

"But it might not only be triggered by the tip," Renee said

Vince stared at her like she couldn't tell a cat from a caterpillar and he needed to explain it to her in simple words. "That's why we have the masks, remember? Besides, we've already been drenched with the gas. If it was going to kill us, we'd already be dead."

"Yes, but—"

"Hey, wait a minute," Ian interrupted. Clearly bored by the rehashing of arguments they had already covered in painstaking detail, he was staring at the exit. "Look!" Ian pointed at a dark spot on the wall beside the door.

Both pyramid and argument forgotten, they went to investigate. The tiny panel beside the door had slid open. The top half of the area behind it was a smooth, gray plastic surface while the lower part was a dark hole.

"Maybe triggering the pyramid made this open?" Erica theorized.

"Makes sense," Ian said. "Or perhaps our captors just did it." He knelt down to peer into the hole.

Cam reached toward the gray area. "That's probably a button that opens the door."

"No!" everyone shouted, but they were too slow. Cam pushed it with his index finger. It didn't move, and the door remained shut.

Cam froze. "Oops. I guess that was a bad idea. I could have set off another trap." Everyone seemed to exhale at the same time.

"At least we know now that it doesn't do anything," Renee said ruefully.

"It has to do something," Denise said. "Otherwise, why have a panel at all?"

Erica was about to suggest poking something into the hole when Cam arrived at the same conclusion. "Maybe there's a latch," he said. He stuck in his finger.

A loud click resonated throughout the room, and Cam cried out. "Something stabbed me!" He jerked back his hand, held it up, and peered at his index finger. A drop of blood quivered on its tip. He thrust his finger in his mouth.

"Look," Vince said, pointing at the hole. The gray area was apparently an LCD panel because upon it were the words:

Healthy
1/6

"Interesting," Erica said, rubbing her lips together. "The door thinks you're at one-sixth health."

"That doesn't seem very healthy," Cam dolefully said.

"No," Ian agreed. He frowned. "I wonder why the message says 'Healthy', then."

"There are six of us…" Denise said. She rubbed her index finger against her front teeth.

"Yes!" Vince said. "It's counting how many of us have been tested."

"And when we've all done it, the door will open," Denise exclaimed. She beamed at Vince.

"Wait a minute," Erica said, holding up a hand. "Those are huge assumptions. We don't even know this thing is doing a blood test.

Maybe it injected something into Cam and displayed the message to fool us. And even if it is a test, that doesn't necessarily mean that if we pass, the door will open."

"Yes," Ian said. "We shouldn't all rush to get stuck with needles. Who knows what that thing does?"

"You're right to be cautious, but they could have poisoned us anytime," Denise said, her tone reasonable. "I suspect it's just checking whether the gas affected us."

Ian looked at Renee, pursing his lips. "Maybe we don't need to play this game at all. You hotwired the electronics in the other door. Can you do the same thing to this one?"

Renee stared back at him in disbelief. "Of course not. The last one was an out-of-the-box system with videos on the Internet explaining how to open it. I've never seen anything like this before in my entire life. I can't imagine that you can buy a blood-testing door lock at the corner store. It's got to be custom made."

Ian blushed. "Well, after last time, I figured…"

"Totally different," Renee said. "That said, we shouldn't let that thing poke us without knowing exactly what it does. We're just speculating that it will open the door."

"It's deduction, not speculation," Denise said. "They've had plenty of time to stick us with whatever harmful needles they could dream up. Therefore—"

Denise was interrupted by a loud click as Vince stuck his finger in the hole. He winced as he pulled out his finger, the tip red. He rubbed the blood off on his pants, and the bleeding immediately stopped.

"I'm tired of talking for hours about everything we do. Constantly gabbing about poison or drugs or whatever else they might be throwing at us. I'm not going to live my life like a terrified squirrel," Vince said, looking at Denise, "so I figured I'd save us all some time."

Denise swallowed, shifted from foot to foot, and nervously rubbed her right hand against her leg. She put her left hand on his arm. "Oh Vince. I think you'll be fine, but I wish we had all decided to do it together."

Vince looked back at her with a level gaze. "It had to be done. It's the same as trying the food in the first room and getting past the cougar. Someone had to do it first, so I did."

"I thought I did it first," Cam muttered, peering at his finger.

Either no one heard Cam or everyone ignored him. They stared at the screen, waiting for the verdict.

Healthy

2/6

"That answers that question," Vince said with a smile on his face that implied he never had a doubt. "It's how many of us have been tested."

"But that doesn't mean—" Erica said.

"I'm with Vince. Enough discussion. I want to get out of here," Denise said. She spoke the words fearlessly, but Erica noticed her hand trembling as she shoved her finger in the hole.

The machine clicked, and Denise squeaked. She frowned at Vince, punching him in the shoulder. "Hey, you didn't say it hurt so much!"

"Well, I'm not a girl," Vince explained, his tone tolerant.

Denise examined her finger. Blood welled out of the pinprick, much more than there had been with the others. "A bleeder too, apparently," she said ruefully, rubbing her hand on her pants.

Renee's gasp interrupted the conversation. They stared at her and then followed her gaze. The display had turned red.

Quarantine

3/6

CHAPTER ELEVEN

Everyone studied Denise. She was shaking.

Renee began to put her arm around her and then stopped. "Don't worry, Denise, you'll be fine. Do you feel normal?" She shifted back a step.

"I'm still cold. And my muscles ache," Denise quietly said.

Vince moved closer to her and raised his hand. "Let me feel your forehead."

"Wait," Erica said, grabbing for Vince's forearm. "It's probably a virus from the gas."

Renee nodded. "She could be contagious."

Vince gazed at her and thought for a few seconds. "We've been sitting together for a few hours and we all inhaled the same gas." Erica hadn't, but it seemed like a bad time to correct him. "If she has something contagious, we're all infected by now. I'll risk it." He put his hand to Denise's forehead for a few seconds. "You're warm."

"I don't feel warm. It feels like it's twenty degrees in here."

"Does anyone else feel cold or sick?" Ian asked. Other than Denise, everyone shook their heads.

"We should test ourselves anyway," Erica said. Nervously, she shuffled to the door. She rubbed her index finger on her shirt before sticking it in the hole.

Though she was expecting it, Erica still flinched as the needle stabbed her. The pain was no worse than getting her ears pierced and faded immediately. She stuck her finger in her mouth, anxiously looking at the display.

Healthy
4/6

Erica exhaled. "Thank goodness." She glanced at Denise, her face slightly pink. "Um, I'm sorry."

"Don't worry about it. I'd be relieved too." Denise abruptly sat cross-legged on the floor. "I need to sit. My head's spinning." She placed her elbows on her knees and rested her forehead on her hands.

"Just relax. We'll only be a second," Ian said. He strode forward and shoved his finger into the hole. After a few seconds, the machine returned a healthy verdict.

The result was the same for Renee. She squatted down near Denise, but not so close that she ran any risk of touching the sick girl. "So it's just you."

"Looks that way."

Erica looked down at Denise, frowning. "Can you keep going? We can't wait around. We can still try smashing the door."

Denise sighed. "I'm not sure. I can try." She struggled to push herself up, and then collapsed again. "I'll need a minute."

Ian shook his head. "You can barely move. Let's go downstairs and you can lie down," he said. He looked at Erica. "I know you want to hurry, but we don't have a choice. Besides, if we're quarantined, that door isn't opening until she's better."

Mentally, Erica added, *Or dead.* Sighing, she nodded.

They had a brief discussion over whether they should stay there and avoid the ants. But they decided that, in the short term, dealing with the insects was less risky than being near the pyramid when it went off again. They trooped downstairs, Vince half-carrying the sick girl, and settled Denise on a mattress. The ant counter was up to twenty.

"I find it strange that it's only her. Maybe one of the claw marks from the cougar got infected," Renee speculated as she paced.

"Let me see your neck," Vince said. He lifted Denise's hair. Her neck was garish purple. "Doesn't seem any better." He looked toward Erica. "Are the bruises worse than this morning?"

"They do look darker than before. Maybe the light's different," Erica offered in a low voice, though she knew that made no sense. The light in one part of the room was no brighter than any other part.

"Can I see your back?" Vince said. His voice was wobbly, like that of a twelve-year-old asking a girl to the school dance for the first time.

Her face slightly pink, Denise nodded, rolling over onto her stomach. Vince raised the back of her shirt. He gasped.

"What?" Denise asked fearfully. "Are the cuts infected?"

"No," Vincent said, quickly tugging down her shirt. "They look pretty good."

Denise shook her head in confusion. "So I'm fine?"

"Yes," he responded, the words tumbling out. "You probably have the flu or something. You should cover up and stay in bed until you're better." He dragged the sheets on top of her and grabbed for another.

Ian and Erica exchanged a glance. They both had had a clear view of Denise's back.

"Don't lie to her," Ian said as he knelt down beside her. "She's not a kid. Denise, the cuts are fine. The scabs are starting to come off already. You healed super fast. But there are a bunch of red spots."

Vincent glowered at Ian, but Denise, still prone, wasn't looking at Vince. "What, like chicken pox?" she said.

"No," Vince said. "They're bigger, darker, and concentrated in two groups. Kind of like someone splattered dark red paint across a couple of places on your back. I didn't want you to worry."

Denise didn't respond to the explanation. She turned on her side, raised the bottom of her shirt, and looked down. Crimson splotches were splashed across her stomach too. She gaped.

"I don't know what it is, but you'll be fine," Vince said, his tone unusually bright. "I've had bruises like that before. Under your shirt, nobody will see them. They hurt for a day or two and fade away."

"I'm not sure those are bruises," Erica said. "They're bigger and maroon, not purple."

Denise sat up and weakly said, "What do you think it is? Has anyone seen anything like this before?"

Everyone shook their heads except Cam. Denise looked questioningly at him.

He said, "This kid in my preschool had something like that on his neck."

"What caused it?" Ian asked.

"They said he was born with it. He got the thing fixed in the hospital."

"So it was probably something else, right Cam?" Denise gently asked.

Cam nodded. "Yeah. Maybe."

"Do the spots hurt?" Erica inquired.

"Not the spots specifically. Just my whole body." Denise sounded weary.

"You should lie down and stay warm," Vince said. He pushed her back with perhaps more force than was necessary considering her weakened state. Tugging sheets over her, he said to the others, "And you guys need to stop asking her questions. Go over there. Give her some space and a chance to relax."

Erica and Ian exchanged a quizzical glance. They'd never conceived of Vince trying to take care of someone. It was like a piranha trying to comfort a baby otter.

Erica looked to Denise for confirmation of what she wanted, but her eyes were shut. Ian shrugged and walked with the two girls to the other side of the room. Cam tagged along behind them.

"Does anyone else have those things?" Erica asked quietly, trying not to disturb Denise. Everyone did a quick inspection. They found no evidence of similar marks on anyone else.

Ian sat, leaning against the wall. "So, any thoughts about what it could be?"

"I think Denise is right that it's not a birth mark," Cam offered, joining Ian on the floor. "Maybe that black gas had something to do with it?"

Ian looked like he was resisting the temptation to say something sarcastic. "Yes, that seems likely." He looked at Renee and Erica. "Do you think it's a poison or a disease? Or something else?"

"She has a fever," Renee muttered, half to herself. Her pace had quickened. "To me, that suggests she's sick."

Ian nodded. "That was my first thought too. But those spots aren't measles or chicken pox."

Renee stopped, turning toward the others. "They are kind of like Ebola though. With that, ruptured blood vessels underneath the skin often cause spotting."

Erica knew the word, but that was about all. "Ebola?" she asked.

"It's a disease that's arisen in Africa a few times. Some of the symptoms include vomiting, bleeding, stomach pains, coughing, headaches, and nausea."

"Gee, is that all?" Ian sarcastically said. "It sounds like it basically has every symptom ever created."

"No," Renee quietly answered. "Also seizures, coma, and death. In some outbreaks, the fatality rate has been ninety percent."

"Can we do something? Like, give her medicine?" Erica asked. She knew how ridiculous the question was the instant it was out of her mouth. Looking down, she crushed an ant that was approaching her hand.

"Even in hospitals, they don't have a reliable treatment. Here, there's nothing. Just give her water, I guess."

"Is it contagious?" Erica said, glancing nervously back toward where the girl was lying.

"It's communicated through body fluids. Blood and vomit, mostly. Though in labs, scientists have transmitted it through water droplets in the air."

Ian's shoulders slumped. "The gas…"

Renee sighed. "Yeah, the gas. That is, if it even is Ebola."

A fierce bout of coughing from Denise interrupted their conversation. When she stopped, they saw her lips move. Vince picked her up and raced off into the bathroom. The sound of vomiting came from behind the thin curtain.

"We should warn him," Renee said. She walked over to the bathroom and poked her head through the curtain. "Vince, you should get out of those clothes and wash off. The infection might be transmitted by her vomit."

They heard a muffled curse and the sound of the shower. Renee grabbed Vince's clothes from the previous day, tossed them into the room, and returned to the others.

"So is there really nothing we can do?" Erica asked. It felt wrong, as if they were just sitting there, waiting for Denise to die.

"No," Renee said. "Just wait, squish a few ants, and hope she gets better."

"How long will that take?" Ian asked.

"A week. Maybe two or three."

Erica frowned, glancing at the number on the wall. "We can't wait that long. We have to go. Besides, if this is anything like the last room, by that time, there will be thousands of ants raining down on us."

Ian sighed. "But if the disease is that deadly, we can't risk moving upstairs and getting someone else infected." He shook his head. "Not until we absolutely have to."

After a brief discussion, they reluctantly agreed to live with the ants for now, and, if it became intolerable before Denise was better, they'd consider other options. To reduce the risk of infection, they hauled five of the mattresses away from Denise's.

After a few minutes, Vince returned, carrying the sick girl. He raised his eyebrows when he saw the rearrangements. He put Denise down gently, covered her with the sheets, and walked over to the others.

"So. New living arrangements?" he asked. His voice was dangerously coarse.

Ian stood up. "We're trying to avoid catching what she has. It's safer if we're separated," he soothingly said.

"Why don't you just abandon her? That's your next plan, right?" He glared at Ian and Renee.

"No," Erica firmly responded. "We never even considered leaving. Regardless of what happens, we're all in this together." Everyone else nodded.

"Good," Vince said. He looked accusingly at Erica. "We shouldn't give up on her just because she has the flu."

"It may be more than that," Renee said. In a low voice, she shared what she suspected about the disease.

Vince listened to her explanation and said, "And when did you become a doctor? You're speculating that she has this thing, right?" He glowered at Renee. "That a disease from Africa is somehow here in Idaho?"

Renee pursed her lips. "Well, yes. It's a guess. But her symptoms match."

"So maybe it is, maybe it isn't. But we will take care of her until she gets better." Vince's tone was halfway between a question and an order.

Everybody nodded. "Of course," Ian said. "We've already said that. But we should still do what we can to avoid being infected ourselves."

Vince shook his head. "You know, she puked all over me. And that didn't bother me that much. God knows I've cleaned up enough puke in my life. But if the disease is transmitted by vomit, it's already too late. I'll get it or I won't, and I can't do anything about it now. So I won't leave her by herself while she's going through all this. I'm with her." He marched to his mattress and pushed it over to Denise, not bothering to glance back.

But, if he expected the others to be shamed into following his lead, he was mistaken.

Vince took care of Denise throughout the rest of the day. Erica had never imagined that he could be so considerate of anyone. He carried her to the bathroom, brought water to her using the paper plates, and gave her his sheet when she was cold. She refused any offers of food.

Denise's condition did not improve. If anything, she got worse. Her coughing was much more frequent though weaker. The vomiting stopped, but only because nothing was left in her stomach to come up.

The others talked in low voices and did their best to guard against the ants. Eventually, the lights went out. Erica joined Ian on his mattress, but for the first time, she didn't find his close presence exhilarating. Perhaps Ian sensed the change in Erica's mood or maybe he was in a pensive frame of mind himself because he said nothing. He just pulled Erica into an embrace and held her.

"I don't think we're going to survive this," Erica whispered, struggling to keep her voice steady.

"The disease?"

"Everything. This place. They planned all of this. I was thinking about it this afternoon. Our attempt to escape is exactly what they wanted. I'd say we should just sit here, but then we'll roast or be eaten alive by insects. But is trying to escape any better? It only exposes us to more of these traps."

"We're surviving so far."

"Barely. Eventually, they'll kill us. One by one."

"We'll figure it out, Erica. We'll escape. Don't worry."

"I hope I'm not the last." She swallowed. "I don't want to be here alone."

Ian had no reply to that.

With Denise coughing, sleeping was challenging. But it was worse when she finally fell silent. Was she asleep or dead?

#

The night was difficult. Three times, Erica was woken by the burning bite of an ant, and twice by Ian flinching. Nevertheless, when the lights came up and Erica opened her eyes, she found herself nestled against Ian's neck, still encircled by his arms. She savored the warmth of his body for a few seconds until the events of the previous day flooded over her. She involuntarily cringed. That awoke Ian.

He contemplated her face for a few seconds and gave a slight smile. "Hello, Erica."

"Hi. Tough day yesterday."

Ian grimaced. "Yeah." He glanced at the wall. "Over two hundred ants an hour. We should check on Denise. Or get Vince—"

He was interrupted by Vince's voice. "Denise, wake up!" Glancing over, Erica saw Vince shake her, to no effect. "Denise, it's the morning. You need to wake up now."

Vince looked over at Ian, saw him rise, and said frantically, "Ian, she won't wake up." He turned his attentions back to the girl, becoming desperate. "Denise, wake up!"

He shook Denise so vigorously that Erica was worried he'd hurt her.

Her eyelids didn't even flutter.

CHAPTER TWELVE

"Check her pulse," Ian said as he raced to the bed.

Vince put his fingers on Denise's neck. It seemed like an eternity before he spoke. "Her heart is beating."

Ian knelt beside the bed. "Is she breathing?"

Vincent stared at her chest. "I can't tell."

Renee knelt beside them. It looked like she was about to touch Denise's neck, but then she pulled back. "Put your ear next to her mouth and listen."

Vince did so. "Yes, I can feel her breath. Why won't she wake up?"

Erica glanced toward Renee. "Didn't you say that falling into a coma was one possible effect of that disease?"

"Ebola," Renee replied with frown. "Yes. It is."

Vince seemed lost. "What should we do? How can we wake her up?"

Renee thought for a few seconds. "I don't think there's much we can do. Keep her comfortable. Move her around occasionally. Treat her like someone who's in a deep sleep."

Vince didn't reply. He half-heartedly pulled the sheets up around Denise. His movements were hesitant and awkward.

Ian stood. "We should check ourselves over for similar symptoms again. Especially you, Vince."

Vince stared at Ian dully, then mechanically pulled off his shirt and studied his body. "No spots," he said. The rest of them weren't displaying any symptoms either.

"I guess we were lucky," Cam said.

Vincent glowered at him. "Don't say that! How can you say that when Denise is lying there unconscious?"

Cam's eyes widened, and he began to tremble. He looked from Vince to the floor, to the others, and back to Vince. Finally, he shrugged, giving Vince an empathetic smile.

Vincent leaped to his feet. Cam held up his hands and tried to retreat, but Vince kept coming until he backed into the wall.

Vince seemed ready to throw a punch, but held back. "For that grin, you deserve to be laid out. Any other time, any other place, you'd be flat on your back on the ground now. But Denise said we have to stick together, and that's even truer now that she's sick. But take care. I can only be pushed so far."

Vince was shaking, whether from anger or the effort it took to stop himself from leveling Cam, Erica didn't know.

All the blood had drained from Cam's face. He said nothing, just cowered.

Vince sneered. "Yeah. That's right." He turned around and stomped back to Denise. Sitting down on the mattress beside her, he tucked an unruly lock of hair behind her ear. A trickle of blood dripped out of her nose and ran down her cheek.

Vince beckoned to Renee. "Is this a symptom of that disease?" he murmured.

"Yes. It's common. You can wipe it off, but try to avoid getting any of it on your skin."

Vince dabbed at the blood using a sheet he had taken from one of the other beds the previous day.

The bleeding eventually stopped, but a few minutes later, it began again. It continued on and off for the entire morning and wasn't limited to her nose. At one point, Erica saw Denise weep tears of blood. Erica flinched and turned away, but Vince just wordlessly dried her eyes.

Throughout the morning, Vincent stayed at Denise's side, crushing any ant that came near, soaking up blood, and doing his best to make sure that the unconscious girl was comfortable.

The ants were falling at such a rate that the others spent most of their time dealing with them. Despite their efforts, each of them was bitten several times, mostly on their ankles and feet, but occasionally on shoulders and necks. Luckily, while the bites stung, they didn't seem to leave the fiery bump on the others that they had on Denise. And on her, it was difficult to tell whether the multitude of red spots was an allergic reaction to the ants or another symptom of the disease.

In hushed tones, the group of four debated whether they should relocate to the pyramid room. Renee and Cam were in favor of moving, arguing that they couldn't spend another night with the ants, so it made sense to get it over with. Erica and Ian, on the other hand, pointed to Denise and asserted that it was a terrible idea risking a bloody death to avoid the temporary pain caused by the insect bites. They remained deadlocked, so stayed where they were. One thing they could all agree on was that splitting up was a bad idea.

Other than the ant discussions, they were mostly quiet. It felt wrong to chat as if everything were normal.

With the oppressive silence in the room, the thud of lunch arriving made everyone jump. Vince remained beside Denise while the rest of them collected the sandwiches from the dumbwaiter. Ian crushed an ant and flicked its corpse off the plate. Then, after a moment of thought, he divided the food into six portions. He took two over to Vince.

"Here you go," he said. Vince just nodded, and Ian returned to the others.

"He's looking tired," Renee said in a hushed voice.

Ian sighed. "Taking care of someone like that must be hard." He absentmindedly bit the sandwich.

"And he's got to be worried about catching the disease himself, too," Erica said, "considering how much blood he's been wiping up. Even if he's careful, how could he avoid it?"

Ian shook his head. "I'm not so sure." At Erica's questioning glance, he added, "I mean, I don't think he's that worried about getting infected. He doesn't seem at all squeamish about cleaning her up." Ian finished off the last bit of his food.

"He's probably used to blood from all the kids he beat up in school," Cam said. "One time, he split open my forehead and blood went all over him. He didn't care. He just kept hitting me." Cam's voice was emotionless, as if he were giving directions to the nearest gas station.

"Maybe that's part of it," Ian said, "but remember what he said earlier? If we were going to get it, we would have got it already." He abruptly rose. "And I think that's probably true. We should give him some help."

Renee grabbed his hand. "Please, don't," she pleaded. "I don't want you to get sick."

Ian turned to Erica, raising his eyebrows. Erica chewed on her lip. "I don't know, Ian. Renee seems to know a lot about this disease, and I don't want you to get it. But it's your decision. Truly."

Ian paused for a second, nodded, and walked across the room to Denise and Vincent. Behind him, Renee shot Erica a poisonous look, as if she was responsible for Ian offering to help.

"So how's it going?" Ian asked.

"Same as before," Vince replied, head down.

Ian sat beside him, his eyes on Denise. "That's a good thing. If it's not getting worse, it's probably getting better."

Vince couldn't hide the hopeful expression that flashed across his face. He turned toward Ian. "Do you think?" he gruffly responded.

"Well, I'm obviously no doctor, but I'd guess so."

"I suppose we'll see."

"Yep." After a few seconds of silence, Ian added, "If you want to get up and stretch your legs or have a rest, I'll take care of her for a bit."

"I thought you were worried about catching it," Vince said.

Ian shrugged. "Yeah. I was. But those red spots appeared quickly, after only a few hours. If one of us was going to get it, we'd have seen symptoms already. So I figure the gas infected her, but the disease isn't contagious."

"What, I'm not in a coma, so you're probably safe?" Vince said. His mouth twisted.

Ian smile was rueful. "Well, I wasn't going to put it that way, but yeah, I guess so." Vince frowned and looked away.

A few more seconds ticked by. "What do you say? Do you want a break?" Ian asked.

"No. I don't," Vince murmured.

"You've got to be getting tired."

"Yeah. Don't worry about it. It's not your problem."

"Not my problem?" Ian's brow furrowed. "How is it any more your problem than mine?"

"Well…" Vince paused, took a deep breath, and then continued, "Over the last couple of days, I've had a lot of time to think." His voice was low, barely more than a whisper, and his eyes were glued to Denise's face, even as his words were directed at Ian. "And I've been thinking about what she said—that we need to stick together if we want to escape.

"At times, I haven't always been the biggest team player. The others aren't any better. Your sister's up to something. And Cam seems scared to even make eye contact with me. Maybe he's hung up on the past. Whatever. That's his problem, not mine. But anyway, Denise is right. I need to be the bigger man. Even if those guys aren't always willing to work with me, I should do what Denise says and cooperate.

"But after all we've been through, does it seem weird to you that it only affected Denise? We all inhaled that gas, so why her? It's got to mean something. It can't just be random." He sighed. "I don't know for sure, but it seems like Denise getting sick might be the universe's way of punishing me for not listening to her when I had the chance.

"Kind of a karma thing. And maybe it's superstitious, but I've seen it again and again in my life. If I do something stupid, even if I don't understand it at the time, I get punished. Like in the first grade, how my mom left after reading the note from the principal. I wasn't supposed to fight. But I did. And so she left.

"It happens all the time. Watching TV too loud. Asking too many questions. Waking my dad. There's always a consequence. That's just the way the world works. At least around me.

"So perhaps her sickness is one more thing like that. And if it's my fault she's sick, I should be the one who takes care of her until she's better. Or something worse could happen." He stopped, raising his eyes slowly to Ian's face.

Ian looked down. He took in a deep breath, exhaled, and then spoke in a quiet manner. "I won't claim I understand any of that deep stuff about the way the universe works." Ian, his face solemn, looked back at Vince. "I think people learn those things through life experiences as you have. And I agree with you and Denise that working together gives us the best chance of escaping. So from that perspective, it all fits your theory."

"So you understand why I need to be the one to take care of her?" Vince asked, his eyes pleading.

"Yeah, I get it," Ian said. He put his hand on Vince's shoulder. "My offer stands, but I can see why you don't want to take me up on it." He stood up and walked back to the others.

In response to Erica and Renee's curious glances at his quick return, Ian said Vince had reiterated that he didn't want to put anyone else at risk of infection. When Renee wasn't looking, Erica shot him a quizzical look, wondering if there was more going on than he was saying. Ian responded with a slight shrug.

#

During the afternoon, the rate at which the ants were falling increased from four hundred to over five hundred. They gave up trying to defend the entire room and focused on the mattresses on which they sat. Even then, an hour didn't go by without them being painfully bitten. Despite Vince's best efforts to protect her, Denise was swollen, like someone had stuck her with a thousand needles.

The four of them reopened the quiet discussion about when they should abandon the room. Erica and Ian conceded they wouldn't be able to stay there another night. Yet, after seeing the bloody impact of the disease, they were more reluctant than ever to move to the room above. Renee refused to consider any idea that involved entering the room containing the cougar.

They eventually decided that, if Vince agreed, they'd leave about an hour after dinner—as late as possible, while still having enough time before the lights went out to move everything they wanted.

To Erica, Renee seemed distant throughout the conversation. When Ian and Erica discussed whether they should try to break the pyramid or contain the gas, Renee's eyes would defocus. She'd simply nod whenever someone looked in her direction. It was unlike her to be so deflated.

Erica wondered if it was because of her. She hadn't encouraged Ian to offer to take care of Denise. She'd said it was his decision. Was Renee holding a grudge because of that? Or was it the boyfriend/girlfriend game they were playing?

As if prompted by the direction of Erica's thoughts, Ian adjusted his position. He had been sitting cross-legged beside Erica, but now he stretched out his legs and leaned back on his hands, putting one arm behind Erica's back. He ended up so close to her that she could feel the heat emanating from his body.

It was no more than one would expect from a boyfriend. Intimate and possessive, but still casual, as if he wanted to be near, but respected the fact that his sister might not want to see more extravagant displays of affection. Yet, it was all Erica could do to keep from shivering at his closeness.

She glanced over at Renee, who carelessly turned her head away, as if examining the white wall for ants.

Suddenly, Erica became intensely uncomfortable. In the middle of a normal, quiet conversation, one small movement by Ian had set her pulse racing. And she was certain Renee knew it.

It was one thing to feel that way in Ian's arms at night, concealed by darkness, or grabbing a quick kiss that was over in an instant. It was another thing entirely to sit in front of Renee in the bright light with her body so close to Ian's and his arm around her.

"I need to go to the bathroom," she blurted out, scampering from the room, heedless of the ants crushed beneath her bare feet.

Her pulse still pounding, Erica turned the tap on full and splashed water into her face.

Sometimes it seemed as if Ian's actions were more than just a way to trick their captors. The way he looked at her sometimes, as if she were the only other person in the universe. The way he could tell her so much with just a glance. The way he comforted her that night when everything seemed so bleak. Sometimes, it seemed as if he really cared.

But that was the whole point. He needed to convince anyone watching that he truly liked her. She'd be a fool to take anything he did at face value. Especially with her promise to Renee. She'd been friends with Renee for her whole life, and she'd never let any guy get in the way of that. Even Ian.

Wiping the water off her face with her hands, she shook her head. She knew what she needed to do. Play the game, not get too tangled up in emotions, and, after they got out, make sure that everything was all right with her best friend.

If they got out.

Steeling herself, Erica left the room and rejoined the others. She sat down again beside Ian, studiously looking anywhere but at him. Close, but not too close. She thought she noticed a grin flit across Ian's face, but it might have been her imagination.

He continued talking with Renee, apparently embroiled in a discussion about the strange things that people eat all over the world.

"In Mongolia," Renee said, "they eat horse meat."

Ian raised his eyebrows. "I wonder if it tastes like moose? Maybe if we'd vacationed in Mongolia rather than Canada, you would have said, 'that's one tasty-looking horse.'"

Renee snorted. "Or maybe, 'there are ten tasty…'"

Vincent's gasp interrupted Renee. They looked toward the mattress. Vince had turned Denise's face toward him. He gazed down at her.

"It's over," he whispered.

CHAPTER THIRTEEN

Slowly, respectfully, Ian, Erica, and Renee stood and walked toward the pair. Cam trailed a couple of yards behind. Denise was still.

"It's over," Vince repeated. He was still staring at Denise's pale face.

Ian shuffled around the mattress and put his hand on Vince's shoulder in consolation. Then, he looked closer. "You're alive!" Ian said in surprise.

Vince stared at him with an incredulous expression. "Denise has been asleep for hours and the first thing you say to her is that? Come on, man." He smiled down at Denise.

"Um, h-how do you feel?" Ian said.

Denise croaked, "Really thirsty." Renee grabbed one of the discarded cereal bowls, brushed off the ants, and walked off toward the bathroom.

"You seem a lot better," Erica said. "All the red splotches on your arms and neck are gone. Other than all the ant bites, you look almost normal."

"What a flattering thing to say," Denise said as she glanced at her arms. She looked around the room and shrieked, "There are ants everywhere!"

"I hadn't noticed," Ian said, his tone dry. "You'll be surprised to find out how quickly you become acclimatized to having thousands of biting ants swarming all over you."

Erica shook her head. "You may have had the better deal, Denise, sleeping through all those bites. Though maybe it isn't that easy now, what with your allergic reaction to them."

Renee returned with some water sloshing around in the bowl. Vince helped Denise sit up. They managed to get most of the water into her with only a few drops landing on the sheets.

"That's so much better," Denise said in stronger voice. "I felt awful last night, but maybe I just needed a good night's sleep to shake it off. No sign of breakfast yet, I guess?"

"You missed breakfast," Ian replied.

"Oh. How long 'til lunch?"

"And lunch," Cam said.

Vince nodded. "In fact, dinner will come soon."

Denise stared at Vince. "Seriously? I was asleep for that long?"

"Yeah," he replied. "We couldn't wake you up. I guess your body needed to rest."

Cam added, "And bleed."

Denise's eyes widened. "Bleed?"

Vince scowled at Cam and turned back to Denise. "Yeah, you got a couple of nosebleeds while you were sleeping. I wiped away the blood. No big deal."

Denise considered his words for a moment. "Wow. I guess it can't have been that bad though. I feel almost normal now, except for being super hungry." Vincent passed her the sandwich he'd saved from lunch. Her eyes narrowed as she saw the ants on it, but then she shrugged, flicked them off, and bit into it.

"I'm glad you're fine," Renee said. "I was worried it was Ebola."

"What? The African disease from that movie?" Denise stared at her with raised eyebrows.

"Yes, but it can't have been. You wouldn't have recovered from it so fast."

"They probably put some sort of twenty-four hour flu thing in the smoke to see what we'd do," Ian said.

"The flu?" Erica said, doubt clear on her face.

"Well, not the flu exactly," Ian said, casually squishing an ant that was trying to make his way onto his foot. "I meant to emphasize the twenty-four hour part, not the flu part."

"That does fit with that whole 'mess with our minds' theory," Erica said as she thought it through. "Find a disease that has some bad symptoms, but ultimately isn't very dangerous. Give it to one of us, drop a dump truck load of biting ants on us, and see what we do."

"Yes," Ian said, nodding. "Do we panic? Do we take care of her or leave her behind?"

"Only a test," Vince spat out. "These are our lives they're playing with. What sort of sick person does something like that?" He glowered at Renee. Erica was unsure if he was angry and just happened to be looking in Renee's direction, or if he still thought she was working with the enemy.

Renee ignored him. "I think it's clear what sort of sick bastards they are. They've abducted us and nearly killed us as well. It's way more than a test. The cougar easily could have got us, and I doubt the disease was harmless. Even in the worse Ebola outbreaks, one in ten survives. I think they tried to kill you, but you were just lucky, Denise."

Denise, who had finished her sandwich, didn't bother joining in on the speculation. She struggled to her knees and stood.

"Whoa." Vince jumped to his feet, ready to catch her if she seemed at all unbalanced. "Are you sure you should get up so fast?"

"I'm fine. The faster I get up, the faster we get away from all these ants. And I really need to go to the bathroom." She walked to the curtain, with Vincent tagging along behind. Denise glanced back. "You're not planning to come in here with me, are you?"

Vince blushed. "Um, no."

Denise arched one eyebrow and smiled. "Good." She pulled back the curtain and froze as she saw the big pile of bloody rags—now swarming with ants—that Vincent had thrown in the shower. Eyes wide, she stared back at him. "Just a couple nosebleeds, you said?"

"They were big ones?" he replied. "Don't worry about it. I took care of it. It probably looks way worse than it was."

"I hope so. Because it looks like a slaughterhouse in here." She shrugged, stepped into the bathroom, and closed the curtain behind her.

They were so desperate to escape the swarming ants that when Denise returned, they didn't even discuss what to do next. Despite having only just regained consciousness, Denise was surprisingly energetic, able to walk up the stairs unaided. Some ants had made it into the stairwell, but Erica didn't see any of them in the pyramid room yet.

Ignoring the pyramid, they gathered around the exit. "Well, I guess you should go first, Denise," Erica said. "That way, if it still wants to quarantine you, we don't all have to have the painful poke."

"Darn," Denise said, sticking her middle finger between her teeth. "I really don't want to, but it makes sense. I think I'm still traumatized from how much it hurt the first time."

"It'll be fine. It's just for a second," Vince said.

"Yeah, the prick's just a second, but the vomiting, bleeding, and coma lasts for hours," Denise returned with a wry twist of her lips. Vince gave her a half smile in return.

She stuck her middle finger into the hole. They were prepared, but nevertheless, everyone jumped at the click and Denise's yelp. This time, they didn't talk as they waited for the verdict from the gray LCD.

Healthy
1/6

"Oh, well, isn't that nice of you to say!" Denise said acerbically to the machine.

Erica nodded. "Very nice. I hope this means there will be less puking this time."

One by one, the rest of them inserted their fingers and each of them got a healthy verdict. After Cam made it 6/6, the door slid open.

"Much easier the second time," Ian offered.

"Yeah, because you suffered *so* much," Denise said, rubbing the tips of her fingers against her leg, as if to massage away the sting of the needle. Her finger was still bleeding.

"I did," Ian agreed. He was grinning, but he sounded half serious. "While you were curled up in your comfortable bed, dozing away the hours, I must have been bitten by eight hundred ants." Denise smiled at him.

Vincent frowned at Ian. "Enough talk. Let's go."

Once again, behind the door was the standard white room with the same mattresses, bathroom, and dumbwaiter. On the wall, the digital display read zero.

The only noteworthy difference compared to the other rooms was the floor. It had wire-thin, shiny brown lines, running parallel, separated by about an inch, going from wall to wall. When Erica ran her fingers over a line, she could feel a slight ridge, though they appeared to be part of the floor. Ian speculated that the lines were related to the number on the display—and the others agreed—but there was no way to be sure what they did.

The dumbwaiter already had food waiting. After dinner, Renee offered to go with Denise to the bathroom to check on the cougar wounds and to see if there were any remaining signs of the disease before continuing to the next room. Erica joined them.

The scratches had healed completely. Only faint white scars remained. The red spots from the disease had also disappeared, and the swelling from the ant bites seemed to be rapidly receding. Denise looked so healthy that it was hard to believe only a few hours earlier, they had been concerned about having enough sheets to mop up all the blood.

They returned to the others and were about to continue to the next room when the lights dimmed. To Erica, it felt like someone was deliberately messing with them. After waiting for so long for Denise, she was ready to go. But they couldn't stumble forward blindly in total darkness.

Instead of sleeping right away, they sat together in the dim light and filled Denise in on what she'd been through. Vince clearly wanted to spare her the worst of the details, but Erica and Ian were completely truthful.

When they told her how Vince had taken care of her, Denise crawled across the mattress and thanked Vince with a spontaneous hug. He stiffened, awkwardly patting her back, his face turning red. Looking over Vince's shoulder, Denise's eyes roamed to Erica and Renee's faces. Erica was pretty sure that Denise's knowing smile was intended for them, not Vince. Beyond that brief squeeze, neither Vince nor Denise made a big deal about it.

They went to bed when they started yawning. By this point, Erica and Ian settling in beside each other didn't even merit a glance from the others, though Erica suspected from the tension in Renee's jaw that it took some effort for her to avoid looking at the two of them.

Ian wrapped his arms around Erica, causing all thoughts of Renee to slip from her mind. With him so close, she was suddenly conscious of how their bodies moved as they breathed. Should she breathe in at the same time he did, or as he exhaled? How could something so trivial seem so important?

"So what was with the running away earlier, when I sat down beside you? You do remember that we're supposed to like each other, right?" Erica could hear Ian's good-natured smirk as he whispered in her ear.

Why was he always so aware of everything she felt? "I don't know what you're talking about," she said, though blood was rushing to her face. "I just needed to go to the bathroom."

"Is that right?" he replied with a smile. "Do you realize when we're this close, I don't even need to look at your face to know you're turning red? I can feel it. Why are you blushing?"

Erica was flustered. "It's still strange being so close to you, like this. With how it is between us."

"Yes. It can be confusing. You're such an actress. It's sometimes hard to tell what's real and what's pretend."

She wanted to say, "None of it's pretend," but instead, she settled for, "Well, that's the point." Erica cast around for a way to change the topic. "So did Vince say anything interesting when you talked with him?"

"It was a strange conversation. He's so up and down. One day, I think I understand him—and frankly, had kind of written him off— and then he surprises me. He seems sincere about not wanting to fight with us anymore. He doesn't trust Renee, but he's seeing the bigger picture now, that we have to work together to escape. Denise helped him with that."

"How could she help him? She was unconscious most of the time."

"It's complicated. He said it was a karma thing. Like, because he wasn't cooperating enough, Denise got sick."

Erica frowned slightly. "By that logic, shouldn't the gas have infected him, not Denise? I don't get it."

"Neither do I. But I like this Vince more than the one we had two days ago. So I'm not going to question him too deeply about it."

Erica nodded. It made sense. The relationship between Denise and Vince was getting more confusing every day that passed—but why mess with a good thing?

"Do you think he likes Denise?" Erica asked. "He took care of her all day."

"I don't know. Maybe. What do you think?"

"Oh, I'm sure he does. I was just curious if you knew it." Erica's smile was impish.

"Yeah, well, I'm a guy. I'm not supposed to see romance everywhere I turn like you girls do," he teased.

"Oh right, I forgot. You're only supposed to club the occasional animal to eat and leave the emotions to the experts."

"Not all emotions." Ian moved his face back, then forward, and then his lips were touching hers, somehow both gentle and demanding. The kiss must have only lasted a few seconds, but it seemed like hours.

Ian brought his lips back to her ear, lightly brushing it as he whispered, "See? I can play this acting game too." She heard his smile fade. "Well, enough to fool an infrared camera, anyway." He lay his head down on the pillow beside her. "I guess we should get some sleep…"

After that, sleep was the last thing on Erica's mind.

#

It took Erica a while to doze off, and morning came far too soon. Cam was the first one up. He giggled as he stood. "My feet are tickly," he said.

Erica rolled over, placing her hand on the floor. It felt like feathers caressing her skin. She hastily pulled back, and the sensation stopped. "Something's wrong with the floor."

Ian touched the floor hesitatingly, jerked his hand away and then put his palm down once more. "It's an electric current. Very mild, coming through those lines on the floor." He pointed to the display on the wall. "Apparently, this is a one."

Denise sighed. "That's not good at all. Let's eat and get out of here." Overnight, she seemed to have recovered completely, without even any sign of the ant bites.

They ate quickly, oddly eager to see what they'd encounter in the next room. Afterward, they ascended a familiar staircase to stand front of the next door.

By now, they all knew their roles, but they talked through it in whispers anyway to refresh their memories. After the last experience with the "tiger", Ian took over the scouting duties. He opened the door a crack and peered through. After a couple of seconds, he shut it, as they had agreed.

"Is anyone there?" Vince whispered. He was beside Ian, but he had a limited view through the thin crack.

"No," he replied. "It's an empty room with some strange ramps on the wall."

"I don't get it," Denise said. "What do you mean? How can a

ramp be on a wall?"

"See for yourself." Ian opened the door wide.

Renee's eyes widened. "That's one ugly jungle gym."

Ian's smile was wry. "No. It's one beautiful medieval torture chamber."

This room's ceiling was much higher than any of the other rooms, a hundred feet at least. Set into the wall were two rough, cast iron ramps, sticking out roughly a foot and a half. The lower one started about twelve feet above the ground, ran the full length of the wall, and ended about thirty-five feet up. The second began another twelve feet above where the first ended and ran all the way back along the wall. About twelve feet above the end of the second ramp was a platform and a door.

Halfway along each ramp was a gap of about six feet. On the lower ramp, railings blocked both sides of the opening as if the designer was concerned about someone walking along the ramp and blundering into the hole.

The higher ramp had a similar railing on one side of the gap. However, the far side was blocked not by a railing, but by an iron wall. The wall had a hole cut out of it, about the size of a car tire, but surrounded by irregular twisting spikes. The rust on the spikes reminded Erica of blood, as if they had already impaled someone and dried blood was all that remained.

Ian turned back toward the others. "If anyone had any doubts about this being some sort of demented test, you might want to reconsider."

"I see a door up there," Vince said, pointing to the platform near the ceiling of the room.

Erica's eyes traced a route along the wall. "So somehow we're supposed to climb up to that ramp, walk along it, jump over the railings and a six-foot gap, climb up another wall, jump over another six-foot gap, through a hole the size of a shoebox that's surrounded by knives, and finally climb up another wall to reach the door?" Her voice sounded a little hysterical.

"Sure, no problem," Denise said, rolling her eyes. "I don't know who created this place, but they're clearly insane. There's no way I can do any of those things. Heck, those ramps are narrow and don't have handholds. I'd have a hard time even walking along one without falling off." Her shoulders slumped.

"And I wouldn't fit through that hole," Vince said, frustration coloring his voice. "We may as well just give up."

"After all we've been through, do you really think we have that option? The voltage in that electric floor is going to increase," Renee said.

Vince eyes narrowed. "Probably, but I don't see that we have a choice. It has to be a hundred feet up or more. We can't get up there." He sat down with his back against the wall, shaking his head.

"I think something is on the platform near the exit," Cam said, squinting at the other door.

"Wood and rope," Renee said. "It might be a rope ladder."

Ian stared upward. "That changes things." He looked to the others, his expression brightening. "That means only one of us has to climb up there, and they can toss down the ladder for the rest of us."

"Except that it makes no difference at all, because it's impossible for even one of us to get to the platform," Vince said, crossing his hands over his chest as if he were settling in for a long wait.

"We could probably boost someone to the lowest part of the ramp," Erica mused, not because she believed there was any hope of reaching the door, but because of morbid curiosity about whether they could actually get high enough to be impaled on the spikes.

"I might be able to jump across that first gap. Maybe," Ian said. Then his face fell. "But I couldn't climb to the second ramp, not without help. And the second gap with the wall seems all but impossible. Look at those spikes."

Renee put the tip of her index finger in her mouth, then walked up to the wall, staring up at the gaps in the ramps. "Hmm, let me try something." She did a handstand and returned to her feet.

"I didn't know that you could do that," Erica said.

"I haven't tried since I was six." Renee looked back at the wall, opening and closing her hands in front of her face as if she were grabbing for invisible bars. She glanced back to the others. "Have you heard of parkour? It's where people run through the city, jumping and climbing over obstacles. They always make it seem so easy. One of those guys could do it."

"I saw some of those videos online," Ian said. "But it's got to be harder than it looks."

"I'm not so sure," Renee said, her voice confident.

With no warning, she ran toward the corner with the low end of the ramp. Jumping, she pushed a foot off one wall, then a foot off the other, and grabbed the edge of the ramp. She hauled herself up.

"What? That's got to be over twice your height," Erica said, wide-eyed.

Renee shrugged and began running along the ramp while the others followed along with her below. She didn't even slow when she reached the railing, but put one foot onto the rail and leaped. Her momentum carried her over the gap, barely higher than the railing on the other side. She grabbed the rail with both hands and swung her body between her arms to land in a crouch.

"Be careful, Renee!" Ian said feebly.

Renee continued running and, when she reached the end of the first ramp, bounced up the walls to the second ramp, just as she had with the first.

There, she paused for a few seconds, studying the railing, gap, and barrier beyond it.

"Wait, Renee. You should stop and think things through now," Erica cautioned, her breath coming quickly as if she had been the one running.

"Yes," Ian said. "You're forty feet up. Even if you don't get skewered, a fall would kill you. Let's talk about what to do next." His face was pale.

Renee ignored them. She sprinted recklessly toward the rail, holding nothing back. Erica wanted to close her eyes, certain she was witnessing her friend's bloody death. But she couldn't look away.

This time, Renee planted her hands on the rail, raised her body into a handstand position, and pushed off with both hands. She sailed over the gap and went feet-first through the hole in the wall. She didn't even graze the spikes.

"That impossible!" Vince said, jumping to his feet, his jaw hanging open.

"As long as I live, I don't think I'll ever see anything as amazing as that," Denise murmured. She looked at Vince and grinned.

Renee smiled. "Well, it's way less scary than a cougar. It really is as easy as it looks in the videos." She began the final sprint toward the wall near the platform.

A vision flashed through Erica's mind.

Renee leaping off the wall. Grasping the bottom rung of the rope ladder. The ladder slipping off the ledge. Panic in Renee's eyes.

"Wait! Renee, be careful!" Erica shouted, suddenly certain that a disaster was about to occur.

Renee continued to ignore Erica's warnings. As before, she pushed off one wall, onto the other, stretching both arms above her head. But this time, as Erica had imagined, instead of gripping the secure edge of the platform, her hands closed around the bottom rung of the ladder.

Renee's weight pulled the ladder off the platform, and she began to fall.

CHAPTER FOURTEEN

Erica ran forward while keeping her eyes on Renee. She wasn't sure what she could do. Maybe try to catch her.

She saw Renee twist her body around and reach out to grab for the higher ramp. But her jump off the wall had already pushed her a foot away and her hands got tangled in the ladder.

As Renee plummeted by the lower ramp, the back of her head clipped it, causing it to ring out.

Erica realized that there was no way she'd be able to reach her in time.

The thud as Renee hit the ground was as a fifty-pound sandbag hitting concrete.

Erica reached Renee seconds after she hit. She was unconscious on her back, blood dripping out the back of her head. Her left leg was bent mid-shin at an acute angle.

Erica skidded to a stop on her knees beside Renee. Before Erica drew a breath to speak, Denise began to shriek. Renee's broken leg straightened as if it were a bent spring returning to its original shape. Denise's cry gurgled to silence, and Erica heard a heavy thump behind her.

Renee opened her eyes. "Wow, I had to have landed perfectly. I feel almost normal. I think my breath got knocked out of me, but—"

"Denise!" the anguished roar from Vince was enough to make Ian, Erica, and Cam tear their eyes away from Renee's face and glance back toward him.

About six feet away, Denise lay sprawled on her stomach. It was as if she had fallen asleep, until Erica looked closer and realized that the back of her head was misshapen, like an orange squeezed on a juicer. Her skin seemed to be largely intact though a few trickles of blood oozed through her hair.

Renee sat up. Her eyes widened as she saw the girl lying prone. "Help her!" she hissed at Ian.

The words spurred everyone out of shock and into action. They gathered around Denise.

"Quick, roll her onto her back," Vince said. He grabbed Denise's arm.

"No, wait. We can't let the back of her head touch the ground," Ian said. "Put something on it to stop the bleeding."

Vince tore off his shirt and pressed it against the wound.

"Can you hear me, Denise?" Erica said, kneeling beside her head. "How are you doing?"

There was no response.

"Denise, wake up," Vince begged, tugging on her arm.

"I don't think she's breathing!" Erica said. She put her hand on Denise's wrist for a few seconds, and then up to her neck. "I can't feel a pulse."

"Do CPR!" Vince shouted in Ian's face.

"I don't know how," Ian said. His face was frozen in shock.

"Turn her over," Renee said. She had crawled over to them and pushed between the two boys. "Keep the shirt on the back of her head." As they did, Erica numbly noted that Denise's left leg was flopping like a puppet's, bending in three places.

Renee stacked her hands on Denise's sternum and pumped. For several minutes, she alternated between chest compressions and plugging Denise's nose while breathing into her mouth. It seemed to have no effect.

The blood saturating Vince's shirt made a garish red streak on the white floor as Denise's body shifted in response to Renee's CPR. Denise still hadn't moved or shown any other sign of life since she had first collapsed.

Ian said quietly, "That's enough, Renee."

"No!" Vince shouted. He threw a wild punch, connecting with Ian's chin and sending him skidding backward across the floor. "Keep going!"

"No, Ian's right," Renee said. She sat up, closed her eyes, and wiped a hand across her forehead. It left a red smear. "She's gone."

"I said keep going!" Vince demanded hysterically, sweat pouring down his face.

"You saw her head," Erica said, trying to be gentle. "There's no way she could survive that." She put her hand on Vince's shoulder. He batted it away and glared at her with unchecked rage.

"You're not trying!" he yelled at Renee and Erica. "Do something!"

Renee sat back on her heels. Tears ran unchecked down her cheeks. "I'm sorry, Vince. There's nothing left to do."

"Aaah!" Vince shouted. "But I took care of her! She lived! How can she die now?" He stood, turned away from them, and smashed his forehead against the wall, hard enough for Erica to wonder if he hurt himself.

Spinning around, he turned on Renee. "You killed her!"

Renee's face collapsed. "I didn't kill her. Or at least…"

"You did kill her. How else could she have got those injuries except from you? They're what should have happened to you. Just like the cougar. You didn't put a gun to her head and pull the trigger, but we all know you killed her."

Suddenly, Renee rose, fury in her eyes. "Stop harassing me, Vince. I don't care what you think. Denise was my friend, and—"

"Wait a second!" Ian stepped between the two. "Do we really want to have this discussion while standing over her body? Show some respect, guys."

Vince stared at Ian and looked about ready to take another swing at him. Shaking his head in defeat, he looked down at Denise and swallowed. "Yeah, yeah, you're right, Ian," Vince said. He took a step backward as if he were fighting against an invisible current, then he pointed at Renee. "But we're going to talk about this later!" He turned back to the wall and hit it with the side of his fist, then put his head against the cold concrete.

"Yes, I'm sure we will," Renee mumbled, her shoulders slumping as if the brief moment of anger had exhausted her last reserves of energy.

Erica went over to Renee and put her arms around her. Ian joined them while Cam just sat on the floor with his head against his knees. As the adrenaline drained from her body, Erica realized the magnitude of what had occurred. She began to shake and then weep.

She had only known Denise for a few days, but they had lived together and struggled together. Erica came to trust her. She didn't have the conflicted feelings toward Denise that she did with both Ian and Renee. Even more importantly, Denise never overreacted the way Vince did or tried to solve her problems using violence.

On the contrary, more than anyone else, Denise seemed to recognize that they were all in this together. Though she sometimes seemed callous, Erica always felt that Denise was simply doing her best to take care of the group.

Even when they disagreed, Erica knew she could count on Denise to express her point of view in a clear and calm manner. She had a way of making everyone comfortable and bringing them together. It wasn't so much that she was leading, but rather listening to what people were saying and easing their worries.

Even Vince seemed to recognize and respond to that. Erica glanced at him. Denise was the only one who seemed capable of getting him to change his mind. It was she who finally convinced him to cooperate. But what would happen without Denise's stabilizing influence? For the moment, he was calm, but he clearly blamed Renee.

And if he did, maybe that was fair. It did seem like her fault. This was just the latest odd occurrence in a series of odd incidents that had been happening for days. And so much of it revolved around Renee. Maybe Denise needed to die because it was the only way for Renee to survive. And if that was true, Renee was the one to blame.

And perhaps Erica would have been content with that if it wasn't for the visions. Renee had climbed the wall and accidentally grabbed the rope ladder exactly how Erica imagined. It was like her visions of the cougar and the gas in the pyramid. The mauling vision hadn't come to pass, but it was as vivid as the one of Renee falling. Just as real.

So even if something strange was happening to Renee, it was equally clear that something strange was happening to her too. If she'd done something differently, said something else, could she have saved Denise as she had saved Renee with the cougar?

And if that was true, maybe she deserved part of the blame for the death. Though there *was* a difference between failing to warn someone of a runaway train and pushing them in front of it to save yourself. Renee, it seemed, did the latter.

But was that really the case? She didn't control her visions. Maybe Renee didn't control the way her injuries were transferred to Denise. And in that case, how could Renee be held responsible for Denise's death?

Denise's death. The finality of the phrase hit her again.

Blame didn't matter now. Denise was dead. A friend, someone she had trusted, gone through no fault of her own. One moment, she was alive and healthy, and then the next, she was a lifeless object on the floor.

Tears rolled down Erica's cheeks, and she felt as if she were drowning.

#

It seemed an eternity before they exhausted their tears. Then they were confronted with the cold reality of Denise's body. After a brief, quiet discussion, they decided to leave her.

There was nothing else they could do. Despite the tragedy resulting from her attempt, Renee had been successful in pulling the bottom of the rope ladder from the platform. But there was no way to take the body with them, and nobody suggested it.

Vincent went downstairs and retrieved a sheet. He placed it gently over Denise.

"Should we say something?" Erica asked.

"I suppose so," Ian replied. He clasped his hands, gazing down on the sheet. "Denise," he said, his voice raw, "before this, I didn't know you that well. I saw you a few times with my sister, but we didn't really talk. But getting to know you here was one of the bright spots of this whole situation. I'll miss you."

There was a pause and Vincent spoke, his voice shaky. "Denise, it wasn't right that you died today. You were different than everyone else here. You didn't judge people based on rumors or appearances, but took the time to understand them and see their best qualities." He paused and then said in a voice scarcely above a whisper, "More than anything, you didn't deserve to die."

Renee waited a few seconds to see if Vince had any more to say, then began, "Denise, I probably knew you better—"

"Shut up, Renee," Vince said, his tone brooking no argument. His voice had gone cold and totally changed. It was as if he were someone else.

"What?" Renee was clearly thrown off balance.

"You have no right to speak. You killed her."

Ian nodded, putting his arm around his sister's waist. "Yeah, Renee. Maybe you should sit this one out."

Renee's eyes widened. She threw Ian's arm off her hip. Spinning around, she climbed up the rope ladder. She glared down on them from the platform before going through the door, slamming it behind her. Ian sighed and looked at Erica, his eyebrows raised in question. She shrugged almost imperceptibly.

Erica and Cam mumbled a few quick words of goodbye to Denise, feeling out of place after Renee's exit.

Afterward, they climbed the ladder, leaving Denise behind. Ian and Vincent were the first to the top. With no guardrail and an eighty-foot drop, the platform seemed crowded even with the two of them. So, they moved through the door with Erica and Cam on their heels. As they expected, the door opened into a room that once again contained six mattresses on the floor, a dumbwaiter panel, a digital display reading zero, and an exit.

"Home sweet home," Ian flatly said.

Vince scowled at him.

The others soon joined them. They took a few minutes to wash and verify that the room was the same as the others, and then tacos arrived for lunch.

"We should tackle the next room now, before the number starts increasing," Ian said as they ate. By now, none of them believed that the exit would lead to a way out, only the next life-threatening encounter.

Erica shook her head. Did Ian think that they'd all forget what had happened to Denise? Obviously, it was risky even being in the same room with Renee. They couldn't just ignore that.

"We need to figure out what to do with Renee first," Vince said, his face dark.

"I'm right here, you know," Renee said. "Don't speak about me like I'm not in the room."

Vincent ignored her and spoke to the others. "Let's not argue about why it took so long for us to figure out Renee was a threat," he said in a deceptively reasonable tone. "We can't go back and change that now. But Denise paid for our negligence with her life. It's time to correct that mistake."

Erica said, "I agree that we have to discuss this. What are you suggesting we do?"

"Isn't it obvious? She killed someone. An eye for an eye." Vince was still trying to sound logical, but his underlying anger made his voice shake.

"What!" Renee shouted. She stared at him in disbelief. "Have you gone completely insane?"

Ian put his arm around his sister's waist. "We are not murdering Renee."

"It's not murder. It's justice!" Vince growled.

"No, justice involves a trial, a jury," Ian said, and Erica nodded. "And you can only get the death penalty for first-degree murder. For deliberate killings. Nobody can argue that Denise's death was deliberate. I'm not even sure how it happened."

"She's working with the people who put us in this death trap!" Vince shouted, raising hands with fingers outstretched as if he were about to grab Ian and shake him until he agreed. "She has something that enabled her to survive the fall by killing Denise. That's close enough to 'planned' in my book. In anyone's book!"

Erica shook her head. Why did Vince always jump to extremes? "You can't seriously believe that we have evidence of any of it. All this 'someone is a spy' paranoia came from your interpretation of a note from our captors. From that one note, you've built this whole conspiracy about Renee."

"Yeah. I'm no more guilty than you," Renee said, pointing a finger at Vince's chest. "Less, actually, since I don't beat up kids at school for their lunch money."

"You murdered Denise. You have to pay for that!" Vince said, his eyes wild.

"I didn't. I have no idea how that happened," Renee said.

"I agree," Ian said. "And we wouldn't have been able to escape that room without you."

Vince was aghast. "Don't pretend she's a hero. She helped us get out, but only by killing Denise."

"By accident," Ian said firmly, emphasizing the second word. "You can't even explain what happened. If you want to blame someone, blame our captors."

"It doesn't matter that I can't explain everything. We know she's responsible, and that's enough." Vince examined Ian's face to see if he was making any headway, but Ian clearly wasn't buying the argument at all. He sighed in exasperation. "So what do you think we should do? Just keep going and pretend it didn't happen?"

Ian thought for a few seconds. "Well, not pretend it didn't happen. If any of us were under any illusions that our captors wouldn't kill us, we know better now. But when it comes to Renee, we shouldn't do anything. I wouldn't condemn her for her actions any more than I'd condemn a police officer for accidentally killing a bystander during a shoot-out with a drug dealer. I don't know how she survived and Denise died, but it's clear that Renee has no clue what happened either."

"Police officer? Shoot-out?" Vince shook his head, frustration written across his features. "What are you talking about? Why are you trying to complicate something so simple? She killed Denise. She should die."

"Don't be ridiculous," Erica said. "Obviously, she was trying to help us escape. Sure, the outcome was tragic, but we can't blame her for that. But we should figure out what to do to minimize the risk to the rest of us."

Vince looked as though he was trying to formulate a response, but at the break in conversation, Cam jumped on the opportunity to speak. "Ah, guys? If we think she's guilty…"

As if on cue, Erica, Ian, and Renee all glared at him.

Cam held up his hands and looked at Renee. "I… I'm not saying you're guilty… It's just that if we believed that you should be punished… Well, if we hurt you, wouldn't we get hurt instead? Like Denise?"

Ian contemplated him, his expression thoughtful. "Yes. I guess that's true."

Vince wasn't buying it. "Denise is dead. If it will give her justice, I'm willing to take the chance," he growled.

"Well, none of the rest of us are, and what you call justice, the rest of us call murder," Erica said. "It's a moot point anyway. The rest of us want to stand by Renee because it's the right thing to do. The fact that her injuries seem to jump to someone else simply gives us another reason to do what we'd do anyway."

"We should test it," Vince said. "Break her finger, or something."

Renee backed up a few steps. "You're not breaking my finger!"

"Don't worry, it would only last a second, and you'd be healed," Vince sarcastically said.

"How about something else?" Erica said. "A scratch."

"No!"

Ian turned to face her. "Renee, it's a reasonable thing to ask. We need to understand the risks. Please?"

Renee shook her head. "Fine." She stretched her right arm toward Ian. "Do it."

Cautiously, he drew the nail of his index finger down her arm. It left a white mark that faded quickly. They all looked at their own arms, but there was nothing to be seen.

"See, you're safe," Renee said caustically, glaring at Vince.

Vince shook his head. "Come on. That was barely anything."

Erica nodded. She reached out, grabbed Renee's wrist, and dragged her nail down her forearm hard enough to break the skin.

"Ouch!" she yelled, pulling her arm back. "What are you doing?"

"It had to be a real test. Look."

A four-inch bleeding red scratch ran down Renee's arm. They waited about fifteen seconds. Renee continued to bleed.

"There. See?" Renee's smile was triumphant. "I'm innocent."

"You're not innocent. This just means we can deliver justice," Vince said. "Besides, you could be faking." He turned to the others. "We should break her arms—to be sure she's not hiding what she did somehow—then kill her."

Erica sighed. "Think about what you're saying, Vince. We don't need to act rashly. If Renee isn't a risk to the rest of us, we don't need to do anything." She looked around at all the others. "Agreed?"

Ian nodded right away while Cam was slower. Renee gulped and blinked back tears. She hugged Ian, putting her face against his shoulder.

"Well, I don't agree," Vince said, glaring at them. "And I'm not going into another one of those death-trap rooms with her. I'll probably be the next one she kills." He spun around and marched off to the bathroom.

Erica looked at Renee. "Don't worry about him. He's just upset. He's a bully, not a murderer," she whispered.

"I don't know," Renee said in a low voice. "I feel like he's been on my case ever since we got here. Anything that happens reinforces his belief that I'm untrustworthy."

"That's his issue, not yours." Ian grabbed her hand and squeezed it.

Renee rolled her eyes. "Well, yes. Except that I'm stuck in the same room with him and he wants to kill me. That kind of makes it my problem."

"He's just saying that," Erica said.

"He seemed pretty sincere."

"Let's give him some time by himself." Erica glanced at the curtain and then back to her friend. "Denise died an hour ago, and he's still trying to process that. We can have a better conversation later when he's calmed down."

"I guess. What else can I do?"

They sat on the mattresses and talked. After a few minutes, Vince returned, pointedly lying down on one of the other mattresses without saying a word. Ian's attempts to convince him to get up so they could move on to the next room were met with sullen silence. Eventually, he gave up and left Vince to sulk alone.

The rest of them were eager to leave and discussed whether they should proceed without Vincent, but none of them, not even Renee, was willing to abandon him yet.

#

When dinner arrived a few hours later, Erica noted that, as she predicted, Vince had cooled off. He was civil throughout dinner, sitting and chatting with them on the mattresses as they ate, treating Renee no differently than the others. He didn't even mention the earlier conversation. Erica suspected the solitary meditation over the course of the afternoon had helped him come to peace with Denise's death.

After the meal, Renee got up to collect the plates and tray, to move them away from the mattresses to their garbage corner. Vince stood to help, picking up several plates in his left hand.

They were almost at the corner, about as far from the others as possible, when a vision flashed through Erica's mind.

Vince spinning to face Renee. His fist impacting her temple. Her head jerking back. Renee on the floor, her neck at an unnatural angle.

Erica looked up to see Vince's right hand curl into a fist.

124

CHAPTER FIFTEEN

Erica shouted, "Watch out, Renee!"

Renee reacted quicker than Erica would have thought possible, but still not fast enough to avoid the blow entirely. Vince's fist hit her jaw, and Renee staggered to the side.

Vince seemed surprised that his blow didn't land solidly and paused for a fraction of a second, giving Renee enough time to regain her balance. But then he moved forward to attack again.

Ian and Erica leaped to their feet and started toward them, but Erica realized it was hopeless. Renee was tiny. Vince was twice her weight and he worked out all the time. There was no way they'd be able to reach them before Vince did some serious damage. If the two of them could even stop him....

Vince jabbed a second time at Renee. She barely moved her head out of the way and hopped back as Vince followed up with his other fist. It, too, hit nothing but air.

Vince kept on coming, throwing punch after punch. Each one missed Renee so narrowly that Erica was certain that the next would land.

But then Erica saw the expression on Renee's face. She'd been friends with Renee since before they were in school. She knew how Renee looked when she was scared or panicked. This expression was neither. She was focused.

Suddenly, Erica saw the fight in a whole new light. Renee wasn't in trouble, barely able to dodge each blow. Rather, her movements were economical, only expending enough energy to avoid being hit.

As the notion occurred to Erica, the fight changed. Vince, getting impatient, lunged toward Renee, overextending himself in a futile attempt to hit her. But this time, instead of backing off, Renee stepped forward and to the side, ducking under Vince's outstretched arm. She planted her left foot and kicked back with her right.

She caught Vince in the back of his leg, and he fell to his knees. Before he recovered, Renee leaped onto his back, wrapping her legs around his torso and putting her right arm under his chin. Vince instinctively grabbed at her forearm, trying to avoid being choked.

As he did, Renee released his neck and pushed him to the side while swinging her leg over his head. In an instant, they were both on their backs, their bodies perpendicular. However, Renee's legs were draped over Vince's chest and neck, with his left elbow trapped between them. She had a firm grip on his hand.

She pulled down slightly on that hand. Vince grunted and writhed, hopelessly trying to free his wrist. After a few seconds, as if by an unspoken agreement, they both went still.

Erica and Ian finally reached the pair, but paused, worried they would upset the equilibrium.

"Vince," Renee said, "you've probably figured out that I can snap your elbow right now. Do you realize that?"

Vince said nothing for a second, so Renee exerted the tiniest bit of extra pressure. "Yes," Vince squawked.

"Good. Because I don't want to hurt you any more than I already have. I believe, like Denise did, that we all need to work together to get out of here. Breaking your arm won't help with that. So I'm going to release you. But you should know that this wasn't a fluke. I may be smaller than you, but from the moment you first swung at me, I knew that I could take you down. I released that choke because I chose to, not because you made me.

"From now on, you will stop being a jerk to me. Heck, by now, even you should have realized that I can help us escape. But, if you try something like that again, I will break you."

Vince nodded.

Erica and Ian exchanged startled glances. The slightest of smiles danced across Ian's lips, but Erica's eyes narrowed. Renee's gymnastics while climbing the ramps had been astounding, but had been overshadowed by Denise's death. This fight only reinforced how Renee's earlier performance wasn't luck. The ease with which she had taken down Vince seemed impossible. Was this truly the girl she'd grown up with? And if she could defeat Vince so easily, were they really safe around her?

Renee released her grip and rolled away. She let Ian help her to her feet while keeping watch for any aggressive move from Vince.

But he was done. Erica had never heard of him losing a fight to someone his own age, let alone to a tiny girl like Renee. He staggered to his feet. Though the fight had lasted less than a minute, sweat poured down his face as if he'd run a marathon on the hottest day of summer.

Vincent glanced at Renee and turned toward Ian. He spoke directly to him as if the others didn't exist and Ian was the ultimate arbiter of all decisions. "There, now that proves it. Renee is working with them. She has martial arts training."

"No, I don't. Or at least," Renee frowned and looked toward Ian, "I don't think I do."

Ian shook his head. "No, you've never shown the slightest interest in martial arts."

Vince's triumphant smile seemed slightly desperate to Erica. "So she's clearly not Renee. She's an impostor. Sure, I went easy on her. I only needed to prove that she isn't who she said she is. But even with me not trying, she shouldn't have been able to put me down like that. Not if she was truly Renee."

"I'm not someone else," Renee vehemently denied. "I'm me. I don't know why I could do what I did." She directed a pleading look at Ian and Erica. "Somehow, I knew how to fight. I'm not saying it's normal. Nothing about this whole situation is normal! I'm just saying that I'm still Renee. The same Renee you've known for years."

"I believe you, Ren," Ian said soothingly, looking at her and ignoring Vince's outraged gasp. "But how do you know all this stuff? You quit gymnastics when you were six and certainly never took jiu-jitsu, or whatever that was."

Renee scanned his face, and a faint smile flickered across her mouth. Glancing at Ian, Erica understood why—she'd seen that expression before. Ian trusted her, and Renee knew it. He wasn't questioning because he doubted. He just wanted to understand what was going on.

"I don't know how I did it. It's not like I planned it. I saw him trying to hit me and did what came naturally to defend myself. It all seemed effortless." She turned to Erica, who was looking at her, chewing her lower lip. "What? You don't believe me? I don't understand how it works, but I'm explaining it as well as I can."

Erica was unsure how she felt. She wished she could be as loyal as Ian seemed to be. Maybe she was Renee, but this Renee was dangerous. And if that had changed, perhaps something else had as well. But she couldn't exactly tell Renee that. Besides, even if she was different, there was no evidence she had done anything wrong. Should Erica abandon her friend out of fear of what might be?

Erica shook her head. Regardless, she couldn't share her doubts with Renee. "No, it's not that. You're bleeding."

Blood dribbled down Renee's chin. She wiped it away with the back of her hand. "Yeah." Her mouth twisted. "While Vince was 'going easy' on me, he punched me in the face. Hard." Another drop of blood trickled from the cut.

"I saw," Erica replied. "It's more evidence you can be hurt."

"Well, that's no surprise to me," Renee said as she began to pace. "I don't know how I healed from that fall."

Vince sneered. "Yeah, you're just a helpless girl. One who can fight almost as well as me, magically crack an electronic lock, and, what else am I forgetting? Oh, right. Kill Denise. I don't trust you, and we should be done with you."

"And what do you suggest we should do with her?" Ian said levelly. Erica recognized the tone—Ian was barely holding back his temper.

"I've already said what we should do," Vince said. "Dispense justice. Throw her off the ledge again. Lock her in the room with the cougar. Whatever. Justice."

"I thought you were just upset when you said that earlier. That you said the words, but didn't realize what was coming out of your mouth. But now—"

"It's the only way," Vince interrupted. "The only way."

"What the heck is wrong with you?" Ian exploded. "It's not the only way. I can understand being upset about Denise's death. We're all upset. But murdering my sister isn't an option. It's not even close to being an option!" His face was red and his fists clenched.

"But—" Vince protested.

"What's more, it's obvious to me—and should be blindingly obvious to you after the beating you took—that she's totally capable of defending herself. But even if she weren't," Ian continued while putting his arm around his sister's waist, "you'd need to kill me first. There's no way I'm going to let you hurt my sister again. And if you try, I'll do the same thing she did to you, but I won't be nearly as merciful."

"I'd like to see you try." Vince walked to within a foot of Ian and stared him in the eye. "Do you remember last time? I went easy on Renee because she's only a girl, but I'd be quite willing to smash in your face. Let's do it now."

Erica stepped between them. "Stop it! We don't need another testosterone-dripping, chest-pounding session between you guys." She shook her head, rolling her eyes. "Renee's already proven that she can beat anyone in this room, so let's all calm down."

"I was going easy on her," Vince muttered.

Erica ignored him. "I admit, something about you is odd, Renee." She raised both hands as Renee appeared ready to protest. "But your martial arts skills give us a better chance to win if we need to fight our way out of here. We're lucky to have you on our side."

Vincent scowled and whined, "But she's not on our side!"

"Saying the same thing over and over again doesn't make it true. She's my best friend, and you'd need to have some persuasive evidence to convince me that our friendship is a lie. And frankly, she's done way more than you to help get us out of here. So give it a rest already."

"I'm beginning to think I'm the only one in the room who isn't in on a secret," Vince muttered.

"Oh, don't even go there," Erica said, glaring at him.

"Whatever." Vince threw up his hands. "You guys always stick together. Of course you won't acknowledge what's going on. I'm done with you." He turned his back and marched off to the bathroom. Erica sighed.

"So how are you doing?" Ian said as he looked at his sister's face. "He went at you hard. Is it only your lip?"

"Yeah," Renee said. She stopped pacing and sat down. "He flailed about a lot. But only his first punch landed."

"How did you manage to avoid being hit?" Erica asked. "That was impressive."

"He made it obvious whenever he threw a punch. He'd always pull back his hand, rotate his shoulders, and stare exactly where he was aiming. Plus, he only targeted my head, and he's kind of slow. So I just stayed out of the way."

"And what about that arm thing?" Cam asked. "How did you do that?"

"He's way stronger than me and has a longer reach. I figured I couldn't make him give up by hitting him. At least not without hurting him or getting clipped myself. So I decided I had to get him off his feet. After that, it seemed like the natural thing to do."

"I liked the speech you gave him at the end," Ian said, smiling.

"Thanks. Didn't do any good though. I was hoping he'd realize that he needs to respect me, and I can help us escape." Renee scowled. "But now, if anything, he's even more serious about wanting to kill me."

"He always said that whenever he bugged me, too," Cam said. He hugged his knees to his chest. "For a long time, I was terrified. But I figured it out. It's just something he says. He doesn't really mean it."

"Maybe," Renee said, her tone clearly indicating that she wasn't convinced. "He seemed furious, and it didn't look to me like he pulled any punches."

"In the middle of the fight, it might not have seemed that way, but maybe he did," Ian said.

Pulling punches? Erica frowned. In her vision, Vince wasn't taking it easy. Without her hasty warning, Renee would have been seriously hurt. Erica was sure of it.

It was impossible, but Erica was convinced she was seeing the future. A changeable future maybe, but a future nevertheless. She wanted to tell Renee she was right, that Vince really had tried to maim her. But she couldn't say that her visions had shown her the truth. They'd think she was mad.

"I'm with you, Renee. He looked serious to me," Erica said. "He was swinging hard."

Ian sighed and muttered, "I wish we could figure out a way to calm him down and let him see sense. I think he's simply making threats. But even if he's just blowing off steam, he shouldn't be blowing it off in your direction. If we're going to get out of here, we need to be working together. And I thought he understood that."

Erica shook her head. "I don't trust him. Even if he was coming around, Denise's death seems to have changed everything. He was closer to her than any of us, and he blames Renee."

"So maybe we should just leave him alone," Cam suggested. "Avoiding him worked good for me."

Renee looked at him and her lips thinned. "Yeah."

#

Vincent returned a few minutes before the lights went out. He didn't speak. Everyone studiously avoided any discussion about the fight or whether he was ready to leave the room with them, sticking to safer topics such as what would be served for breakfast tomorrow.

When the lights dimmed, Erica cautiously crawled into the bed beside Ian, more determined than ever to keep her promise to Renee to control her emotions around him.

Denise's death and the fight had made her realize that any feelings she had for Ian weren't helpful. They were in a life-and-death situation, and her infatuation with Ian would just complicate things. At minimum, it would distract her from the matter at hand. And in the worst case, it could seriously hurt her relationship with Renee. Besides, there was no sign that Ian felt anything toward her, so it was a waste of time anyway.

Her resolution vanished the moment Ian pulled her close to him and brushed his lips across hers. It was as if the warmth of the kiss radiated through her whole body. Nothing existed but the two of them.

Ian whispered in her ear, "How are you doing?"

The brief moment of calm vanished, and the world came crashing in once more. The wave of grief that rolled over Erica was no less intense than the emotions she felt from his kiss. "Oh, I can't believe Denise is gone."

"I know," Ian solemnly whispered. "It hurts." His voice was hollow.

He said nothing more, just held her. After the tumultuous day, Erica longed to fall asleep in Ian's arms, but the events kept spinning through her head. Her visions were real. They had given her the opportunity to save Renee from the fall if Renee had just listened. And something like that might happen again. She needed to make sure that Ian and Renee would listen to her when she needed them to.

Could she tell Ian the truth? Sure, he accepted Renee's abilities, but she was his sister and the amazing things she did were visible to everyone. Her visions though? There was no evidence at all. He'd say she was nuts, three steps down the path Jen took a year earlier. He'd recoil, treating her nicely, but holding his distance. Their nightly conversations would end.

But how else could she be sure he'd listen when she needed him to, when their lives were at stake? Even if he doubted her now—in the moment that mattered, it might make him pause. That second might be enough to save his life. It would have been with Renee.

Though it might cost her Ian, she needed to take the risk. She swallowed, pushed Ian's hair aside, and whispered, "You know, Vince could have seriously hurt Renee today."

Ian frowned. "Maybe. But I think you're overestimating his chances. Even if her healing ability comes and goes, she seems deadly in a fight."

"I wanted to talk to you about that," Erica said. "About the way she can do all this amazing stuff."

"What? You're buying into Vince's theory that she's an impostor?"

"No, not that. Kind of the opposite, really. Her ability is amazing. A bit intimidating. But I think she's who she says she is, yet somehow has other skills as well. Skills she never learned."

"I don't get it. You have an explanation for it all?"

"Not an explanation for it. I'd guess it's something caused by us being here. But that's not what I'm getting at. I'm absolutely sure it's her. Just changed."

"Stop beating around the bush, Erica. I don't believe what Vince says, but—and don't tell Renee this—I can't dismiss his arguments entirely. She doesn't seem to remember a bunch of things we did together in the past and she can do things that seem impossible. How can you possibly be sure that it's her?"

Erica took a deep breath. "Because something similar is happening to me."

CHAPTER SIXTEEN

Ian listened in silence while Erica recounted each of her four visions. When talking about Renee's fall, she could barely get the words out.

"You foresaw Denise's death?" Ian whispered. Erica didn't need to see the shocked expression on his face. She could hear it.

"No, not that. Only Renee grabbing for the ladder and pulling it off the ledge. I saw her fall."

"Why didn't you do something?"

"I did. I yelled at Renee to wait." Erica's eyes began to sting. "She didn't listen. I might have saved her. Or saved Denise. But she didn't listen."

Ian somehow sensed the tear trickling down Erica's cheek and wiped it away. "You tried. You couldn't have done anything else."

"I know, but that doesn't make me feel any better."

"I know."

"Please tell me that if I tell you to do something, you'll listen to me!" Erica said desperately, her voice cracking. "Trust me!"

"I will," he whispered. "I promise."

She buried her face in his shoulder, as if he could keep away the image of Renee falling, the raw terror in her eyes.

Ian held her.

After a minute, Erica was ready to talk again. She swallowed. "That's it. Four times." She pushed Ian back, so she could study his eyes in the dim light. "Do you believe me?"

"If this were any other situation, I'd say you were nuts," Ian said. "That you were just seeing signs subconsciously. You know. Body language. The end of a rope ladder. And your imagination was converting those subconscious thoughts to something you understand and making you think that you were seeing the future."

"It's more than that. The visions are as real as life. I see details."

"I know, I know." He paused as if considering it and then nodded. "I believe you." Erica let out a breath she didn't realize she had been holding. "How far in the future do you think you're seeing?" Ian asked.

"Not very far. Maybe five seconds at most."

"In some situations, five seconds can be a long time," Ian mused. "Have you tested it?"

"What do you mean?"

"Well, these visions just come to you, right? Have you deliberately tried to get a vision?"

"Um, no. If you leave illegal drugs out of the equation, I'm not sure what I'd do to 'try' to get a vision."

"Yeah, I don't know either. But suppose you were able to do it whenever you wanted. We're opening doors with no idea what's on the other side. Imagine if you could tell us what we're about to see before we even look in."

"It hasn't worked like that so far," she said, her doubt clear. "I've only had visions when it was a matter of life and death."

"Except for the gas," Ian pointed out. "Only Denise got sick from the gas."

"Well, yes, but we didn't know that at the time. And who's to say I wouldn't have gotten sick if I hadn't held my breath?"

"Good point. In any case, we should try. Maybe you need to think really hard about what the future is and it will come to you."

The theory seemed reasonable to Erica. "How about an experiment? Pick a number between one and ten thousand and tell me in ten seconds. I'll try to determine what it is before you say it."

"Between one and ten thousand? With such a huge range, you'll never be able to guess it."

"Well, yes. That's the point. I'm not actually guessing, remember?"

"Oh. Of course." Ian sounded abashed. "Okay, ready. Got one."

Erica focused on the future, reaching with her mind, trying to determine what was going to happen. What number would Ian choose? He wouldn't select a number randomly; there would be some reason behind it. Would he choose a low number like three to be perverse? Or choose a pattern? Or someone's phone number? There were so many options.

"Well, what's the number?" Ian said.

"3,333," Erica guessed.

"No. It was 8,765," he replied. "Not very close."

"Well, that's because I didn't have a vision. I guessed," Erica said.

"Oh. Yeah. Let's try again. Do something different from what you did this time."

"Yeah, something different," she said with a touch of friendly sarcasm. She couldn't see Ian's face, but she knew him well enough to know he wore a wry grin, recognizing how unhelpful his suggestion was.

They played the game for about fifteen minutes, with Erica thinking about the future in various ways and becoming more and more frustrated. The closest she got to the answer was within about fifty, but it was still only a guess.

"This isn't working," Erica said. "I'm just getting annoyed. We should stop."

"Yeah, perhaps you can't control it. That's too bad."

Erica nodded. "Plus, it's hard to prove I can do it, if these visions only happen at random times. I feel like an idiot."

"Don't worry about it. We knew it was a long shot when we started."

"Yeah, but it's still frustrating."

"I know. Should we tell anyone else about this?"

"I'm not sure," Erica said, rubbing her lips together as she thought about the others. "Maybe Renee? Are you at all worried about her being a spy?"

"I wasn't really worried before, and I'm even less worried after this conversation. Even if you can't see the future whenever you want, it's still evidence that all this strange stuff isn't only related to Renee."

"So you think we should tell her?"

"Yes, but I'm not sure how. I can't exactly whisper in her ear while we're hugging in bed," Ian said.

Once again, Erica was glad the darkness hid her warm face. Deep in discussion, she had forgotten how close Ian was to her. But his words brought it all back and made her stomach tighten. She pushed the thought aside, trying to focus on the conversation.

"Well, the next time I hug her, I could try," Erica suggested. "It worked last time. However, I guess this might need a longer explanation than the last conversation we had like that."

"Seems like a plan. But what should we tell the others?"

She cringed. "I'm not sure I could explain it to Cam. And Vince scares me. His reactions are so extreme. I don't trust him."

"In here, I think we have to."

"Look what he did with Renee. He didn't hesitate to attack her. She's tiny. Without her ability, he could have killed her. I can't trust him. If he knew I can do this, he'd probably think I'm a traitor too. Like he does with Renee. And I can't defend myself like she did."

"I don't know," Ian said. "If you get these visions whenever you're threatened, you might be a better fighter than you imagine."

"That's not a theory I'm eager to test," she said. Vince was so strong and had been in so many fights that even if she could foresee exactly what he was about to do, Erica was certain she wouldn't stand a chance.

"Okay. It's your decision. We won't tell him for now."

After a few moments of quiet contemplation, Ian leaned back and looked at Erica in the dim light. "Sleep now?"

"Yeah, I guess so."

Suddenly, the vision tore through her consciousness.

Ian's warm voice caressing her. "Goodnight, my visionary girlfriend." His lips moving gently against hers. His right hand touching her hair, sliding past her ear, caressing her neck, finding a path down her side to her hip.

"Goodnight—"

"Wait!" she urgently whispered.

"Um, yes?"

She pulled him closer and whispered in his ear. "'Goodnight, my visionary girlfriend'. A kiss. Your hand touching my hair, my ear, and my neck. And my side."

Ian's quiet gasp sounded loud with his mouth brushing against Erica's ear. "I was going to say that. And do that. Well, actually I was just about to touch your hair and go from there. But whatever."

"Yeah. I had a vision. Obviously."

"What did you do? What were you thinking about?" Ian spoke rapidly, as if they only had an instant to grab hold of the moment before it faded.

Erica cast her mind back. Concentrating was difficult with the vision so fresh in her mind. "Nothing important. About sleeping and hoping tomorrow would be better than today." And about him, in bed, beside her. But she didn't want to admit that.

"You know I'm not trying to kill you, right?" Ian whispered. His tone wasn't serious, but Erica suspected he wanted to make it clear nevertheless.

"Yeah, you don't seem like the murdering type. So I guess this means these visions don't only happen when someone's in danger."

"Yes. That's a good thing. I'd admit the danger thing is useful in here, but in the real world, it's much more practical if you can see more than people's imminent deaths."

"I suppose," Erica said, distracted. She considered Ian's earlier question. What had changed, compared to the number guessing game? The circumstances around each of the visions were so different. She hadn't been trying to see the future on any of the occurrences. So it wasn't only mental. It must be related to what was happening somehow.

She went through the incidents in her mind, one by one, searching for a connection. What did the risk of death and Ian kissing her have in common? It seemed very little. Renee's fall was the most horrifying thing she'd ever seen. On the other hand, kissing Ian—even when she knew that he was only playing a role for the cameras—set her soul aflame like nothing ever had before. The two incidents were complete opposites.

Suddenly, it hit her in an almost physical way. The thing in common was emotion. Undeniable, overpowering emotion.

Ian sensed the shift in her thoughts. "What's up, Erica?"

If that was the explanation, she couldn't tell Ian. It would reveal far too much about her feelings. Still, perhaps she could test the theory without divulging any sensitive information.

"I'm just trying to figure out what might be causing it. Let me try something," she whispered in his ear. "Kiss me."

"For science," he replied. He brushed his lips against hers, tender at first, but then more demanding.

Erica was so focused on what she was feeling, straining to have a vision, that she didn't experience the familiar surge of emotions. She barely noticed the hand caressing her cheek that normally would have sent her heart racing.

Apparently, it was hard to become emotional when one was focusing on becoming emotional. Kind of like trying to avoid thinking of a purple rhinoceros when someone said, "don't visualize a purple rhino."

"Didn't work. Complete waste of time," she said disgustedly as Ian pulled back and looked at her questioningly in the dim light.

"What?" he said with mock outrage. "My kisses are a waste of your time?"

She smiled involuntarily and pulled him close so her lips once again brushed his ear. "You know what I mean."

Clearly, she needed to try something else. Her reaction to his touch wasn't strong enough when she scripted everything. But this was the first time she'd had a vision with Ian. Several had resulted from her fear when lives were at risk. Maybe fear was easier than bliss. But it was hard to be afraid lying in Ian's embrace. She needed something real.

Suddenly, she realized what she had to try. The idea that had been worming its way around her thoughts all day, but she'd been trying to ignore. "Think of a number. When I tap your arm, wait a few seconds and tell me."

Erica cast her mind back to the room where Denise died. Renee was running on that final ramp before the big drop. She had the vision, what, five seconds before Renee jumped? And what did she say? "Be careful"? Ian had said it earlier. Five seconds is a long time. Why didn't she use that time to come up with something better than *be careful?*

She knew Renee was impetuous, and she'd already ignored their cries earlier. Why did she think that *be careful* would be enough to stop Renee? She could have said a hundred things. *The ladder isn't attached to anything* or *there are spikes on the ledge.* Even—*watch out for the man up there.* Any lie would have worked. She just needed Renee to stop sprinting for a moment and listen.

But, with Renee's life hanging in the balance, she shouted the most inane thing she could possibly say. No matter how much she'd like to blame it all on someone else, she was responsible. She'd had the power to stop Renee, to save a life, and she had utterly failed.

She had killed Denise. The blood on the floor. The broken girl. It was all her fault. Because, when the moment mattered, she chose the banal.

Tears brimming in her eyes, the vision struck Erica the instant she tapped Ian's arm.

Ian leaning back from her. "7,328. What's wrong?" A hug.

"Don't worry. You'll figure it out."

"7,328," she whispered, her voice cracking.

"That's right!" She heard the grin in his voice.

"I know."

He must have sensed something in her tone. "What's wrong? You figured it out." He pulled her close to him.

"I... I don't want to talk about it. Please. Just hold me."

"I will."

#

She didn't mean to, but Erica fell asleep that way, overcome by exhaustion from the events of the day and the warmth of Ian's embrace. Despite the turmoil in her thoughts, she slept soundly.

A shout from Cam awakened her. As Erica's eyes opened, a vision flashed through her mind. Right away, she knew what was wrong.

Ian rubbed the sleep from his eyes and struggled to sit up. "What are you yelling about, Cam?"

Erica pre-empted whatever Cam was going to say.

"Renee's missing, Ian. She's gone."

CHAPTER SEVENTEEN

Ian was instantly awake. He leaped out of bed, scanned the room, and ran to the bathroom, nearly ripping the curtain off in his haste.

"I already looked there," Cam said.

Ian strode to Vince's mattress. "Where is she?" he demanded, looming over Vince with his hands on his hips.

"I have no clue. I woke up when Cam shouted, just like you," Vince said, pushing back the sheet and sitting up.

"Give me a break. You've wanted her gone for days and threatened to kill her several times. What did you do to her?"

"I swear, I didn't do anything. I admit that we had our disagreements, and I believe we're better off not having her, but I didn't touch her. Now, though, we don't need to worry about her jumping off a cliff and killing one of us."

"Then where is she?"

"How would I know? Maybe she was scared and ran away on her own. Or, more likely, our captors realized that we figured out she was a spy and pulled her out."

To Erica, Vince seemed genuinely surprised at the disappearance. Besides, he'd had no hesitation before about saying they should kill Renee. Why would he deny doing something now? If anything, he'd probably be proud of it and want to brag. But Ian didn't seem to be buying the story. He seemed about ready to take a swing at Vince.

It hadn't worked out well last time he did that, so Erica searched for a way to distract him. She stepped forward, placing her hand on Ian's arm. "I doubt she was a spy. I see only two options. She either left voluntarily or was taken. If it was voluntary, she would've left a note or something. And if it was involuntarily, she would have put up a fight and may have left some clues."

Ian turned to her, his face intent. "Yes. We should look." They spent the next few minutes searching the mostly empty room for messages on the backs of paper plates, in the bathroom, or in her bed. Erica noticed in passing that the display on the wall now said 0.5, but other than that, nothing seemed to have changed. There were no signs of a fight. That didn't surprise Erica. If Renee had left a note, she would have made it obvious and if there had been a struggle, surely Renee would have made enough noise to wake them.

When breakfast came, they paused to eat. Nobody commented on the fact that there was even less food than on the previous days. They were missing two people, so less was needed.

Afterward, they resumed the search for clues, though nobody held out much hope. Eventually, Erica maneuvered Ian into the bathroom with her. Once there, she turned on the water to wash her face and pulled him into a hug, seemingly to support him in his hour of need, but really so that she could talk privately.

"I don't think Vince did it," she whispered.

"He must have. There's no sign of her here," he said. Even whispering, his voice sounded strained.

"Could he murder her without any signs of a fight? You saw how she beat him yesterday. Even if he attacked her while she was sleeping, I doubt he'd be able to kill her without waking up the rest of us. And how would he hide the body? It can't be him."

"So what, she walked out of here on her own? Or do you think she was a spy?" His tone was halfway between curious and accusing.

"Of course not. I told you that last night. I'm leaning toward the abduction theory. Because she would have left some sign if—"

Vince chose that moment to walk into the room. "Come on. Remember what I said? Crying never solves anything. And particularly not crying on your girlfriend's shoulder. She'll leave you for a better man."

Ian broke the hug and straightened. "I'm not crying, Vince, and if you had any speck of decency, you wouldn't harass a guy who just lost his sister."

Vince held up his hands. "Hey, I'm only trying to help."

"We don't need your help," Ian said, glaring at him, his fingers curled into fists. "You're useless here, just like you're useless at school, and probably worse than useless at home."

Vince stared at him for a few seconds, blinking. Swallowing, he turned his back and walked away. "Man, you're just like your little sister." He glanced back at Erica. "And you too. I'm starting to think that you guys have been playing us this whole time." He shut the curtain behind him.

Ian looked at Erica. "What's *that* supposed to mean?" he spat out.

She shrugged. "Renee's gone, so he now needs to pin his paranoid delusions on someone else? Even so, probably not the best idea to call him useless. That was cold." She grabbed his hand and intertwined her fingers with his to show that she still supported him, despite the criticism. "And we are trying to work together."

"We are?" When Ian saw Erica's raised eyebrows, he sighed and stared at his feet, the anger leaving his posture. "Yeah, I know we are. I'm just tired of his constant sniping. With Renee gone, you'd think he'd give it a rest, but it seems worse than ever."

Erica suspected that Vince had actually been serious about the advice not to cry and that, in Vince's book, getting a comforting hug was the equivalent of crying. But she didn't want it to seem as though she was siding with Vince, so she settled for, "Well, he is who he is. You can handle him."

"Yeah," he said, sighing. "I can. But he keeps flip-flopping. Yesterday morning, I really believed that he was coming around. I guess Denise's death ruined all that."

Erica flinched. As if Denise's death wasn't enough, she was now responsible for Vince's callousness as well. Her eyes stung.

Ian misinterpreted her reaction and squeezed her tightly. It almost made it all seem okay. Almost. "I know," he said. "It hurts whenever I remember her."

"Yeah," Erica said and then changed the topic. "But we need to focus on Renee now."

"Of course." Ian took a deep breath. "I know you believe someone grabbed her, but to be completely sure, we need to retrace our steps and see if Renee's there. If she was trying to escape from Vince, that's the only direction she would have gone."

Erica blanched. "But that would mean..."

Ian finished her thought. "We'd have to go through the room where Denise died. Where she is."

Erica wanted to refuse, to say that there was no way Renee would have gone back in the middle of the night, through the room with the body. But if there were any possibility, however slim, that they could find Renee, Erica wouldn't abandon her friend. Nor deny Ian the chance to find his sister. "Okay," she quietly said.

Together, they returned to the main room and explained their thoughts to the others.

"I'm not going back," Vince said. His tone was firm, shoulders set, but his eyes seemed a bit red. "Not to look for Renee."

"Why not?" Erica said quickly before Ian said anything. She didn't want the earlier nastiness between him and Vince to spill into this discussion.

"Isn't it obvious?" Vince said.

"Not to me."

"Oh, come on! Denise died yesterday because of Renee. I'm not going to stroll past her body in a futile search for her murderer."

Ian's eyes snapped to Vince's face. "What do you mean by futile? How would you know it's futile?"

"It's obvious. You really think she'd climb down that ladder in the dark and walk right by the body? There's no way!"

Ian's lips twitched. "Maybe it's unlikely, but she's my sister. We have to eliminate every possibility."

"Well, you can do it without me," Vince said.

"Fine then! You stay here then, and we'll go check. Come on, Erica!" Ian grabbed Erica's hand and tugged her toward the door.

Cam glanced at Vince and back at Ian, clearly trying to figure out whether he should remain there with the boy who had tormented him through all those years of school or follow the others down the ladder and past his friend's bloody remains. Erica sympathized. It was hard to imagine two less appealing options.

Cam never had a chance to make the decision. Ian opened the door and then stopped. The rope ladder was gone. Only the two posts to which it had been attached remained, each sticking up six inches from the floor.

"I guess we should see if it's fallen," Ian said tentatively. He swallowed, looking like he wanted nothing more than close the door once more.

Erica nodded, though she couldn't imagine how the ladder would have become unhooked on its own. Still holding hands, they crept toward the edge, dreading the sight of Denise's bloody shroud, but needing to understand what had happened.

A vision raced through Erica's mind, causing her to gasp. Ian stopped and looked at her, a question on his face. Her heart racing, she shuffled forward, gesturing toward the floor far below. "Look."

The ramps looked exactly as they had the previous day, but otherwise, the room was empty. There was no sign of Denise, the sheet, or the ladder. Not even a bloodstain remained.

They surveyed the scene silently for several seconds.

"Someone must have cleaned up," Ian said, stating the obvious.

"It supports the theory that someone grabbed Renee." She paused for a second and then added, "We can't get down there safely."

"And even if we did, we couldn't get back up," Ian said. His face drooped. To Erica, this was the downside of Ian's optimism. He'd clearly half convinced himself that they had a real chance of finding Renee here.

Erica looked at Ian, sighing. "I'm sorry," she said. She put her arm around his waist and her head against his shoulder.

"It was a long shot anyway," he replied despondently.

Cam arrived at the door with Vince trailing a few steps behind. After taking his strong stand against searching for Renee, Vince's gait was casual, as if he was strolling in the park and not at all curious about Ian and Erica's reaction.

"Did the ladder fall?" Cam said.

"No, someone took it. And Denise is gone," Erica said.

Cam and Vincent hurried forward and stared down on the empty room while Ian and Erica retreated to give the others space on the ledge.

"So someone was prowling around here last night," Vince pointed out.

"Yeah," Ian said. "It makes it more likely that Renee was abducted. Again." His shoulders slumped.

"Or she moved Denise and the ladder when she left to join her buddies." Vince's tone made it clear that, in his view, this was almost certainly what had happened.

Ian wearily rolled his eyes and walked slowly back to his mattress in the other room. He collapsed there. Erica sat down beside him.

Renee was probably dead or being tortured alone in some cell. Erica's fears were coming true. One by one they were dying. First

Denise, now Renee. Marching smartly in single file to oblivion.

If they were all going to die, she hoped she'd go before Ian. She didn't want to watch him die or wander around for days in here by herself. That would be too much to bear. She wondered if Ian would grieve when she died. Her eyes felt prickly.

The others returned to the room and stood before them. Erica sighed. Though they seemed to be getting nowhere, they had no choice but to keep going. They needed to escape.

"So what do we do now?" she said. She stared up at Vince and Cam, although she intended the question for Ian. She knew the search for Renee was hopeless, but wanted him to recognize that himself.

"We say good riddance to Renee and continue our journey," Vince said.

"Why can't you show some respect? Or at least just leave it alone?" Ian said. He had red eyes, as if he'd been crying, though Erica hadn't seen any tears. "She's gone who knows where, and we wouldn't have gotten this far without her."

"Because we didn't *all* get this far without her. I look around, but I don't see Denise anywhere." He scowled at Ian. "And that was all Renee's fault."

The future flashed through Erica's mind.

> *Ian's eyes narrowing. "You know, Denise didn't even like you. You're pathetic, obsessing over a girl who didn't even care about you." Vince's face twisting in anger. His knee coming up, connecting with Ian's head.*

"You know—" Ian began.

"We are all grieving for Denise," Erica said, her voice loud even over her pounding heart. "But we have to put Denise and Renee behind us and move on."

Ian looked at her. She rarely interrupted him. "Please?" she quietly said.

He blinked, and the anger drained from his face. "You're right, Erica." He turned back to the others. "We have to keep going. There's nothing left for us here." He sighed.

"No kidding," Vince said, and Cam nodded.

"Should we wait for lunch before heading out?" Erica said.

"I don't think so. It's only been an hour, and by now, we can be pretty sure that after we get through the next room, we'll be fed.

Besides," Ian said, gesturing to the display on the wall, which now said 0.7. "The longer we wait, the more likely we'll figure out what that means." Everyone nodded.

The exit was unlocked. When opened, it revealed the expected staircase up. They ascended and gathered in the tiny room above.

"I guess we use the usual strategy?" Ian asked Vince. The disagreement seemed to be forgotten, now that they needed to confront the next challenge.

"Yep. You open the door. If someone's there, we'll attack. If not, close the door and we'll discuss it."

Ian turned to Erica. "Are you ready?" he pointedly asked.

He clearly wanted her to try to use a vision to see behind the door as he'd talked about last night. "Just a sec," she said, closing her eyes.

She cast her mind back to Denise's death, trying once again to focus on the pain and guilt. But it was different in the day, standing there in the light with everyone gathered around her. Less safe and too many distractions.

She couldn't do it. After what felt like a minute, but was probably a few seconds, she gave up. "I'm ready," she said, shaking her head slightly, a movement Ian would know how to interpret but the others wouldn't even notice.

"Done saying your prayers?" Vince said, sarcasm dripping from the words.

It was as good an excuse as anything. "Yes. We're all just trying to deal with Denise's death in our own ways," she replied. Vince had nothing to say to that.

They turned back to the door. Ian opened it, peeped in, and closed it again.

"Cubes. The room has a couple of big cubes in it, and nothing else as far as I could tell," he said.

"Cubes? Why would they bother with cubes?" Cam said, his expression halfway between disbelief and outrage.

Erica shrugged. "Yeah. What's with these rooms with the geometric shapes?"

"Still better than the cougar," Ian said. "The cubes are probably like the pyramid, with something hidden inside. We should be careful not to touch anything."

"Obviously," Vince said, rolling his eyes. "Can we go now?"

When everyone nodded, Ian opened the door. Just like

everywhere else, the room was white. In its center were two white cubes, separated by about ten feet. Each was about ten feet high and roughly twenty-five feet from the closest wall of the rectangular room.

Cautiously, the group crept forward in a huddle toward the closest cube. They were about six feet from it when the vision crashed through Erica's head.

Dark-uniformed soldiers leaping out. Pronged devices pointing. Crackling. Ian and Vince collapsing.

"Someone's back there!" she shouted. "They have Tasers!"

"Go! Go! Go!" yelled someone. Four soldiers jumped out from behind the two blocks. As in Erica's house, the soldiers were dressed in high-collared black uniforms with matching caps, high boots, gloves, and utility belts. They look huge and muscular, like heavyweight boxers, and their faces were grim and businesslike. Each soldier pointed a pronged device about the size of a small flashlight at them down the corridor between the cubes.

Vince didn't have time to react. A red dot appeared on his shirt and moments later, a dart on the end of a cable shot from one of the Tasers, hitting him in the chest. Electricity crackled, and there was a smell like the laser printer from school. Vince's legs turned to jelly, and he fell prone.

Ian had been half expecting Erica to warn him, so he moved in an instant. He dodged the first cable that shot toward him before charging at the soldiers, interposing his body between Erica and the attackers.

Clearly recognizing Ian as the biggest threat, the remaining two soldiers trained their weapons on him and fired. One cable missed and sailed between Erica and Cam. The other didn't. A surge of electricity coursed through Ian's body, and his momentum carried him heavily into the cube on the right. He lay on the floor unmoving.

CHAPTER EIGHTEEN

With a faint whirring sound, cables snaked back to the weapons. The soldiers refocused their attention on Erica and Cam.

Cam scampered behind the left cube before the soldiers finished reloading. Erica, stunned at how hard Ian had hit the cube, took a quarter of a second to decide whether she should follow Cam or help Ian.

It was a quarter second she didn't have. She turned to follow Cam, but the soldiers were ready to fire again.

Two buttons being pressed. Cables shooting out. A prong in her shoulder. Her knees buckling.

Instantly, she decided to stop running to avoid being hit in the shoulder, and another vision crashed through her brain.

The first cable missing. The other hitting her neck.

Instinctively, she cast around for another option and considered dropping down to one knee.

The first two missing. The third cable snaking out. Her arm.

Like a perfectly choreographed dance, Erica's plan stretched before her. Stop. One knee. Somersault.

The fourth cable. Her leg.

Stop. One knee. Somersault. Jump.

Cables striking around her. Safe behind the cube.

It had taken only an instant for the different scenarios to sift through Erica's mind and for her to find the four-dimensional path through the twisting cables.

Erica appeared to slip and fall onto one knee, causing the first two shots to miss her by inches. With a tumble and a desperate leap, she barely avoided the next two and took shelter behind the same cube as Cam. She heard the cables retracting and knew that the soldiers would soon be ready for another shot.

Fear distorting his face, Cam looked at Erica in desperation. "What should we do?"

Erica thought quickly. They could run for the exit as they had with the cougar. But unlike the animal, soldiers wouldn't be thwarted by a closed door.

But did they have any other choice? If they tried to retreat the way they came, the soldiers would probably pursue them. And besides, there was still Ian to consider. She couldn't just abandon him. Not to mention Vince.

Her visions were the wild card. It had been close, but she'd been able to dodge. If she kept seeing the trajectories of the cables, would they be able to hit her? But she didn't want to rely on the visions, considering how inconsistent they seemed to be. And even with them, she couldn't evade the soldiers forever. But nor could she and Cam run away. And that left one option.

"We have to fight," Erica answered, her eyes hard.

"What? Are you crazy? Those are soldiers! With weapons."

"There's no other option. They'll cut us down from behind if we run." A vision coursed through her mind. "Here they come! Fight!"

Two soldiers jumped out from one side of the cube and two from the other. The two closest to Erica, in the corridor between the cubes, aimed at her and fired.

Once again aided by the visions, she turned sideways and let the two cables sail by harmlessly on either side of her. Deciding that they'd have a better chance if they both attacked the same pair, she turned toward the soldiers targeting Cam.

Unfortunately, Cam was not as good at dodging as Erica. He stood rooted to the floor. One of the shots struck him in the chest and the second in his right forearm. The electricity crackled. But unlike Ian and Vince, he didn't fall.

Astounded, Erica paused for a second to look at him. All of Cam's muscles were tense. Veins popped out on his neck and forehead, and he wore an expression of intense concentration. She stared down at the cable embedded in his arm.

At the end of it was a prong. As she watched, Cam's flesh rippled, then rose and enveloped the entire dart. She looked up to see both of the soldiers who had shot Cam collapse. The laser printer smell permeated the air.

Erica didn't know what had happened, but she was willing to take advantage of the opportunity. "Grab the Tasers," she said, acutely aware of the low whirring sound of the remaining two soldiers reloading.

She sprinted toward the nearest fallen soldier, picked up one of the weapons, and glanced at the soldier's face. His eyes were vacant, but clipped to his ear was an earphone with a small integrated microphone. On a whim, Erica grabbed it as well.

Aware that the other two soldiers would almost be ready to fire again, Erica stepped behind the edge of the cube and looked back toward Cam. He had only just reached the other unconscious soldier, having paused to pull out the dart from his chest. He was still tugging against the cable sticking out from his right arm.

Erica poked her head out quickly to see what the remaining two soldiers were doing. There was no sign of them. She assumed that they had moved back into the gap between the cubes for cover while they planned their next attack.

She examined the weapon she'd grabbed. Two prominent buttons were near its tip, one black and one red. Guessing that the black one meant reload—and at this point halfway confident that if she were about to press the wrong button, she'd get a vision preventing her from doing so—she pressed it.

She was right. The cable snaked back into the weapon, much faster than she expected. Unfortunately, she didn't consider the implication of retracting the cord with the dart still trapped within Cam's arm. The jerk when the cable became taut tore the weapon from Erica's hand.

"Ouch," Cam said, "that hurt!"

Erica winced in empathy. "Sorry."

The weapon reeled itself in toward Cam. He reached for it, but, before he grabbed it, the skin on his forearm surged up and absorbed it, like an orca devouring a salmon in a single gulp.

"What the heck?" Cam said. He pulled his hand away from where the weapon's dart had been embedded. The arm looked misshapen, swollen, its skin distended.

Erica didn't have a chance to comment before she was struck by another vision of a red dot on Cam's back, followed by a dart. Not trusting Cam to react quickly enough to a warning, she hauled him to safety behind a cube. The cable harmlessly shot by.

They had some temporary cover, but still no weapons. Erica debated whether she could trust her visions enough to try to retrieve the other weapon, well aware that another soldier was out there ready to fire, just waiting for her to show herself.

She had just decided it was worth the risk when it occurred to her that she was still holding the headpiece she had taken from the fallen soldier. She stuffed the bud into her ear.

Cam looked at her in confusion. "What's—"

A voice from the earbud interrupted him, so Erica ignored whatever Cam was going to say.

"*Focus on Cam. Be careful. He took out the other two.*"

"*Are they armed?*" crackled a whisper in reply.

"*No. They went for the Javelins, but I don't see them holding anything.*"

Instinctively, Erica scanned the room, looking for someone watching them, but with the soldiers on the other side of the block, there was nobody to see.

The earpiece crackled again. "*Wait. Erica has a headset. Go radio silent.*"

Now that they realized that she was listening on the headset, there didn't seem to be any reason to be quiet. But Erica bent the microphone away from her mouth and covered it anyway. "They're targeting you, Cam," she hurriedly whispered.

"What?" He shot her a fearful glance.

She pointed at the earpiece. "They said they'll focus on you."

"What should I do?" he whispered back. He was trembling, looking wildly around the room.

"Fight."

"I don't know how to fight. If I did, I wouldn't let Vince bug me all the time."

"Well, it's time to learn. Just do whatever comes naturally," Erica said. She gestured to her left. The soldiers had doubled back to surprise them from the other side. "Get ready! They're coming around from over here. As soon as they turn the corner, attack. They won't expect it."

Cam stared at her for a second as if weighing his options, then darted off in the opposite direction. Erica cursed under her breath and followed. She heard the heavy footsteps of the soldiers sprinting behind her.

"This feels natural," Cam said.

"We have to fight. They'll catch us if we keep running around these blocks!"

"I'm pretty fast."

Right before they turned the next corner, Erica was hit by a vision of a dart embedding itself in the back of her neck. By now, she was becoming more comfortable reacting to the visions. Almost casually, she moved her head a few inches to the left, letting the dart fly over her shoulder.

She turned the corner as one of the soldiers, who had reversed direction again, leaped into view from the opposite side of the cube.

Cam skidded to a halt, unsure what to do. The soldier raised his weapon and fired, hitting Cam in the center of his chest.

As before, Cam didn't fall. Instead, once more, there was a crackling sound, and the soldier collapsed.

"What did you do?" Erica asked urgently. "That's the second time that's happened."

"I don't know," Cam said, looking even more lost and frightened. "Those cables shoot electricity. They really hurt." He ripped the electrode from his chest. Erica saw blood on its tip.

Erica's headset clicked. Apparently, the enemy had a message worth breaking radio silence to convey. "*The Javelins are malfunctioning when they hit Cam. Don't use them.*"

A second voice answered, "*Repeat.*"

"*No Javelins. Knock Cam out.*"

"*Roger.*"

Erica thought about the implications of the exchange. The Javelins must be the Taser-like weapons. If they were out of the picture, it was two against one, and they had a hope. A slim one, considering he was a trained soldier and Cam was more of a trained punching bag. But more of a hope than when it was four against two.

Erica knew next to nothing about fighting. What was the best strategy for two against one? Probably for them to attack him at the same time. Get him in the open so they could see him coming and he couldn't use the tight quarters near the cubes to isolate one of them.

Erica grabbed Cam's arm and tugged him toward the wall with the door from which they had entered.

Cam gave her a look of confusion. "Over there, we can't hide behind the cubes," he said.

Erica nodded. "I know." She tapped on the headset in her ear. "Their weapons are malfunctioning. They told him to disable us without using it. We need to be able to see him coming and have enough room to dodge. It's a fistfight now. Us against him."

Cam still seemed dubious, but Erica was insistent. She pulled him away from the cube, and they both turned and waited for the soldier to appear. In a few seconds, the soldier peered around the corner of the cube, about thirty-five feet from the pair. Erica and Cam awkwardly raised their fists, trying to appear threatening. The soldier smiled maliciously, an expression made all the more malevolent by the scar that ran across his left cheek and onto his nose.

Erica reconsidered whether it was a good idea to fight. The soldier must have been close to twice their combined weight, with a much longer reach. Even if he had no experience in hand-to-hand combat, he'd likely be able to beat them without breaking a sweat. Would it hurt being knocked out?

The soldier brought up his hands and strode forward, rapidly closing the distance. Erica inched sideways a bit to put some space between her and Cam. The soldier ignored her movement, continuing to focus on Cam as he'd been instructed.

Cam swung his left fist when the soldier was ludicrously far away, still at least six feet. He had no hope of landing the blow. The soldier chuckled, whether at the distance or Cam's poor form, Erica didn't know. Both maybe.

Then Cam swung his right. It was a still a ridiculously long distance. But it didn't matter.

As Cam's arm reached its full extension, a cable shot out of his wrist and the dart on the end embedded itself in the soldier's abdomen. The man stared down in wonder for half a second before a now-familiar crackle heralded the surge of electricity through his body. He twitched and crumpled to the ground.

Cam's eyes went round. He jerked his hand back as if he'd touched a hot burner on the stove. The cable snaked into his arm and vanished.

"Um, Cam, what did you just do?" Erica asked in a deliberately understated tone, trying to understand what had happened without freaking out Cam any more than he already seemed to be.

Cam studied his arm and experimentally shook it. "I'm not sure," he murmured. Using his left arm, he held up his right for inspection as though it was a dead rat.

Gently, Erica took his hand and scanned one side of his arm and then the other. The bulge she had seen earlier was still there, though the skin was unbroken. "The weapon's inside your arm. Does it hurt?"

"It feels strange," Cam said.

There was a groan from near the entrance to the room.

Erica had forgotten the others. "Ian!" She ran toward the cube where he had fallen. She only made it a step before a vision struck her.

> *A hissing sound. Reaching Ian's side. Blood on cube. Falling into darkness.*

She took a deep breath, then, as the hissing started, remembered Cam. Erica shouted, "Hold your breath!" back to him and continued toward Ian.

She could hear Cam running behind her, but ignored him and rolled Ian over onto his back, smearing the blood from a cut on his forehead across the white cube.

Ian's eyes opened. "Erica. What happened? There were soldiers." Erica, afraid to talk lest she inhale the gas, made quick "stand up" gestures with both hands and pointed to the door.

"What's wrong?" His head lifted a few inches off the floor. "I don't think I can get up."

Erica stood up, grabbed his hands, and tugged at them.

"I'll try but…" Ian's voice trailed off. His head bobbed and then sagged. He was out cold.

Erica hauled on his hands, but realized that she couldn't drag him out of the room on her own. She'd need Cam's help. She turned to look for him.

Instead of following her toward Ian, Cam, who had survived four years of high school by consistently choosing flight over fight, had raced back to the door from which they had entered. He yanked the handle, but it wouldn't open.

Their only chance was to advance. Erica clapped her hands to get Cam's attention and pointed vaguely in the direction of the other door. Uncharacteristically, Cam deciphered her gestures at once and set off at a run.

Erica bounced to her feet. Saying an apology in her head for abandoning Ian and promising that she'd return as soon as the room was safe, she turned to follow Cam between the cubes.

With less warning, Cam hadn't been able to take as deep a breath as Erica before the gas descended. Erica was several yards behind him, but was still close enough to hear his gasp as he gave in to his need for oxygen. Almost immediately, he stumbled and slid on his chest across the floor.

Erica didn't spare him a second glance, just kept running. A half a second later, she realized that she wasn't going to make it either.

With about ten feet remaining, she pulled the bottom of her shirt over her mouth and nose, praying without any real hope that it would act as a filter against the gas. Fighting against her body's demands to fill her lungs, she took a shallow breath. She was within five feet of the door when her head began to spin.

Her hand on the door handle. Desperate tugs. It didn't budge.

The vision told Erica everything she needed to know.

She stumbled to the floor and gave in. The ubiquitous white walls seemed to turn gray, and then black.

CHAPTER NINETEEN

"Wake up, Erica."

The voice was gentle, but it was persistent in her ear. A hand on her shoulder urged her to consciousness.

Cautiously, Erica opened her eyes and slightly turned her head. Ian knelt to her right, gazing at her with a worried expression. She gave a slight grin, and the wrinkles around his eyes smoothed.

"Hey, beautiful. I was worried about you. Those Tasers pack a serious kick." Ian helped Erica roll over and sit up. As he did, the peripheries of her vision shrank and the world narrowed to a small circle. It was too soon.

"Not shot. Gas," Erica croaked. She struggled to pull the thoughts together to form full sentences. The floor had never before seemed like such an enticing place to rest. Trying to pull herself together, Erica shook her head as if, with enough vigor, she might toss the last remnants of the drug from her brain. That was a bad idea.

After a few seconds, Erica's eyes opened a second time. She looked up at Ian and blinked, wide-eyed. A second ago, she was sitting, and now she was lying on Ian's lap, with his legs stretch out on either side of her.

"I think maybe you should just rest there for a while." Ian brushed a stray strand of hair away from her forehead.

"Oh," Erica said. She didn't seem up to saying anything, but lying for a few minutes on Ian's lap didn't seem like the worst thing in the world.

"There's no need to rush. When you tried to get me up after being hit by those weapons, the same thing happened to me."

Red blood on a white wall. Erica suddenly remembered.

Worried, she tilted her head back to peer at Ian's face. There was a dark smear on his forehead and a prominent bump, but the cut seemed to have clotted. Erica instinctively raised her hand toward it, and then realized it would probably hurt him if she touched it.

"Yeah, I hit the cube pretty hard when I fell. It still feels like my brain is bulging out of my skull, but at least it's stopped bleeding."

Erica let her hand fall back down to her side.

"Don't worry. I've been through worse. I'll be fine," Ian said. "How are you doing?" His voice was gentle and his eyes worried.

Erica paused as she mentally assessed how she felt. "I'm not injured. Other than a bit of fog, I'm good."

"I guess you were wise enough to stay away from the blocks as they shot you. You almost made it to the door. A few more feet…" He gestured behind him.

Erica didn't bother looking. She knew exactly how close she'd come. "They didn't shoot me. They piped knockout gas into the room."

Ian looked at her oddly as if he wasn't sure whether electricity had addled her brain. "That's strange. They only shot Vince and me?"

Erica described to Ian what had happened, although she glossed over the part about Cam's arm absorbing the Javelin. Instead, she just said that some of the Javelins were malfunctioning and Cam used one against one of the soldiers. She figured that, if anyone was listening, it might be better not to converse about the strange abilities in front of them.

"So failing with the Javelins, they used the gas…" Ian said, his tone thoughtful.

Erica nodded. "Piped it into the room somehow."

"Where's your headset now?"

Erica touched her right ear. It was gone. She looked around for it and flinched when she saw Vince standing back near the cubes, staring at them. She sat up.

"Oh. Hi, Vince, how's it going?" Erica said casually, like they were meeting in the school hall. How long had he been listening to them?

"I'm great. What's that about headsets?" He walked slowly toward them, staring at Erica.

"Oh, the soldiers wore them. Didn't you see them?" Erica asked guilelessly.

"No, I got shot right away. I didn't see much of anything."

"I guess not." Erica's mind spun. She didn't want to get into a big discussion with Vince about how Cam had knocked out all four soldiers. After everything they'd gone through with Renee, who knew how Vince would react this time? She didn't want him to set his sights on Cam.

She glanced toward the door and blandly said, "Cam and I made it farther than you, but they took us down too." Erica's cheeks felt warm.

When she looked back at Vince, his eyes were narrow and his lips flat. "Yeah. Where is Cam?" he asked.

Erica's eyes widened. The drug must have addled her brain more than she realized. Despite talking about him, it didn't actually occur to her to check on Cam. "I thought he fell just behind me." She looked around. "But it was so fast. Maybe he's behind one of the cubes."

They explored the room. There was no trace of him, the soldiers, or any of their equipment. The only sign of the fight was Ian's blood, still smeared across the cube and on the floor.

Vince walked to the door from which they had entered. "Maybe he went back?"

"No, he couldn't," Erica replied as Vince tried the handle. It opened.

"Couldn't?" Vince asked, his eyebrows raised.

Now that she'd implied that she and Cam had been shot like the others, she couldn't say that they had spent a few minute dodging soldiers, running around cubes, and trying to open doors.

"I mean, he wouldn't," Erica said, biting her lip and looking away. "Even if he woke up before us, he wouldn't go off on his own. He wouldn't abandon us."

"We should probably search for him anyway," Ian said. "Or at least let's check the last room. That's really the only place he would have gone."

Everyone nodded, though Erica was almost certain the search was hopeless, that Cam had been taken away. Silently, they retraced their steps to the lower room. Cam wasn't there, and the room was how they'd left it. The number on the display had increased to 0.9. They decided to ascend once more.

"So now we've lost two people, Renee and Cam," Ian said at the foot of the stairs.

Vince stopped, scowling at him. "Two? We started with six. Are you going to pretend Denise didn't even exist? Try to pave over the fact that Renee killed her?"

Ian turned toward him and said, "She didn't kill her. But what I mean to say is we know she's dead." Erica saw Vince's mouth twitch. "Renee and Cam were alive when we saw them last. So two of us are unaccounted for."

"And they both vanished while we slept," Erica added.

"Or at least while *I* was sleeping," Vince said, his tone dripping with implication.

"What's that supposed to mean?" Ian asked. "We were *all* sleeping. Or unconscious, or whatever you want to call it when you get hit by a Javelin."

Vince looked at him flatly. "I'm saying that all I know is that *I* was unconscious. I never saw you get hit. All those soldiers fired at me and took me down. And when I regained consciousness, you guys were just hanging out, chatting."

Ian raised his hand. "That's not how it was. We had just woken up ourselves." His voice was defensive.

"Well, you looked pretty relaxed to me. Erica lying on your lap, not a care in the world. You didn't even check if I was okay. Or look for Cam, for that matter."

Ian dropped his eyes and turned pink. "I woke up first. I looked up and noticed Erica lying face down on the floor. So I went to her and woke her up, but she felt unsteady and had to lie down. I was making sure she was fine, but I still planned to check on you as soon as she was better."

"I was woozy," Erica explained, and Ian nodded.

Vince stared accusingly at Ian. "If that's true, why are you pretending to be ignorant about the soldiers? Don't lie to me. Why did you say, 'your headset' to Erica? And what's with calling the weapons 'Javelins' rather than 'Tasers'? How do you suddenly know everything about the soldiers and their equipment when this is supposedly the first time you've encountered them?"

"It was, for me," Ian defensively said.

"And I told you on our first day in here that soldiers grabbed me from my house, but you didn't believe me," Erica pointed out. She crossed her arms and stared at him. "Maybe you should listen to me more, rather than just freaking out all the time."

"Yeah, I was wondering about that too," Vince said, looking back at her with heavily lidded eyes. "The soldiers exist. But what makes you so special? Why did the soldiers grab you, while the rest of us go to sleep at night and wake up here?"

"I don't have an explanation, but I do agree it seems strange. I don't know why they'd treat me differently."

"Of course you don't." Vince's voice dripped with sarcasm. "Or maybe you got instructions over your headset to tell the rest of us about the soldiers so we wouldn't be surprised when we entered this room."

"I don't have a headset," Erica said. "Look at my ears." She turned her head to either side and moved her hair out of the way so Vince could see.

"You misheard me when you thought I said something about a headset," Ian said. "Or maybe I misspoke. I'm not sure." At Vince's skeptical expression, he continued, "When you woke up, we were talking about the soldiers. Erica said one of them had his headset knocked off. I meant we should try to find it. That's all."

"And the Javelins?" Vince said.

"That's just what the weapons are called," Ian responded.

"I heard a soldier say it," Erica added.

Vince smirked. "What, you heard them say, 'Let's shoot the Javelins at Erica now'? They seemed pretty quiet when they were behind those cubes."

It wasn't going well. When she first woke up, it had seemed much easier to lie than tell the whole truth to Vince. But he suspected they were hiding something and had jumped to the wrong conclusion. She needed a way to turn it around. To find a story that Vince would empathize with and believe. Perhaps stroke his ego a bit like Denise used to do.

Back in the seventh grade on the way to school, Erica saw Vince trip Cam. The moment Cam got up, Vince pushed him down again, taunting him, relishing the moment. Cam had tried to stand four or five times. His knees and hands, chewed up by the unforgiving asphalt, were bloody. And the worse it got, the more talkative Vince became. He had reveled in exerting his power over Cam. Would he understand someone else doing that too?

"They grew chattier after they knocked out the only two guys they considered a threat," Erica said. "They might have been scared of you, but with you down, maybe they treated it as more of a game. I could see how it might be fun to zap someone with ten thousand volts. I suspect after they took out the big guy, they realized they were in control, so they relaxed and started talking. We played cat and mouse in the cubes for a minute or two before they got us. But they weren't really trying."

Vince nodded, so Erica kept speaking. "Maybe that's why I saw the soldiers back when we were abducted. You scared them. They knew you'd fight, so they needed to grab you while you slept. But I wasn't a threat, so they did it the old-fashioned way."

"They have done everything they can to avoid a real fight," Vince said. "Hiding in some room, watching us with video cameras. Or using those weapons. I just wish they'd come in here and fight me like a man."

Erica nodded. "Yeah. They're pretty cowardly."

Vince appeared to consider her story for a few seconds before shaking his head. "I don't know. This isn't that convincing."

"What isn't?" Ian said.

"This explanation of yours. You overheard soldiers talking about the lances—"

"Javelins," corrected Ian.

"Whatever. A soldier had a headset knocked off, and that's the headset you were talking about. You were lying down to recover from the Javelin, and that's why you didn't bother checking on Cam and me. It seems hard to believe."

Ian said, "Is it more reasonable to believe that we're working with the enemy? That two people you've—"

"Three people," Vince interrupted. "You two and your sister."

"Three people," Ian amended, his frustration showing on his face, "that you've known since grade school have been plotting against you to imprison you and a couple of your friends in a death trap?" He gazed thoughtfully at Erica, "Though, it's interesting that we all got hit by the Javelins, but didn't die. Just like Denise didn't die when she got sick. Maybe these aren't all death traps."

"Denise is dead," Vince said, his tone menacing. "You seem to keep forgetting that."

Before Ian could respond and rekindle the fight, Erica jumped in again. "Vince is right. We shouldn't fool ourselves. These rooms can kill. We didn't die this time. But maybe Cam did. How can we be sure?"

"What? We failed the test, so he got taken and killed as punishment?" Ian said.

"That's what a psychopath would do," Vince said with authority. "Why create this tower and bring in six people if you're going to just kill everyone in one trap? You have to punish someone in the group for failure, but let the rest keep going."

"It makes sense, in a twisted sort of way," Erica said. "You could be onto something, Vince." She smiled at him appreciatively.

"So if that's our best theory, what should we do?" Ian asked.

"It's probably a waste of time searching for Cam," Erica said. She rubbed her eyes.

"If that's what's going on, it's simple. We continue and try not to die. If that's really what's going on," Vince said, his voice much calmer than it had been before.

Had they convinced him? Erica was unsure. They had certainly made him consider alternatives to his paranoid "everyone is a spy" theory. But was it enough?

Ian, on the other hand, seemed to have concluded that Vince believed them. "How about we go get lunch first? Or dinner? I have no idea how long we were unconscious. There's probably a mattress and food room through the other door of the cube room. So let's eat and then keep moving."

Erica and Vince nodded. They resumed their way up the stairs with Ian leading. Ian continued to talk inanities while Vince stepped silently behind him, his muscles strangely tense and the back of his neck growing progressively redder.

They almost reached the upper room when the vision cut through Erica's thoughts.

"You're playing me." Vince's fist slamming into Ian's kidney. Ian staggering. Vince heaving him over the railing.

CHAPTER TWENTY

Erica spoke rapidly to interrupt what she knew was about to occur, saying the first thing that popped into her head, stopping Ian mid-sentence. "Hey Vince, I was just thinking about Denise."

Vince paused near the top of the stairs and turned to look at her. "Yeah, what about her?"

"Well, I think she kind of liked you."

Vince's face froze for an instant, then, with excessive casualness, he turned back and continued following Ian. "Oh really?" he tossed over his shoulder. "What makes you say that?"

Erica's mind spun, trying to justify what her mouth was saying. "Well, she spent a lot of time talking with you compared to the rest of us. She always chose the mattress beside you when we were sleeping. And she told me the way you took care of her when she was sick really touched her."

They passed the danger point, reaching the landing. "Not that any of it mattered," Vince said, shaking his head. "I was so nice to her. I took care of her, but now she's dead. All my efforts meant nothing. It was such a waste. I shouldn't have bothered."

Erica blinked. The idea that one could waste kindness was foreign to her. "I don't see it as a waste. I mean, life has been terrible for all of us these last few days. But having you there with her made her life a bit better than it would have been otherwise. That's got to be worth something."

"Yeah, to her, of course. But that was for her, not me. I deserved more," Vince said pointedly as he opened the door at the top of the stairs.

"Yes. I can see why you'd feel that way," Erica said even though she didn't at all. She bit back the temptation to ask Vince what he thought he deserved but didn't receive.

As they walked into the cube room, Erica continued, "Still, I imagine the way you took care of her really cemented in Denise's mind the importance of cooperation. If you're right about this place being a test created by psychos, we'll need that more than ever. It's us against them, and we have to figure out how to win." Internally, she winced as the sentences came out of her mouth. She needed to keep Vince on their side, but her words seemed so heavy-handed.

Ian, who had been listening bemusedly to the conversation, jumped in. "It's true. But I wish we could change the game somehow."

"How do you mean?" Erica said.

"Well, we're in a tower designed for these sorts of tests." He gestured toward the door they were approaching. "You can be sure that through that door, we'll find another room with mattresses and a bathroom. And when we leave that room and go up some stairs, there will be another room with another trap."

"But what about the exit?" Erica asked. Privately, she had her doubts whether they would find an exit simply by climbing, but she was curious what Ian would say.

"Well, maybe the exit is at the top of this tower and we just have to keep climbing. But on the other hand, maybe there isn't an exit. Who knows? Perhaps the tower is only a few stories tall. When we get too high, they drug us when we're all asleep, take us down a few levels, and change the traps."

Erica's brow furrowed. "But the rooms aren't identical."

"Sure, they're a bit different, but they're similar overall. All the same dimensions, except for the one where Renee fell." Ian shrugged. "After a certain point, the building would have to be as tall as a skyscraper and there aren't any skyscrapers anywhere near Battlefield. I'm not saying that's what's happening, just that it could be, and we'd never know."

Erica nodded. "Yeah, the pieces don't fit together, do they?" She chewed her lip. "Unless we're underground. There are all those old copper mines east of town. They might have used one of those to build this thing."

Ian's eyes widened. "That totally makes sense. Way better than the tower idea." He paused, shaking his head. "But our location is beside the point. What I'm getting at is, we're doing exactly what they want us to do—trying to escape, ascending through trap room after trap room. We're rats hoping if we climb high enough, we'll find some cheese. But that's really stupid. We should be smarter than rats. Why are we doing what our enemy wants? Can we find a way to change the game?"

"What—like a hunger strike or something?" Erica offered.

Ian's lips narrowed, and his eyes grew clouded. "No, not suicide. Something else. I don't know what, and I've been thinking about it for a while. Maybe there isn't anything. But let's at least think about it."

Ian turned the handle of the door. It opened, though the door had been locked in Erica's earlier vision. She wasn't surprised. She was beginning to understand how this place worked. Beyond the door was yet another mattress room with a display reading zero on the wall, barely noteworthy.

"Yeah, that's a good idea. We should all think about that," Vince said in contemplation as they strolled into the room. "Maybe we'll come up with something. Change the rules of the game…" His eyes were narrow.

"Ready for the next room?" Erica said.

"No," Vince quickly said. "I have no idea how long I was out. It could be close to nighttime already."

"I have no desire to have the lights turn off when we're in one of the trap rooms," Ian said. "But we shouldn't wait. Maybe if we rush through several trap rooms, we'll surprise them."

He was cut off by the thump of food arriving from the dumbwaiter on the wall.

Vince opened it, revealing a dinner of roast chicken, potatoes, carrots, and broccoli.

"Well, we get some decent food, at least," Erica said.

Ian contemplated the meal. "I guess this could still be lunch."

"I'm way too hungry for this to be lunch," Vince said.

They ate on the mattresses, and the lights dimmed as soon as they finished.

"I guess it was dinner," Ian said.

"It's early," Erica said, looking at the ceiling. "There are usually a couple of hours between dinner and lights out."

"They probably delayed the food until we got here," Ian said.

Erica said, "Yeah. Or maybe they just heard your idea to go through several trap rooms quickly. I guess they don't feel the need to pretend they're not spying on us."

"Obviously, they know everything that's happening, one way or the other." Vince said, his eyes narrow.

"Yep," Ian and Erica agreed in unison.

#

After the stress of the day, Erica was exhausted and wanted nothing more than to fall asleep in Ian's arms. But she had too much she needed to share with him.

It still felt simultaneously wondrous and uncomfortable for her to start anything with Ian. Hesitatingly, she leaned forward to kiss him. Ignoring her racing heart and the rush of warmth through her body, she nestled against his neck with her head tilted up so her lips barely brushed his ear.

"I think I messed up," she began. Her throat was dry.

"How?"

"I shouldn't have hidden the truth when talking with Vince about what happened in the cube room."

"Yeah," Ian agreed. "I was wondering about that. Why didn't you tell him about the malfunctioning guns and the gas?"

"Because of our discussion. I was trying so hard to hide what I knew to throw off anyone spying on us. And it accidentally carried over to our conversation with Vince."

"What didn't you want eavesdroppers to hear?"

Erica told him in detail how she had dodged the weapons. After that, she haltingly tried to explain how Cam had absorbed the Javelin into his arm and knocked out the soldiers.

She could hear Ian's grin as he said, "I guess Cam won't have to worry about Vince anymore."

"If he's even alive."

Ian went back to connecting the dots. "I would guess he is, regardless of what we said earlier with Vince. I figure they had to use the gas to save their soldiers. And, most likely, they grabbed Cam at the same time."

"Yes. It seems parallel to what happened with Renee. She beats up Vince, and then vanishes while we're asleep. Cam beats up the soldiers, and then disappears while we're unconscious."

"Hmm. If that's what happened, it's probably good for Renee. It makes it less likely Vince did something to her while she slept." Ian paused. "So to get back to where we started, I don't understand why you lied to Vince about Cam. Our captors must have seen how Cam took them down. So why lie to Vince?"

The question hit Erica like a weight dropped on her stomach. "I was worried that getting into the details about how Cam eliminated the soldiers would make him freak out. After how Vince reacted to your sister, I didn't want to put Cam in his crosshairs."

"But Cam was gone by that point."

"Yes. But I didn't know that yet. And I couldn't exactly backpedal when we discovered him missing." Erica's face was warm. The truth was, if she hadn't been so comfortable resting in Ian's lap, she would have figured out much sooner that Cam was gone.

"That makes sense," Ian said.

"Do you think he realized I was lying?"

"Yeah, for sure. He might not know what happened, but he definitely knew you were being evasive." Ian smiled against her cheek. "Don't take this the wrong way, but you're not very good at lying."

Erica blushed. Was that just an innocent comment? Or was he saying obliquely that he understood how she felt about him, how her pulse quickened whenever he was near?

Somehow, Ian sensed her reaction. "Don't be embarrassed. It's kind of cute."

Perhaps the comment was intended to reassure, but it only deepened her self-consciousness. Luckily, Ian paused. Erica sensed his thoughts shifting directions. "So Renee goes all ninja, you see the future, and Cam's arms eat Tasers for breakfast. Clearly, you guys aren't normal."

"Um, yes," Erica said.

"That's got to be the reason we're here. Perhaps they put something in the air that does it. Perhaps it's in the food. It could be anything. But what about Denise? Remember how Renee's wounds appeared on her? And how fast those claw marks healed? We thought Renee did it, but what if Denise was responsible? That would explain why it stopped when she died."

"But why did she only heal Renee? Why not the rest of us?"

"Maybe she did, but we didn't notice. Only Renee got seriously hurt. Plus, Denise reacted to the ant bites while nobody else did. Maybe she wasn't allergic. Maybe all the bites that should have appeared on us jumped to her instead. Same thing with the disease. We all got infected, but she became sick instead of us. When Denise was around, do you remember having any injuries? Even small stuff?"

"No, nothing much. There was the needle. In that case, the pinprick stopped bleeding quickly." Erica started chewing on her lip. "This theory makes a lot of sense."

"Yeah. So if that's Denise, Renee, Cam, and you, what can Vince and I do?"

Amid the chaos, Erica hadn't even considered that. "Yeah, good point." Her brow furrowed. "Feel stronger than usual?"

"Nope."

"Strange urge to fly?"

"No, that's not one of my strange urges."

"X-ray vision? Are you going to look at me naked?"

Ian paused as if considering it. "It's a tempting offer, but I am a gentleman."

"I question that," Erica said. "We've only been dating for a few days... and you've already got me into bed with you. Some gentleman!"

"It's just so I can better whisper sweet nothings in your ear," he replied mock-gallantly, or at least as gallantly as one could be while whispering in someone's ear. "There is so much I yearn to say."

Erica snorted. "Yearn to lay, maybe. Typical boy." She sighed. "There's no way to know what caused this change or what it'll do to you. Your hair might become prehensile or you might transform into some kind of scaly cockroach creature. We can only to wait until whatever's going to happen happens." Erica's voice grew somber. "But I need to talk with you about one other thing. Vincent would have killed you earlier if I hadn't stopped him."

Ian transformed instantly from flippant to sober. "What? When?"

"Earlier on the stairway. Near the top. When I blathered on about Denise and how much Vince meant to her."

"I thought that was odd. I'm not so sure that Denise even liked him. It seemed to me like she just sided with him to keep the peace."

"No, she didn't like him. She told me as much. But Vince liked her, and that's what matters. If I hadn't started talking, he would've punched you in the back and tossed you over the railing."

"That's got to be a forty-foot fall," Ian said, dazed. "What would he have done to you?"

"My vision didn't get that far. I figured it would be best to do something before you fell two stories."

Ian's voice was weak. "Yeah. Thanks."

"No problem."

Ian spoke slowly as if he were assembling a puzzle in his head. "He's a jerk sometimes, but he's not a murderer. Is he? A few days ago, he told me that cooperation was the key to escaping."

"I don't know what to think anymore. Vince is a murderer in all but deed."

"He must believe we're spies. He's been suspicious all along, and he got way worse after Denise died. Then he heard us talking about the headset. When you seemed evasive, he must have become convinced we were working with the enemy."

"Yeah," Erica said. She felt miserable.

"So we need to tell him the truth. Get him back on our side."

"I don't trust him."

"We need to take the chance. Telling him everything is the only way we'll be able to convince him we're not the enemy."

The emotions that Erica had been suppressing all day came bubbling out. "You don't get it, do you? I saw him kill you. Without any warning. Like killing a dog. You didn't stand a chance. And I saw him hit Renee. Hard enough to put her in the hospital, at least. Sure, none of it happened, but only because I stopped it. This wasn't TV. It was real to me. How can I trust him? I saw him *kill* you!"

Ian held her close, his voice firm. "Yeah, he did. But you saved me. And if he tries something like that again, you'll save me again. I trust you. And besides, now I'm ready for him." He smoothed back her hair and gently caressed the nape of her neck.

"But I don't want your life in my hands. Not like that."

"We have no choice. We're trapped in here together. There's no escaping him. We can't leave him behind. The only option is to make him an ally again."

After what she'd seen, she was fairly certain it wouldn't work, but she also couldn't suggest an alternative. She sighed, squeezing her eyes shut. "I guess you're right."

"I am. Don't worry. We'll survive this. Vince and I connected when he was taking care of Denise. He's angry now, but I'm sure I can get him back on our side. We just need to come clean. First thing tomorrow."

"Okay," Erica said. This plan seemed to have serious holes, but they had to make it work. There was no alternative.

They lapsed into silence, reflecting on what tomorrow would bring. Neither one of them intended to fall asleep, but it had been a hard day.

Erica's dreams that night were a troubled mishmash of soldiers with guns, devouring flesh, and Vince transforming into a monster and tearing Ian away from her.

The last dream was the worst, seeing Vincent loom above her in the dark, his fists raised. His first punch hit Ian in the side of the head. His second swing connected with her.

A heavy grunt from Ian ripped Erica from sleep. Opening her eyes, she saw Vince's shadowy form standing above her. Before she could react, his fist swung down like a hammer.

CHAPTER TWENTY-ONE

For the second time in less than twenty-four hours, the sound of Ian's voice pulled Erica out of unconsciousness. This time, though, he wasn't talking to her.

"You have to let us go. You can only escape this place with our help." He sounded frustrated.

Vince's reply was calm. "You'd really like me to believe that. But I don't. You've made too many mistakes, and I'm not stupid. I'm certain you're with them."

"I'm not collaborating with them. How can I convince you?"

"You can't. At this point, I'm just waiting to see what your friends will do. Oh, you're awake too."

The last was directed at Erica. She blinked and looked around. She was still lying on the same mattress on which she had fallen asleep. Ian sat beside her. His arms were tied in front of him with sheets from the bed, and Erica realized her arms were restrained the same way. Moving her legs, she discovered her ankles were also bound.

Erica flexed, testing her bonds. There wasn't much give.

Vince observed her brief struggle. "I tied you up. I figure it'll be easier for us both this way."

"I'm just trying to sit up. Can you help me?" Erica asked.

"Sure." Vince came toward her, grabbed her shoulders, and pulled her into a sitting position.

Erica considered head butting him, but didn't see what it would do. The best possible result would be a little pain for him and a lot for her. She would get better chances. Maybe. "So what's the deal,

Vince? Why did you tie us up?" Erica tried to keep her tone calm, certain that giving voice to her rising fear would only make things worse.

"Me and Ian have been chatting about that. For hours last night, I thought about what Ian said. That we needed to do something different. He makes a good point. So far, I've been doing what my captors wanted, but now, I'm changing the rules of this game."

"Game? What game?" Erica said. She knew he was paranoid and dangerous, but she needed to know what particular flavor.

"The game you, Ian, and Renee have been playing this whole time with Denise and me. Pretending we're all prisoners in here together." Vince looked at Ian. "Pretending to be my friend." He sighed. "You guys did a good job. I believed you for a long time. Longer than I should have, but that's only because I'm more trusting than I should be. And Denise convinced me that we should all work together. But now I know the truth."

Ian opened his eyes wide and said, "You don't know the truth. The truth is—"

"—that we are all in this together," Erica said loudly over him. Perhaps Ian was going to explain what really happened with the soldiers. But perhaps he was going to reveal her secret ability, which—regardless of the discussions last night—seemed like a terrible idea now.

It was one thing to tell Vince while chatting over breakfast. If he reacted the wrong way, they'd at least be able to defend themselves. It was another thing to tell him when they were tied up, helpless. If he reacted badly, they wouldn't be able to fight back. As long as she was bound and unable to move, foreseeing the future wouldn't help her protect herself at all. But if her ability remained a secret, it might help them survive this encounter.

Erica gazed pointedly at Ian. "Ian said he would trust me." She saw in his face that, though she was speaking to Vince, Ian realized her words were a message for him. He looked conflicted for a moment, and then his features smoothed. She knew he'd follow her lead. Erica turned back to Vince. "And you should trust me too, Vince."

"And why is that?"

"Because to get through this, we need to cooperate. With any of these traps, we would have died if the others hadn't helped, whether it was us working together to get by the cougar or you helping Denise with her sickness. We're in a stressful situation, so disagreements like this are bound to arise. But when it matters, we've been able to work together and survive."

Vince contemplated her for a few seconds, and then his face hardened. "Yeah, I'll admit that it's a good story. They certainly chose the right actress to put in here with me. But come on. I'm not an idiot. There's too much evidence of your lies."

"What evidence?" Erica said confidently, though her heart was pounding. "I'm sure we can clear it up."

"Well, Renee was clearly a mole. She did stuff that no sixteen-year-old could ever do. Then when I figured it out, she attacked me and vanished during the night. You can't deny she was working with the enemy."

Erica said, "It might seem that way, but—"

"I'm not done. Yesterday, you two were obviously hiding something. You weren't even very good at it. You completely blew your cover with that one remark about the headset. And you can't explain it away with a story about beating up soldiers. Every one of those guys outweighed you by a hundred pounds."

"Well, I had Cam's help," Erica defensively said. It seemed unlikely that coming clean on her lies about Cam would help them at all. It might even make things worse.

"Cam." Vince snorted. "I've seen how he fights. He'd have less chance of overpowering one of those guys than you."

"What about Cam?" Ian thoughtfully asked.

"What about him?" Vince said.

"Well, if you think Renee, Erica, and I are collaborators, and you and Denise are the victims, what's Cam?"

Vince shook his head. "I'm not sure about him. On one hand, he disappeared, which makes him more like Renee. On the other hand, he's so stupid that it's impossible to believe he could fool anyone for more than fifteen seconds.

"So he likely was the second person you betrayed, after Denise. I figure you used the soldiers to take me out—the one guy left to defend him—and killed him. So the only real question is exactly when you're planning to betray and kill me."

"We weren't planning to betray you. We're on your side," Erica said, trying to put all of her conviction into her voice. Her stomach was queasy, but it was critical she not let that show on her face.

"I thought you were too," Vince said. He looked at Ian and sighed. "But now I know better."

"So what's your plan, then?" Erica asked. "To leave us here and try to get out yourself? You'll never make it."

"Maybe not. But I have to try. I'm not the type to give up, even when the odds are stacked against me. If I'm going down, I'm going down fighting. And, no, I won't leave you here."

"What will you do with us?" Ian asked, his muscles tense.

"Well, I was pretty sure your friends would come and save you when they realized I figured it all out. But they seem to want to continue this charade to the end." Vince pursed his lips and nodded. "I need you out of the picture, so you can't interfere. I'll take you as far back as I can and leave you tied up there. By the time you get out and climb all the way back here, it will all be done. One way or another."

Vincent stepped toward them and crouched down in front of Erica. "Now, I can't carry you both down there, so you'll need to walk. But remember, I can beat either of you to a pulp even if your hands weren't tied up. Please don't make me."

He untied Erica and Ian's feet. Erica considered kicking him or running, but it wouldn't accomplish much. It seemed safer to wait until he left them alone to figure out how to get free.

Vince helped each of them to their feet. Erica could see Ian turning scenarios over in his mind, trying to decide whether he should run, fight, or wait, but he didn't resist. He clearly reached the same conclusion she had.

"Let's go." Vince walked behind them to the door and held it open as they went through.

Erica wondered where Vince would leave them. In one of the mattress rooms? They couldn't navigate the cliff where Denise had died, so perhaps the room before that?

Denise. Vince was convinced they were responsible, and she'd already seen him murder Ian once. Would he really leave them somewhere, all tied up? She was becoming more doubtful by the second.

Suddenly, it seemed very important to convince Vince they were on his side. She had to go for broke.

"There's another good explanation, Vince," Erica said, walking slowly down the staircase, trying to gain time to talk without appearing to be stalling. "Think of all the strange stuff that's happened."

Vince snorted. "Strange stuff? Everything is strange. I've been kidnapped and put in a death trap. And now you feel the need to point out that this isn't your average Sunday afternoon?"

"Well, yes, that's true. But look at how Denise died. What actually happened? She wasn't the one who fell, but somehow, she died. Even in these strange circumstances, you must consider that extraordinary. It seems completely inexplicable, right?" Erica fought to keep her tone level.

"Yeah," Vince replied as he opened the door to the cube room. "It was Renee. Somehow, she had some sort of spy technology enabling her to survive the fall by sacrificing Denise."

"Spy technology?" Erica asked. "Have you ever heard of anything even remotely like that?" She craned her neck trying to catch a glimpse of Vince's face to gauge whether her words were having any effect.

"No, but so what?" Vince said dismissively, not even bothering to look at Erica. "Those guns the soldiers had are pretty unique too. Maybe Renee has bionic implants or something that let her do that stuff. It doesn't matter that much anyway. The only thing that matters is Renee killed Denise to save herself." They left the cube room and continued down the next staircase.

"It does matter how she died. I have a different theory," Erica said. She stopped and tried to look at Vince, but he pushed her forward. "The guys who abducted us did something to us. Maybe they injected us with drugs when they grabbed us. Or maybe they put something in our food. But they did something. And it's manifesting as strange abilities."

"Abilities?"

"Yes, that's why Renee was able to open the lock, do those wall jumps to get on the ramp, and survive the fall. We're test subjects. They gave us drugs with these unpredictable effects, and this place exists so they can see what happens."

Vince frowned as he opened the door to the next mattress room. "Except it's only Renee who's done these strange things."

They were getting close to the room where Denise died and Erica was running out of time. Her mind spun, searching for something else to say. She'd already said almost everything, yet Vince didn't seem the slightest bit convinced.

The only option was to come clean about Cam. "It was Cam too. After you got shot by those soldiers, Cam was hit as well. But instead of him collapsing, the soldiers did. Three of them. And his arm opened and ate one of the Javelins, which he fired at the remaining soldier." She kept her voice calm and spoke at an even pace, resisting giving in to the fear that would make her words sound even more unbelievable.

"Stop," Vince instructed. When Erica glanced back up at him, he was staring at them with a bewildered expression. "What are you saying?"

Erica elaborated on her story and shared how the gas, not the Javelins, had knocked them out.

Vince stared at Erica, wide-eyed. "Really? And you believe that this story is more convincing than your last story that you got shot by the soldiers? This is ridiculous. You say you lied before. Why would you do that if you were working with me? It makes no sense."

"I didn't trust you," Erica said.

"Yeah, right. You didn't trust me! I'm the only trustworthy one in this room. Walk!" Vince barked.

They turned and went through the door to the next room, the room where Denise died. Erica and Ian stopped within a few feet of the edge of the cliff. With three of them on the small ledge, it was somehow dizzying and claustrophobic at the same time, like a single careless movement would send them plummeting to the hard concrete below. The floor seemed miles away.

Ian flinched as he looked over the edge. "Remember that the rope ladder is gone. There's no safe way down. I guess this is the end of the line for us."

"Yes. It is." Vince's voice sounded uncharacteristically introspective. "You know, for most of the night, I was thinking about your betrayal, Ian. How you worked with the enemy. Played Denise and me. And killed her, with no regrets at all."

"Well, now you'll have those regrets. I figured your friends would try to save you. That they'd come and I'd have a chance to fight them, face to face. But they didn't, so this is Plan B.

"I was never going to let you live. I needed you down here so I could kill you the right way. It's necessary. Not only for justice, but also to send a message to the people you're working with. They shouldn't have taken me and murdered my girlfriend. They messed with the wrong guy.

"This is where Denise died, and it's fitting for you to suffer the same fate as her. I figure that on the way down, you'll have the last few seconds of your life to think things over. I suggest you spend that time begging forgiveness for murdering—"

Vince leaping forward. A hand on each of their chests. A shove. Falling.

The vision reinforced with sick certainty what Vince had already told them. In a flash, Erica worked through possible responses in her head, discarding them one after another.

Kicking led to a shove and death. Head butting led to a punch and death. Rushing led to a push and death. Dodging delayed a second, maybe two. Then death.

There seemed to be no alternative. Every scenario ended on the cement far below.

Then she found it. She might not survive. But Ian would. And right now, that was the best she had.

"Ian, trust me." Erica only had time for a brief glance at him, but she saw him relax. He was certain she had found a way out.

Even here, in this impossible situation, he believed in her. Here, where she'd failed Renee. Where she'd killed Denise. How could he trust her here and now after that?

Erica drove her shoulder into Ian hard, at an angle. He bounced off the wall and over the edge.

She jumped.

CHAPTER TWENTY-TWO

Ian plummeted, unable to control his direction. But Erica had planned his trajectory perfectly. Rather than falling all the way to the ground, Ian landed prone on the foot and a half wide ramp about twelve feet below.

Erica wasn't so lucky. As she leaped, she felt Vince's hand on her back, as she knew she would. It wasn't a firm push—it all happened so fast that Vince barely had time to react at all. But it was enough to send her an extra couple of feet farther from the cliff than she would have been otherwise.

Erica twisted in the air, looking down to spot Ian's hands. They were exactly where she expected them to be, sticking out over the edge.

"Catch me," she commanded.

Her bound hands closed upon Ian's wrists, and her legs slammed into the wall. She ignored the pain as she tried to hold on, and then Ian grasped her wrists.

"That hurt a lot more than I thought it would," Erica muttered. She looked up and saw Ian peering over the edge of the ramp at her.

"I don't know how long I can hold you," he said through gritted teeth.

"Can you pull me up?"

"No. Lying like this, I have no leverage. It's all I can do just to hold on," Ian said. "It looks like a long way down to the floor."

Above them, Vince looked over the edge. "Huh," he said, a note of surprise in his voice. "That wasn't supposed to happen. I was going to be the one to deliver justice." His eyes narrowed as he watched Ian's struggles.

"I can't hold her for long, Vince! I'm slipping off the ramp," Ian desperately said.

"That's not quite how I imagined you dying, but it's worked out well. Will Ian drop his girlfriend to her death, or be pulled over with her?" Vince exclaimed in a deadpan announcer's tone.

"Please, Vince. It's not too late for you to help us," Erica said, her voice shrill.

"Late?" Vince mimed looking at a wristwatch. "Now that you mention it, breakfast is late, and I'm getting hungry. Maybe I should go."

"Vince! We need you," Erica pleaded. "We're on your side. If you just give us more time to explain, I'm sure you'll understand."

Vince shook his head. "I'll admit that you're a persuasive girl, Erica. You've been fooling me for days. But I'm smarter now. My dad warned me about girls like you, bringing down men with your deceit. It happened to him, and I swore it would never happen to me. But you're naturally good at the lies and trickery. And if I stay here talking to you for long enough, you can probably figure out a way to fool me again."

Vince gazed down on her with an expression of contempt. "But I'm smarter than that now. I won't give you that chance." He smiled. "It's time for me to go." Vince pretended to touch the brim of a hat. "Bye!"

He disappeared from view.

"Wait, Vincent. Please!" Ian shouted.

They heard the door open, and then close.

"Well, that didn't work too well," Ian muttered.

"Right now, I prefer him not being here. How are you doing?" Erica asked, struggling to remain calm.

Ian winced. "It's hard even staying on the ledge. My arms are going numb, and it will only get worse." He gritted his teeth. "Do you think you could hold onto the edge?"

"Not for long. Not with my hands tied."

"It doesn't have to be long. Five or six seconds?"

"Probably."

"Then we have to take the chance right now before I get too tired even to try. Here we go." Slowly, Ian lifted Erica up, his biceps straining and his face turning red. He placed her fingertips on the edge of the ramp, so that Erica was supporting a significant part of her weight. "Ready?"

"Yes," Erica replied. Her fingers ached and her hands trembled.

"Let's do this." Ian released her arms and scrambled into a squatting position, facing down the ramp with his left hip against the wall. He reached down to his right and grabbed her wrists again.

"Now I'm going to lift you up. You'll need to let go of the ramp and grab my hands again."

The last thing she wanted to do was to release the strong, stable ramp and grab hold of Ian, but Erica forced herself to do it anyway. Ian straightened his legs, painfully raising his torso and pulling Erica up. Eventually, she was high enough to swing her knees onto the platform. The minute she was safe, Ian collapsed on his back.

"That was way harder than I thought it would be," he said, his face bright red. Beads of sweat trickled down his brow. "Not that you were heavy. Just because my hands are tied, and I needed to maintain my balance. It was so hard to get in the right position."

"Thanks for saving me." Then, aware that the cameras were still watching—and wanting to make sure that Ian realized it too—she crawled on top of him and kissed him. It lasted longer than she planned initially, but that wasn't really a problem.

When she came up for air, Ian whispered, "Wow, I should save you more often."

"I'd rather not make it a habit," she replied in his ear. They both lay there together, regaining their strength.

"Next time you say 'trust me', I'm going to turn in the other direction and run," Ian said.

"Well, it worked, didn't it?" Erica said.

"I suppose if you use a loose enough definition of 'worked'. So your visions let you see all of that? Several minutes in the future? The whole conversation and me pulling you up?" Ian whispered

"No," she replied. "Not that far. I knew that if I nudged you just right, you'd land on the ledge. And that when I jumped, Vince would push me hard enough that I'd miss the ramp, but that you'd be able to grab my arms. That's as far as I saw."

"What? You didn't know that I'd be able to lift you up?"

"No. But I knew you wouldn't let me fall."

Ian shook his head. "Why didn't you jump down to the ramp

instead of making me catch you?"

"If I had gone first, I would have landed fine, but I wouldn't have been able to catch you when Vince pushed you over. Going second was the only option."

Ian blinked a few times as he processed the decision she had made. "Wow. Thanks for saving me." He kissed her neck.

"No problem," Erica said casually, ignoring the rush of warmth through her body. She carefully raised her torso by pushing her hands against the ledge above Ian's head, looked down, and gulped. "You know, two minutes ago, after dangling precariously seventy feet above the floor, lying on you like this seemed like a good thing and not risky at all. Now, not so much. Now, it feels like lying with my hands tied on top of a twitchy boyfriend on a narrow ledge above a deadly drop. And I'm getting an elbow cramp."

Ian raised his eyebrows. "Twitchy?"

"Twitchy," Erica firmly said.

"Okay then. Maybe this isn't the best time for romance. Let me help." Ian put his hands on her side, holding her against the wall, and Erica eased herself back into a sitting position below him on the ramp.

"Mmm, better," Erica said. She raised her hands. "Can you open this knot?"

"Yeah." He began to work at it. "It's tight. This might take a while."

"Well, as long as Vince doesn't come back, we've got time." Erica looked at the floor, far below. "Even once we get our hands untied, it will be difficult getting down. Renee might have been able to do that insane leap over that hole," Erica nodded her head at the gap in the middle of the ramp, "but there's no way I'd be able to. And even over there, at the lowest part of this ramp, it's way too high for us to jump down safely."

"I don't see that we have a choice," Ian said. "We can't stay here. Maybe I can dangle, holding on to the ramp, and you can climb down me, using me as a ladder."

"Ugh," Erica groaned. She had enough of clinging to the side of cliffs for one day. "Actually, no, we don't need to do that. After we untie our hands, we'll have two sheets. We can tie them together and use them as a rope to climb down."

"Great idea!" Ian enthusiastically said. "It might not reach to the next ramp, but it'll be close enough."

Erica felt her cheeks become warm at his praise. "There's another option too."

"Another option?" Ian looked puzzled.

"Yeah. If we go down, we're trapped. But, we might be able to climb up instead."

Ian smiled. "Yes! There are those pegs on the platform. We can lasso one of them."

Erica nodded. "Yes. So we have a choice. Would you rather go down to safety or go up and risk encountering more traps, not to mention the guy who just tried to kill us?"

"A safe, white-walled room or confronting a homicidal maniac in a labyrinth of death traps. They're both such attractive offers!" Ian said, pretending to ponder the alternatives. "I believe I'll take door number two."

"I agree," Erica said with a smile. "There's no real safety below. We'll get roasted, or nibbled to death by ants, or something worse. Vince is a huge problem, but we'll just need to deal with him. If we retreat, we'll die. There's really no choice but to advance. Vince or no Vince."

"Besides," Ian said, his eyes narrowing, "Vince is tough, but if he doesn't surprise us like he did last night, I don't think he'll be able to 'dispense justice' as easily as he imagines."

Erica's mouth quirked. "No, maybe not." She shook her arms to relieve a cramp. "Now hurry up with these sheets."

#

It took half an hour before they freed their hands. Considering he was working with sheets, Vincent had been remarkably effective at tying tight knots, and balancing on a narrow ramp didn't make things any easier. But eventually, Ian pried loose the knots on Erica's hands. Soon after, she was able to free his.

Ian knotted the two sheets together into a rope, tying a loop at one end. After testing the strength of all the knots, he walked back up the ramp and tried to lasso one of the pegs.

Throwing the sheet to the top of the platform and hooking a peg that they couldn't see while precariously perched on the side of a cliff proved harder than expected. After a frustrating half hour, Ian took a break and passed the makeshift rope over to Erica.

Erica pursed her lips and closed her eyes. Getting in the right state of mind to conjure up a vision of the future was easier than last time; being in this room helped.

After going through what seemed like hundreds of throws in her head—including a disturbing scenario where she overbalanced, tried to recover by grabbing Ian, and pulled both of them off the ramp—Erica saw and felt what she needed to do.

Her one throw was perfect, firmly hooking a peg.

"Very impressive," Ian said. His mouth kept quirking into a smile as if he was struggling to hold back his glee. "I didn't even consider that you might be better than me at lassoing it."

It was clear to Erica that Ian was speaking in code. He knew what she had done. "Beginner's luck, I guess." She couldn't resist grinning at Ian's giddiness. He seemed more excited with her power than she was.

"Yeah. I'm just glad I don't have to try another three hundred times." Ian finally got his face under control. "Should I go first, just to test the rope?"

"No. You test the rope, but I'll go first," Erica said. "If the loop up there slips or the sheet tears, you'll have a better chance of catching me than me you."

"Makes sense." Ian tugged the rope to test if it would hold his full weight, gave Erica a quick kiss, and passed it to her. She began to climb the swaying sheets, looking only upward.

The sheets held, and Erica finally swung her leg up onto the platform above. She tied the sheets more securely to the peg and waved to Ian to follow. Soon, he stood beside her, a bit winded, but safe.

"I can't believe that worked," Erica said.

"Not as many style points as Renee, but it seemed to do the job."

They cautiously opened the door to the next room, just in case Vince was waiting for them. But nobody was there.

After searching the room, Ian said, "So, now what should we do?"

"We have to go after Vince," Erica said firmly. "But we should be smart about it. Make sure we have a plan. Surprise is one of our only advantages, and I'd hate to squander that by recklessly barging forward."

Ian nodded. "We shouldn't be reckless, but I don't want to delay too much either. Vince has an hour's head start. So, he's almost certainly entered the next trap room and could be past it. I don't want to lose him."

"I agree. Just a few minutes to catch my breath, and then we'll go. Okay?" Erica grabbed Ian's hand, turned him toward her, and began to nuzzle his neck. She turned pink as she imagined what any observers might think. They'd barely survived the cliff, their attempted murderer was still roaming around, and, as far as anyone watching could tell, all she cared about was making out with her boyfriend. But they needed to speak privately somehow, so it fell to her to be the besotted airhead.

At least Ian understood.

Through a combination of speaking in code and whispers, they designed their strategy. At each room, Ian would get ready to rush in as soon as Erica opened the door. Seconds before she'd do so, she'd attempt to peer into the future to look behind the door. If she saw Vince, she'd whisper "Okay?" to alert Ian. For some other threat, she'd say, "Ready?" and for anything else, she'd make any other random statement.

They disagreed about what to do if they encountered Vincent. Erica wanted to attack him immediately while they possessed the element of surprise. Ian, however, was steadfast in his assertion that they needed to give him another chance. There was no guarantee they'd come out of a fight with Vince unharmed, and they might need his help to get out.

After seeing the set of Ian's jaw, Erica finally conceded. They would only fight if Vince made them, and, if it came down to that, they would try to disable him, tie him up, and leave him behind. They weren't murderers.

After they worked out the plan, they crept back to the room where they had slept the night before. Vince was nowhere to be found, although they discovered the remnants of his breakfast.

They had no reason to delay, so they ascended the staircase outside the room. Side by side, they stood before the door at the top. It seemed odd for the two of them to open the door of a new room without Vince and Cam at their side.

Spontaneously, Erica gave Ian a quick kiss. She turned away and focused her thoughts on how she had failed Renee and Denise.

"Ready?" she murmured.

CHAPTER TWENTY-THREE

Erica flung open the door, scanning the room to verify what she'd already seen in her vision.

It was almost empty. No cubes. No pyramids. No ramps. It had white walls and a door just like every other room in this place.

But the starkness of the room only made the vertical crimson streaks on the far wall near the exit door stand out more prominently. The color stretched from the floor to about four feet up the wall. The air smelled faintly of iron.

Ian took a few seconds before he vocalized his suspicions. "Is that...?"

"Blood," Erica said, completing his thought. "Yes, I think so."

They inched forward, alert for any possible threat. As they neared the wall, it became clear their initial judgment was correct. "Definitely blood," Erica said.

She could make out the thin cracks of a six-inch tall square panel set flush with the wall. While the panel itself was spattered with partially congealed blood, most of it seemed to have dripped from behind it. A small puddle was at the base of the wall.

Erica gestured at the panel and the few drops that were still lazily making their way down the wall. "It's leaking out of there."

"Yeah," Ian replied, his voice faint.

Erica glanced at him. "Are you okay? You're very pale."

Ian began to sway on his feet. "I'm fine. I'm just... I don't know. There's a lot of blood."

"It's not that bad. Worse than a typical cut, but there was more when Renee split her forehead open on that branch. That really gushed."

It was the wrong thing to say. Erica noticed Ian's knees shaking. She grabbed his arm. "You should sit down. Now."

"Yes. Sitting is good," Ian listlessly said. He sat, well away from the pool of blood on the floor, and blinked a few times.

"Interesting. I've known you my whole life and never knew you had a thing about blood," Erica said, bemused.

"I didn't either," Ian said. "But until now, I've just seen skinned knees and paper cuts. And Denise, but I was too busy trying to help her to even see the blood." Sitting seemed to help. Color seeped back into Ian's face. "What do you think is behind the panel? And why is the blood only coming from that one?"

"That one?"

"And not those other panels." Ian gestured at three almost invisible panels along the wall spaced at intervals of about six feet.

"I hadn't noticed them," Erica replied. "But the one on the end is open."

Ian frowned. "Do we really want to see what's inside?"

"I sure don't," Erica admitted and then sighed. "But we probably need to." She offered her hand to help Ian up. "Let's go look."

Ian rose, and they walked over to the open panel. It revealed a hole in the wall about eight inches deep. At the back was a small, smooth metal knob that reminded Erica of a handle on a kitchen cabinet. Or was it a crocodile pretending to be a log?

"Am I crazy, or was this designed for us to put a hand into the hole and pull the knob?" Erica said.

"You're not crazy. But whoever made this thing is. What sort of idiot would stick their hand in this hole after seeing the blood dripping from the other one?"

"Yeah. The hole with the needle in the other room was one thing. But this is completely different." Suddenly, Erica realized what might have happened, and her eyes widened.

"What?" Ian said.

Erica was so stunned she could barely speak. "I've been looking at this all wrong. I was so distracted by the blood that I forgot. We're not the first ones to be in this room."

"Vince."

"Yes," Erica said. "Perhaps when he first came in here, the room didn't look like this."

"The blood…"

Erica nodded. "It might be his."

"But then, where is he? Wouldn't he still be here? Could Vince really lose so much blood and walk out of here?"

"It's not that much. It looks bad, but I bet it's less than a pint. Maybe he was able to get through the door."

Ian shrugged. "I guess. If that's true, the exit might already be unlocked."

They walked over to the door and tried the handle. It wouldn't budge.

"So much for that theory," Erica said.

"Yeah. Figured we had to check though." Ian gestured toward the panel. "There's no blood over here. Surely if he'd walked out, he would have left a trail of blood."

Erica knelt down and peered at the floor near the door. "I see something though. Not blood. It looks like water."

"Odd," Ian said, squatting beside her. "Could Vince have brought water from the other room and spilled some?" His tone was doubtful.

Erica had another idea but didn't want to discuss it. "I don't know. I'm not touching it though."

"Yeah," Ian said. He stood up. "Maybe he didn't walk out of here. Maybe he was injured, collapsed from a lack of blood, and they took him away. Like Renee and Cam."

Erica nodded. "Of course, that's assuming the blood is Vince's and not someone else's." She rubbed her forehead. "But that seems like the most likely scenario. In that case, what do you think we should do?"

Ian frowned. "I hate to say it, but I think we need to reach into that hole and pull the knob."

"Didn't you say three minutes ago that we'd have to be idiots to do that?"

His grin was rueful. "Well, yes. But I don't see another option. Do you?"

Erica considered the idea. Despite what they had said earlier, they both knew that, with the advantage of Erica's visions, it was a reasonable risk to take. She sighed. "I guess not. We can't stay here." She pursed her lips. "But instead of using our hands, let's wrap a sheet around the knob and use that to pull it. If a trap is triggered, then the sheet will bear the brunt of it, not us."

Ian nodded. "That's assuming it doesn't go off the instant one of us puts a hand in there."

"Still seems better than nothing."

"I agree."

Together, they trudged back to the door to the staircase down. It was locked.

"You know," Erica said, "the next time we enter one of these rooms, we should prop the door open."

"One of those things that seems obvious, in retrospect," Ian agreed. He stripped off his shirt.

"Um, what are you doing?" Erica asked, a hint of a smile coloring her voice.

Ian grinned back at her. "Well, seeing as we're trapped, I figure we need to do something to pass the time..." Erica felt her face turn pink, and Ian's smile grew. He continued, "No, I mean, we don't have a sheet, but we can use my shirt instead. It's not as long, but it should still work."

Erica's thoughts involuntarily darted to other, longer items of clothing they could use, and the mental image made her blush even more furiously. To her relief, Ian didn't comment.

Together, they walked back to the hole in the wall. Ian stretched the shirt out, examining it with a critical eye. "Even with this, I'm not looking forward to putting a hand in that hole," he confessed.

"Can't blame you. Let's poke something in there first. Just in case."

"Yeah, we can use this." He folded the shirt in half and rolled it into a tight tube. "Perfect. A nice fake hand." Ian experimentally jabbed Erica in the abdomen a few times. "Yep, seems to work," he said.

"I prefer your real hand."

Ian raised his eyebrows. He poked her gently in the stomach with his index finger. "Me too." Erica giggled.

Ian turned back to the wall. "Let's try this." Cautiously, he put the tip of the rolled-up shirt into the hole. Nothing happened, so he poked the knob, to no effect.

"That's reassuring. As long as it doesn't have a heat sensor or something, we're fine," Ian said.

"Yeah. Shall we try it? I think maybe I should do it."

Ian looked like he was about to argue, and then reconsidered. "Are you sure?"

"Yes. It might need a delicate touch."

"Hey, my touch is delicate."

"You can prove that later. This one's mine."

Ian shrugged. Unfolding the shirt, he rerolled it into a rope, passing it to her.

"Thanks," she said.

Erica stuck her hand in slowly, ready to withdraw in an instant if she had a hint of a vision. Nothing happened, so she rapidly wrapped the fabric around the knob and jerked her arm back. The shirt was barely long enough. Several inches hung outside the hole.

"I'm glad that's over," she said, exhaling.

"Maybe. Maybe not. Let's see what happens when we pull it."

Erica nodded. She counted to three and tugged on the shirt.

The fabric pulled the knob out several inches. For a second, nothing seemed to happen. Then, a loud click echoed through the room as a panel several feet away slid up.

"Great," Ian morosely said. "Another hole."

"This one's different," Erica said. She wrinkled her nose as she caught a whiff of something unpleasant, like raw chicken that was left too long in the refrigerator. "Look."

Unlike the last compartment, this one was covered in transparent plastic, with four lines, each about five inches long, intersecting to form an eight-pointed star. Behind the plastic, the hole was almost filled with a red substance. As Erica got closer, she realized it was moving. Her eyes widened. "Oh man, what is that?"

"Rotting meat."

In the hole was something that had once been alive, but no longer remotely resembled any sort of creature. Maggots wriggled around while feasting on a noxious soup of blood, pus, and rotten flesh. When Erica looked closer, she could see a dark red tube that might have been an artery, and a yellowish-white sphere that could have been part of an eyeball. The smell alone made Erica want to retch.

Ian stared at the mess, revulsion twisting his features. "That's totally disgusting."

Erica examined the cover. "Those lines on the plastic are cuts. There's probably a knob behind all that stuff."

Ian sighed. "Are you sure?"

"Hmm," Erica said. She peered at the hole and reached toward the red gloop, moving her hand until she touched the plastic.

Her hand parting red flesh. Maggots wriggling against her fingers. Hard metal.

She pretended to ponder the question for a few seconds. "The only way to find out is by feeling around," she said with a touch of irony in her voice that only Ian would pick up on. "But I'm pretty certain there is. Other than that stuff, the hole looks the same as the first one. And why bother with the hole at all if there weren't?"

Ian nodded. "That does make sense."

Erica's stomach recoiled. The stink was so intense that she tasted it in her mouth. "I better do it before I puke." She meant it as an exaggeration, but then realized it wasn't.

"You're okay with rotting meat?"

Erica half-smiled before wincing.

"Yeah, I thought so," Ian said. "I'll do it. What's a boyfriend for, if not to grab the things you need out of a putrid, maggot-infested soup?"

"I was thinking it was more about the smooching." Erica regarded the hole for a few seconds and nodded. If something went wrong, she could likely warn him in time. "Yeah. You do it."

Ian glanced back at his shirt, which was still on the floor. "Without the shirt is better." His mouth curled. "Maybe a cool, maggot-infested meat bath will be refreshing."

Erica enthusiastically nodded. As long as she was smiling, she could keep from vomiting. "Oh, I'm sure it will be. That's how Cleopatra kept her skin so young looking, you know."

"I'll use my left hand. Let's get this over with." Ian readied his hand before the plastic, gritting his teeth. Plunging his hand into the goop, he quested for the knob.

There was slurping sound when pulled back his arm as if the muck was reluctant to relinquish its hold. In total, Ian took less than two seconds to finish the task.

"Such speed. Such finesse," he said, holding his hand far away from his body.

Erica nodded. "From now on, for any task involving maggots, I know where to go." Several of the writhing worms were stuck to his arm, still questing for rotting food.

Ian ignored the panel that had opened, but ran back to grab the shirt he had tossed on the floor. He wiped his hand, trying to get all the blood and pus off his arm without dripping it on any other part of his body. He mostly succeeded.

"I guess we're stuck with the smell until we're able to get to a sink," he said, casting the shirt away.

Erica heard a steady, faint humming. "Yeah, well, that's not that bad, considering," she said. She turned from Ian to examine the panel that had opened. This one was covered in plastic too, but from a distance, it looked dark yellow rather than red. She walked toward the hole and peered in. "Oh wow. Bees."

Ian's eyes widened. "You've got to be kidding me." He put his face down in front of the hole, right beside Erica's.

Though there seemed to be hundreds of writhing insects, the alcove wasn't completely filled. Most of the bees seemed clustered around the back of the hole and on the sides, with only a few flying from one wall to another. One landed on the plastic. If anything, it seemed bigger and darker than a normal bee. The brick-red, barbed stinger sticking out from its abdomen twitched as the insect moved.

Erica's mouth felt dry. She tried to keep her tone light to squelch her fear. "They look huge. I wonder if they're wasps, not bees. How do you tell them apart?"

Ian shook his head and shrugged. "Not a clue. At least the plastic is keeping them in."

"I guess. That's odd that they're not flying, right? That they're just sitting at the back?" Erica asked. Dispassionate observation, like in biology. That was the way to handle the situation. Not shrieking and running as far away as possible.

"Perhaps they cluster like that in their hive." Ian shivered. "They're probably all on the knob."

Erica nodded.

"The shirt might offer some protection," he said. He looked to his left and grimaced.

Even from where she was, twenty feet away, Erica could see maggots writhing on the shirt. "We can use mine," she said. Before she could change her mind, she slipped it over her head. Really, the sports bra she was wearing underneath the shirt was no more revealing than a bikini. Nevertheless, her face felt warm.

"Yeah, that'll work," Ian said. Was it her imagination or did he seem a bit pink too? "You know, I've never been a big fan of insects," he casually said. "Especially ones that sting."

Erica began wrapping the shirt around her left hand.

Ian shook his head "I didn't mean that." He reached for the shirt. "I can do it."

"No, I will."

Ian's mouth quirked. "You're fine with bees?"

"A bee flying around the room? No problem. With sticking my hand in there? Absolutely terrified." Her lips flattened. "But it's my turn. I can handle it." Now if only she could stop trembling.

Ian scanned her face and nodded. "If you're sure. Let's just hope that bees are all we have to worry about. That they weren't put in that hole to distract us from an even deadlier threat."

That idea hadn't occurred to Erica, but she figured that her ability would warn her regardless. "Do you think I should try to push the bees aside or go right for the knob and crush anything in the way?" she said in a business-like tone, not even considering that her visions might be able to answer the question for her.

Ian winced. "I'd try to leave my hand in there for as little time as possible."

Erica nodded. "How does this look?" She raised her wrapped hand.

Ian took her hand in his and slightly readjusted the shirt. The flimsy fabric seemed like it would offer almost no protection against the swarm. "I think it's good," he lied.

Erica nodded and spun around. Without pausing to reconsider and ignoring the visions that were bouncing around her skull, she plunged her hand through the plastic and into the writhing mass.

For a fraction of a second, all she could feel was the popping of insect bodies as they were crushed under her fingers. Then, it felt as if she had shoved her hand under an industrial-strength sewing machine. She could see bees writhing on the back of her hand where the shirt offered the least protection, frantically plunging their abdomens into the fabric.

Tears streaming, she grasped for the knob. Finding it, she hysterically pulled at it, ripping her hand from the hole.

The plastic cover scraped off most of the bees, but not all. With her other unprotected hand, Erica frantically crushed the bees clinging to the shirt.

Finally, she finished. She tore off the shirt and flung it to the floor. "It hurts so much!" she panted.

Ian was white. "Let me see," he said. He took her palm in his hand. Numerous fiery welts pulsed on the back, many still containing stingers. "I need to get these out."

Erica gritted her teeth. Nodding against the pain, she looked away. She no longer felt the individual stings. It was as if her hand had been ground down under an electric sander.

Using his fingernails, Ian removed the stingers. "From the bumps, I'd guess you were stung almost twenty times, mostly on the back of your hand."

"It seemed like a hundred." Erica's voice was ragged.

"I'm not sure what we should do now. My mom always used to put some kind of lotion on it, but we don't have anything like that." Ian frowned. "Your hand is swelling."

"My mom used ice. But don't worry. I'll live. Let's just get out of this room. I'll run some cold water over my hand in the next one." Although it burned, Erica pulled her hand from Ian's grasp, placing it firmly at her side. Wiping her arm across her face to brush away the tears, she strode away.

Ian looked at her, swallowed, and followed.

The final panel—the one from which blood was dripping—had opened.

CHAPTER TWENTY-FOUR

Perhaps her mind was shying away from the truth or the pulsing pain distracted her, but at first, Erica didn't realize what was in the hole. There was no plastic this time, just an irregular red oval a few inches in diameter, with two spots of pinkish white. Erica moved forward for a better look.

The dripping blood forced her to connect the dots.

Erica stopped. Her eyes widened, and she blanched. "It's a hand. A severed hand."

Ian came up behind her. "Yeah," he said flatly. "I thought it might be." He knelt down below the hole, avoiding the blood, and peered up at where the panel had retracted. He pointed at the upper edge. "This looks the same as the others, but if you look closely, you can see a blade."

"You mean…"

"Yes. If we pull the knob, the blade will come down and the panel will close. Quickly." Ian's face was grim.

The steel blade looked wickedly sharp and heavy, like a cleaver. One that would easily cut through bone, let alone soft flesh.

"So… you stuck your hand into that other hole, believing it might be chopped off?" Erica involuntarily shivered and then winced as the movement set her injured hand aflame. Ian nodded.

"I should have been more careful looking for traps. That hand…" Erica's voice was rough. "It has to be Vince's."

"That's the most likely explanation," Ian said, "but I'm not totally sure." At Erica's questioning glance, he continued, "I mean, if he got his hand cut off, blood would have spurted all over the place, particularly on the panel. Why isn't there more blood?"

"Yeah, even if he fainted, he still would have bled out."

"That's what I mean," Ian said, his brow furrowed. "So, maybe it's fake. Or someone else's hand. Maybe they left a hand in the hole to alert us to the trap."

Erica was dubious. She examined the hand in more detail. "It looks real to me. Where would they find a fresh hand?"

"I *am* stretching," Ian conceded. "But the lack of blood is so strange." He gestured at the wall. "So much dripped out of the hand. Why not the body?"

"Perhaps they cleaned the room before we got here. Maybe they grabbed Vince, quickly hosed down the area, and ran out of here before we came. That would explain the water near the door. And remember how clean the room was where Denise died? They could have done the same thing here."

"But forgot the hand?"

"I guess. If they were in a hurry because we were about to come in." Erica's tone implied she wasn't at all convinced by her own words.

Ian shrugged. "I suppose it's more likely than my theory that it's someone else's hand. Would you recognize Vince's hand?"

Erica winced and bit her lip. "I don't know."

"Me neither." Ian took a deep breath. "We need to move the thing. Not only to determine if it's his, but also to pull the knob."

Erica's eyes widened. "What? After seeing that, you still want to stick a hand in there?"

"I don't want to, but what else can we do? The doors are locked, and nothing else in this room seems likely to open them. If we wait, they'll figure out a way to make us do it. Something very unpleasant."

Rubbing her forehead, Erica squeezed her eyes shut. "How bad would it need to be for me to believe putting my hand in that hole is the better option?"

"I don't want to find out. I guess we can use your shirt to remove the hand." He picked it up from the floor and spun back to the opening. "I figure we should do a test first."

Ian rolled up the shirt as he had before and poked it into the hole, touching the hand and each surface. "Seems safe enough." He draped the shirt over his left hand. "I'm going to try taking the hand out now," he said, wiping away a drop of sweat from his forehead. "Tell me if you see anything suspicious."

"Of course."

He positioned himself carefully and raised his hand until it was inches away from the hole. "Fast or slow?" Ian mumbled to himself. "Fast."

His hand darted out. He grabbed the severed appendage, pulled it out of the hole, and flung it away, all in a fraction of a second.

"Wow, that was super fast," Erica said.

"Thanks, Erica. I've always dreamed of having my girlfriend say that to me," Ian said in a bland tone. "Is it his?"

Erica knelt to examine the hand. "It's definitely a man's. And about the right size. But I can't be sure."

"Yeah, I'm the same." He turned back to the wall. "Man, now that the hole's empty, other than the blood, it looks exactly like the first one. The empty one. Vince must have come through here, did the first one with no problem. Managed the rotting meat and the bees. Then he saw this one, identical to the first. He must have thought he was home free."

Erica shivered. "Poor Vince." Shaking her head, she pursed her lips. "What am I saying? He tried to kill us."

Ian shook his head. "Yeah, even so. Poor Vince," he murmured. "Anyway, we still have to do it ourselves."

"Yeah. Shall I do it?"

Ian shook his head. "You did the last one. It's my turn."

Erica nodded.

Ian pivoted and stood solidly in front of the hole. He took in a few deep breaths. "You know, I am fast," he said, mostly to himself.

Ian's hand shooting out, swifter than ever. The panel slamming shut. A waving stump. Crimson walls.

"Stop!" Erica shrieked.

Ian froze and then slowly turned his head toward her.

"Sorry, you scared me for a second. The way you're standing..." Erica realized she was close to hyperventilating and deliberately slowed her breathing. "You look the same as you did when you grabbed the hand, and I was worried you were about to do the same thing. But we should use my shirt on this one like we did on the first one, don't you think?"

Ian nodded. "That makes sense." Reaching down, he pulled

Erica's shirt out from beneath the hand. Twisting it into a rope, he repositioned himself in front of the hole.

"I figure it's triggered by pulling the knob," Erica said. "If that's the case, speed isn't as important as making sure you don't jar the knob. So don't hurry."

"Why would I rush?" Ian said, his expression wry. "It's only a guillotine, and my left arm has always seemed a bit too long. And besides, it stinks."

"Yes, but I have big plans for that hand," she said with a smile, "and I can imagine the looks I'll get if the rest of you isn't attached to it."

"I definitely wouldn't want to spoil your fun," Ian said. He turned back to the wall. "Now, let's try this again."

Ian grasped the middle of the shirt and reached into the hole. He paused for an instant, holding his breath, as if waiting for the blade to fall.

When nothing happened, he draped the shirt over the knob and warily wrapped it around once. The instant he finished, he jerked his hand back.

"Nicely done," Erica said, finally exhaling.

"Never worried," Ian said with a smile. "Now let's see what happens."

Only an inch of the shirt hung outside the hole. Ian gingerly grasped the ends of it, careful to ensure that, in doing so, his fingers didn't break the plane of the panel.

"Here we go," he announced and tugged the shirt.

The panel swept down almost faster than they could see. Ian was left holding a few inches of fabric in his hands.

All the blood drained from his face. "I had no idea it would be so violent," he whispered. "A minute ago, my hand was in there."

Erica pulled him into a hug. "Yeah. Somehow, this one seems more... personal." She leaned back to gaze up at him. "Are you okay?"

"I'm fine," he said in a robotic manner. His eyes were distant. "You know, right before you stopped me, I was thinking that if I was fast enough at grabbing the knob, I'd be able to get my hand out before it came down." He glanced down at his left hand, flexing his fingers.

Erica brushed the back of his hand with her fingertips. "Well, I'm glad I said something then."

"I was joking about all this, but I was that close to losing a hand. I should have been smarter. Realized that I should use the shirt."

"It's an easy mistake. You probably saw the shirt as a way to get rid of that hand, not to pull the knob."

"I suppose so. But without you—"

"But you do have me," Erica said. Her fingers intertwined with his. "We're a team. And I'll take care of you, like you take care of me."

Ian sighed and then gave a tentative smile. "You're one hundred percent right. Thanks." He blinked a few times, shaking his head as if to flick away a mosquito. "Let's see if we accomplished anything." He scanned the room.

All the panels except the first had slid shut, but the door seemed unchanged.

"It's exactly the way it was when we came in," Erica said in disbelief. "We did all that for nothing."

"If I risked my hand for nothing, I'm going to get very grumpy. Let's at least try the door."

They walked over to the door, still holding hands. Erica turned the handle, and the door swung toward them. "Good, I wasn't looking forward to the new grumpy Ian," she said.

The room beyond was in disarray. Always before, the mattresses had been arranged with crisp white sheets in two neat rows. This time, however, one mattress had been rotated and shifted a few feet. Drops of blood had showered the floor and much of the bedding. Two of the sheets, bunched up beside one of the mattresses, were almost completely red. Even the face of the digital display—which read zero—had a blood smear.

As in the prior room, water pooled in several puddles on the floor, as if someone had begun mopping up but didn't bother finishing the job.

"I guess that answers that question," Ian said. "Vince made it here, at least." He gestured at the sodden sheets and said in a shaky voice. "Looks like he was trying to staunch the blood flow." He swallowed.

"He might still be here," Erica whispered. She gestured at a trail of blood leading to the bathroom. "Check behind the curtain."

Ian pursed his lips, then raised his voice and said, "Vince, we're here. We don't want to fight. We saw what happened to your hand, and we know you need help. Come out, and we'll do what we can."

The curtain door hung motionless in the dead air.

Erica whispered, "If he's in there, he's not coming out. Let's get on either side of the door and pull back the curtain."

Ian nodded and crept to the far side of the doorway. When they were ready, she cast her mind out.

"I don't think he's here," Erica said. She yanked the curtain aside so they could both see into the room.

The bathroom looked like a crime scene. There were blood spatters on the walls and the edge of the sink was scarlet. Water streamed out of the faucet.

"Perhaps he tried to clean out the wound?" Ian said. He frowned. "Does that even matter for something so severe?"

"Or he needed to drink. He lost a lot of blood. That makes you thirsty, right?" Despite the mess, Erica held her swollen hand in the cold stream of water. It dulled the sharpest edge of the pain.

Ian shrugged. "I don't know, but it makes sense. Get back the fluid you lost. I guess it explains all the water on the floor out there, at least."

"Yes." She sighed. "What do you think we should do now?"

"If your hand is up to it, we have to keep going. We need to find Vince. If he's bleeding like this, he'll need help."

"They probably grabbed him, like Renee and Cam."

"I'm not so sure. Look at all this blood. He was here for a while. If they were planning to take him, wouldn't they have done it right away, instead of leaving him here to bleed?"

"Maybe," Erica said. "But he lost so much blood that I'm not sure he'd be able to leave here under his own power." She bit her lip. "Besides, do we really owe him anything at this point? He did try to kill us."

"Erica, he's not the enemy," Ian said quietly. "They kidnapped him just like us. He went through the same gauntlet we did, and he might bleed to death if we don't help him. Sure, he got angry, but it's understandable after everything we've been through. He just wanted to fight someone and, frankly, we looked suspicious.

"I think that, after we fell, he even regretted it and changed his mind about killing us. Why else would he leave us alone on that ledge? He could have just as easily waited until we fell. And besides, there's nothing to lose. Even if he is still hostile, there's no way he'd be able to fight us now."

Erica shook her head. She'd already seen Vince kill Ian once. That still mattered even if she had been able to stop him. "Maybe he's not the enemy, but it's hard to tell the difference. After what he tried to do, I feel no need to risk my life to save his." Ian looked at her flatly, and Erica sighed. "In any case, it doesn't matter." She gestured at the room. Every surface had at least some specks of red. "He must have been carried out of here."

"That does seem likely. But how about this then? This room's disgusting. There's not even any clean bedding. What say we go to the next room and see what it's like? If the trap seems beatable, we can go through it to the next bedroom, where we will at least have somewhere to sleep. And if not, we can come back here and we'll be no worse off than we are now. It doesn't hurt to check."

Erica glanced through the doorway at the bloody sheets and mattresses, grimly nodding. "Yeah, good point." She shrugged and pulled her hand from beneath the streaming water. It was still swollen and throbbing, but the cold water had helped. "Let's go."

They went out the exit and up the staircase. At the top, Erica hugged Ian. "Remember the drill?" Erica whispered. "'Okay' for Vince, 'Ready' for some other threat?"

"Of course."

Erica turned and stood in front of the door. When she focused on the door handle, the vision hit her.

"Okay? Ready?" she said in a fierce whisper. Ian's eyes widened. He nodded.

Erica opened the door.

CHAPTER TWENTY-FIVE

Vince sat on the green floor in the middle of the room, staring down with an empty expression. His right hand was missing, severed a quarter of the way up his forearm. His shirt encircled his bicep, forming a crude tourniquet.

It wasn't enough. Beads of blood still dripped from the stump.

He had other wounds as well. A crimson slash began at his right shoulder, went diagonally across his chest, and ended at his upper abdomen. Blood spotted his face and clothes.

Lying supine in front of Vince was a humanoid monstrosity. Had the creature been standing, Erica would have estimated it to be at least seven feet tall. Its legs, revealed by ragged shorts, looked mostly human except for several bony spikes sticking out through bloody holes torn in its skin. The placement and direction of the spikes seemed to have no logic. They weren't even symmetrical.

The monster's muscular arms had similar spurs. Instead of hands, both of its arms ended in vicious, barbed prongs.

Its human-like face had a single spike sticking out from a gash above its left eye. Long, sharpened teeth—or tusks—stuck out in random directions, puncturing its cheeks in several places.

Without the spikes, prongs, and tusks, the creature would have passed as human. With them, it was an atrocity from a nightmare.

Ian crept into the room with Erica a few steps behind. The green floor, unlike all the other white floors in this place, seemed sticky. Where Vince's blood had splattered, it was black.

Vincent continued to ignore them as they moved closer, although the sound of the door and their footsteps had surely alerted him to their presence. They stopped about twenty feet from him.

"Vince, are you all right?" Ian said tentatively, as if it weren't blindingly obvious that Vince was nowhere close to all right.

Vincent sighed and arduously raised his head. He smiled bitterly and ignored the question. "I was wondering when you'd show up. I hoped you wouldn't, but I knew you would."

Ian nodded. "Yes, we came after you. We found the hand and realized you were in trouble. We can help you if you let us."

"Help me? You're going to help me now?" Vince's mouth twisted, and he snorted. "Where were you twenty minutes ago when I needed your help against this thing? Or better, where were you an hour ago, when your help could have saved my hand?" He glanced down at the stump, and for a few seconds, his face relaxed and his eyes drifted. "My hand..."

The sound of his own voice snapped Vince out of his reverie. He looked up at them again. "You seem to have your hands."

"We figured out the trap," Erica said, her voice sympathetic.

"Of course you did," Vince said. "You had nothing to figure out."

"Your hand was still in the hole," Erica said. "That made it obvious."

"You know that's not what I meant," Vince sharply said. His head nodded again, and he said nothing for a few seconds.

Ian broke the silence. "What happened in here? What is that?" He gestured at the corpse at Vince's feet.

Vince's eyes strayed to the grotesque monster on the ground and he jumped slightly, like he was seeing it for the first time. "What is it? I don't know. Just the next trap. The next horror. It doesn't even surprise me anymore. It's no better or worse than anything else in this place. It's just the next in line.

"All I know is that it likes to fight. It's fast and strong." He looked down at the slash across his abdomen. "It likes to rip and tear." Vince's mouth quirked. "And it likes to breathe, although it isn't doing much of that anymore." He looked up at them with a feverish, blood-spotted smile. "I killed it."

"What?" Ian said. "You killed that thing? Without your hand? Come on. It looks like you can barely stand, let alone fight something like that."

"You'd be surprised," he said. "Or really, you wouldn't be. You've seen everything, from the moment your friends saved you from that ledge."

"We saved ourselves," Erica said. "Remember the sheets? We untied our hands and made a rope to climb up from the ledge."

"Yes. Of course," Vince said in a tone of tired sarcasm. "You always have an answer, Erica." He glared at her, the intensity of his gaze belying his obvious exhaustion. "Tell me, did you smirk when those bees stung me? Did you laugh when your trap turned me into a cripple forever?" He spat out the words and raised the bloody stump as if she may not have noticed his missing hand.

"No, Vince. We weren't even certain it was your hand until we came in here. But we thought you might be in trouble. Like Ian said. We want to help you."

The speech felt stale in Erica's mouth. After all she'd seen, she was, at best, indifferent to Vince's potential death. And, in her darker moments, she'd consider it something to celebrate. She also knew that nothing she could say would make any difference. But Ian still believed in Vince, and she had made a commitment to Ian to try. So she said the words.

"Help me…" Vince mumbled. Raising his face, eyes aflame, he shouted, "You killed my girlfriend!" He tried to spit blood upon the floor, but a tendril remained attached to his lower lip. He wiped it away with his stump, leaving a smear of blood across his chin.

"It was a freak accident, Vince," Ian said in a tone intended to calm a rabid dog. "We really want to help. Let's go to the next room and wrap up that arm. We'll eat, rest for a bit, and talk about it." Ian took a few hesitant steps forward. "It'll all be okay."

"It'll never be okay," Vince darkly said. "I won't survive this." He glanced down at his stump. "I'm not even sure I want to." Laboriously, he clambered to his feet. Pain distorted his features. "At this point, death is fine. I won." He smiled, even though the cruel twist of his lips was joyless. "I survived these horror rooms. I exposed your betrayal. I fought you off. And when you realized I was too strong for you to beat me fairly, you took my hand. When you tried to gas me, I kept coming. When you put this in my path," Vince kicked at the corpse at his feet, "I killed it."

Vincent looked back to them. "No matter the friends of mine you murder, the creatures you send against me, the traps you set that maim me, I keep coming. I will die, but I will die undefeated."

"Come on, Vince, you're not thinking clearly. None of that was us. It was our captors," Ian said, his eyes pleading.

Vince ignored him, seemingly mesmerized by his stump. "Even in this state, I'm still strong enough to kill you," he said with a touch of wonder in his voice, like a child discovering new snow. He turned his head toward Erica and showed his teeth in a contorted smile. His voice grew stronger. "Both of you. I'll die, but I will get my justice."

Vince walked toward Ian, his remaining hand clenching into a fist. The realization that he could fight seemed to have revitalized Vince and given him focus.

Ian circled back and sideways away from him. "Come on, Vince. We're not here to fight."

Erica tried to follow Ian and nearly fell. Her feet seemed rooted to the floor.

"Ian," she hissed, "I can't move. My feet are stuck."

Ian and Vince both paused and stared at her. "What?" Ian said. "Stuck on what?"

"Stuck on the floor." Erica pulled on her knee. "It's like glue."

Vince snorted and turned back to Ian. "Huh. A fair fight between you and me."

"I'm not going to fight you," Ian said. He backed away.

"You can run away." He turned his head toward Erica. "But your girlfriend can't. She'll stand and fight like a man." He gave her a manic, blood-speckled grin. "Or a girl."

Ian paused and studied Erica, clearly trying to decide whether her ability would enable her to beat Vince without moving her feet. With bright eyes and a slight smirk, Vince watched the indecision play out across Ian's face.

After a few seconds, Ian walked back and stood between Vince and Erica. "I don't want to fight you, especially like this. But I can't let you hurt her."

"Oh good. I knew there was a man hiding somewhere in there," Vince said. He strode forward, swinging.

Ian blocked the first blow—a wild left haymaker—on his forearm, then leaned back to avoid a right jab. Several drops of blood from the stump flew onto Ian's shirt.

Vince continued to swing, favoring his left hand, but not hesitating to attack with the stump of the right. Ian threw no punches, but simply avoided the flurry from Vince.

Erica shook her head. Ian was nuts. Did he not realize what Vince meant by "justice"? Vince was trying to kill them, but Ian was still trying to save him. It was a risky, almost foolhardy strategy. Although, surely, with those injuries, Vince couldn't sustain that pace for long. If Ian could dodge the worst of it, perhaps Vince would pass out from blood loss.

Just when Erica began to think that Ian's strategy was working, Vince surprised him. He planted his left foot and delivered a hard roundhouse kick to Ian's side. Ian doubled over in pain. The uppercut that followed drove him to the ground.

Ian shook his head as Vince followed up on his advantage. Desperately, Ian kicked Vince in the stomach, making him stagger back and giving himself some backward momentum. He crabwalked away and hastily climbed to his feet.

"Vince, please?" Ian said. He spat. His blood created another dark oval on the floor like all the others.

Vince smiled and continued to advance with his fist and stump raised. If anything, knocking down Ian seemed to give him more energy.

This time, after dodging the first left, Ian stepped forward. He ducked under Vince's right arm and delivered solid blow to his gut. It wasn't nearly as hard as one of Vince's punches, but it was enough to make Vince stagger back a foot.

Ian didn't follow up on his momentary advantage, but hung back, waiting for Vince to come to him. Again, Vince advanced, swung, and missed. In return, he received a glancing blow on the side of the head.

Vince was stronger and more experienced at fighting, but Ian had always been faster. The blood loss only magnified that advantage. None of Ian's blows was particularly punishing, but he could land twenty of them for each glancing blow that Vince landed.

Finally, after a desperate jab by Vince, Ian connected solidly on Vince's ear. He stumbled, tried to regain his balance, and tumbled to the ground.

Once again, instead of following up on his advantage, Ian stayed back. "You can't win, Vince." He offered a hand to help his opponent up. "Now, let's figure out how to get Erica out of here, and we'll do our best to stop that bleeding."

Vince swatted away Ian's hand and stood up slowly under his own power. He smiled like an indulgent teacher. "Look at you. Finally stepping up like a man. I thought I could beat you like this, but maybe I can't."

Ian nodded. "Good. So let's sit down, take care of your wounds, and talk about what to do next."

"No. I can still beat you, just not like this." Vince nodded at the corpse. "You saw what I did to him. Now it's your turn." He stared at Ian for a second, long enough to see the first hint of uncertainty and fear reflected in Ian's eyes. Vince squeezed his eyelids shut.

It took a fraction of a second for the change to happen. In one instant, Vincent looked normal. In the next, he was almost transparent.

He held a human shape for several seconds, then Vince's face contorted in pain. His form disintegrated, splashing to the ground like water poured from a bucket.

Ian's eyes were wide. He turned back to Erica in confusion. "What the heck? He turned to water," he said unnecessarily. He kicked the puddle at his feet. "But he misjudged it somehow. He couldn't hold himself together."

Erica let out the breath that she didn't realize she had been holding. "He must have been hurt too badly. Maybe he didn't have enough energy left." She paused, looked at the expanding puddle, and said, "But you know, it's better this way." At Ian's questioning glance, she continued, "He was too angry, too out of control. He'd never be willing to work with us."

"Maybe," Ian said, his shoulders slumping. "But we should have been able to figure out something. Some way to save him. He didn't need to die. It's such a waste."

Erica nodded, not in agreement, but in understanding. She scanned the area. The dissolution of Vince's body had covered the floor of the room in water a fraction of an inch deep, except near the walls.

Erica glanced at Ian and then twisted her gaze back to where she had been looking. Was it her imagination or was the water peeling away from the edges of the room?

A vision flashed through her mind. She turned back toward Ian. "It's not over."

CHAPTER TWENTY-SIX

The water deepened in the center of the room, then grew into two columns, each about six feet high. About halfway up, they merged into a single trunk. From either side of the trunk, two branches extended. The trunk became more and more refined until Erica could make out a head and torso. Simultaneously, the columns and branches resolved themselves into legs and arms.

Finally, a watery simulacrum of Vince stood in front of them. It looked at Ian and smiled.

"Hi Vince," Ian said, as if speaking to a person made out of water was an everyday occurrence. He swallowed, clearly trying to think of something else to say. "Quite the dramatic transformation."

The watery statue's mouth didn't move, but tiny waves rippled across the surface of his body, creating a whispering speech-like sound. "I can't seem to keep my shape when I liquefy. It hurts." Erica found the incongruity between the voice and Vince's unmoving face disturbing.

"I can imagine that might be hard," Ian said. He looked to the floor and back at Vince. "At least you have your hand back," he awkwardly said.

The watery statue glanced down at his right hand and back to Ian. "Didn't even notice. Interesting conversation. You seemed almost sorry to see me dead." He turned toward Erica. "You, on the other hand, didn't seem so upset. What was it you said? 'It was good I was dead because I'm too hard to control'?"

Erica stammered, "I didn't mean—"

Vince continued as if she hadn't interrupted. "It's nothing more than I'd expect from you. You're too weak to fight, so you manipulate people instead." He turned back to Ian. "But enough of this. Are you ready to experience firsthand how I killed your monster?"

Ian's smile was weak. "Not really."

"Too bad." Vince advanced upon Ian, his fists raised.

This time, Ian seemed to recognize that he couldn't hold back. He struck first, lunging forward, putting all of his strength into the blow. Vince didn't even try to defend. The fist connected right on his chin.

The water offered almost no resistance. His hand passed through Vince's head, and Ian, expecting solid contact, was carried forward by his momentum. His whole body traveled almost unimpeded through Vince's.

They both turned to face each other. Ian swung several more times, more careful to maintain his balance, to no real effect. Each blow did nothing but temporarily displace Vince's liquid.

"If your monster couldn't touch me, why would you think you can?" Vince said. His watery lips curled. "Such a sick joke. I become invulnerable half a second after my hand is sliced off."

Ian stood back and lowered his hands. "You might be invulnerable, but it's a standoff," he said. "I can't hurt you, but you can't hurt me either. Unless you're planning to give me a nasty case of hypothermia, we're at an impasse."

"You don't really believe that?" For the first time since his transformation, Vince threw a jab. Ian jerked up his arm to block it. The weight of the punch landing on his forearm made him stagger back.

Vince continued to ripple. "It's a matter of preserving my body shape when I want to and not when I don't." As if to emphasize the point, he leaped forward and let his arms flow through Ian's. Then, he placed his hands on Ian's chest and shoved.

Ian stumbled backward and then cautiously circled away.

After that, it was only a matter of time. Ian tried to fight back but had nothing to hit, while Vince's fists seemed, if anything, more solid and heavy than flesh. Ian gave up on offense and simply tried to defend himself against the downpour of blows.

It wasn't enough. Punch after punch rained down with Ian remaining on his feet only by dancing back to reduce the impact of

Vince's fists. Finally, he bumped into a wall and couldn't retreat any more.

For an instant, Ian took his eyes off his opponent to find the best avenue for escape. Vince chose that moment to deliver a haymaker. His right hand connected solidly with Ian's ear.

Ian crumpled to the ground, dazed.

Vince looked down at him. "I'm kind of proud of how I beat that monster. I came up with it in the middle of the last fight."

Ian, his face already darkening from the bruises resulting from the overwhelming assault, lifted his head weakly and stared at Vince. "I can do without the speech. Just get it over with already."

"Fair enough." Vince pulled Ian up to his knees and knelt down in front of him. Almost tenderly, he placed his hands on either side of Ian's head. "Take a deep breath."

Vince plunged Ian's head into his own chest.

The shock of the water and the awareness of how he was about to die seemed to give Ian new energy. He struggled to get away, trying to pry the grip away from his head and kicking against the wall with his legs.

At first, Erica thought Ian might escape. But he was too exhausted from the fight. She saw his face turn red and his eyes bulge. The kicking grew sluggish.

"Don't do this, Vince! He's your friend!" Erica screamed as she struggled to tear her feet from the floor. Blood leaked from cracks in her feet.

Vince turned his head and looked at her. "Erica. I forgot about you. Don't worry, your time will come." He turned back to Ian.

With strength she didn't realize she possessed, Erica tore her right foot from the floor. Her bloody sole remained behind. The pain only intensified her efforts. Soon, she freed her left foot as well.

It was like running on razor blades, but Erica didn't hesitate. Leaving black footprints in her wake, she sprinted toward the two combatants and, when she was close enough, leaped.

As she foresaw, she passed through Vince's body. But it didn't matter. Ian was solid enough. Her arms encircled his waist and her momentum tore him from Vince's grasp. Ian collapsed on the floor, gasping for oxygen.

Vince shook his head. "Erica. Always interfering." Both he and Erica climbed to their feet. "So much of this is your fault," Vince said. "I think Ian and I might have been friends, if you hadn't messed with his head. Always speaking. Always lying. Always manipulating."

Vince walked toward her, while Erica circled away. "You know, I've always wanted to try water boarding. Such a simple thing, a bit of water flowing onto a face. In the shower, it's refreshing. Yet, it's somehow so horrific that our government considers it the best way to torture people.

"Now seems like a fine opportunity to try it out. The best thing is that you'll know you're going to drown. But not necessarily the first time. Or the second. If I want, I can do it a hundred times before I finally end it. And each time, you'll be wondering if you've breathed your final breath."

Taunting Vince was about as smart as juggling a hornet's nest, but she needed him distracted from Ian. So Erica smirked. "It will be fun to watch you try. I doubt you can even catch me." Despite the spikes of pain, she kept shifting her feet to make sure she wouldn't become glued again. Vince tried to grab her, but, aided by her visions, she slipped away without him even touching her. He began to throw punches, yet he couldn't land a blow.

Casually, she maneuvered backward toward the door into the room. If Vince followed her out, she'd at least be on a normal floor and Ian would have a chance to recover. It felt like a tightly choreographed tango, turning this way, spinning that way, coming close, but never quite touching her partner. Already, her black footprints on the floor looked like some demented dance lesson.

Finally, Erica made it close to the door. She snorted and didn't even bother with the handle. It was locked. Now they really had an impasse. He couldn't hit her. She couldn't hurt him.

The problem was Ian. Eventually, Vince would tire of this waltz and, when he did, he would realize that Ian was the only vulnerable one in the room. She might be able to save herself, but she couldn't protect him at the same time. Vince would eventually get through.

She had to find another way. She needed to escape. Erica looked toward the room's other exit, and then discarded it as an option. Even if it was unlocked—unlikely—it almost certainly led to another mattress room, another set of traps. And Vince would follow them anyway.

The only real escape was to get out of this gauntlet. But other than Jen and Alex, just Cam and Renee had got out. And that was only because their captors decided to remove them.

Could she do something to get their kidnappers to intervene now? Why did they take Cam and Renee? They had both shown extraordinary abilities, but if that was enough, then why didn't they take Denise? Not to mention Vince.

Perhaps they tried and failed. During Vince's rant before the fight, he mentioned something about them trying to gas him. And maybe, just like her and Ian, their captors didn't understand where Renee's ability ended and Denise's began until she was dead. In that case, perhaps all they needed to do to end this was prove that they all possessed these extraordinary abilities.

Had it been a mistake to hide her ability from their captors? If she hadn't, would she have been whisked away like Renee? Vince seemed to like Ian. Without Erica around, maybe they would have been able to work together. Though if not, she wouldn't be here to help Ian now.

She shook her head. It didn't matter now. Right now, she just needed to end this fight.

After she ducked under Vince's latest punch, she smiled at him. "It's impossible to hit me, Vince. You can turn into water, but I'm extraordinary, too. I have perfect luck. I'm not a fighter, but even dodging randomly like I am, any move I make will just happen to be the right one. We may as well stop fighting now."

Vince's watery face frowned. "Whatever. Your mouth can't get you out of this."

Erica shrugged and stepped back to avoid an uppercut. "Have it your way. Tell me when you're ready to stop." It was what she expected. Though she directed her remarks at Vince, she spoke them for any observers. She simply needed to make it blindingly obvious to anyone watching that she had an ability.

Ian was the bigger problem though. Strong emotions brought out her visions, but had done nothing for him. She needed to force him to do something extraordinary. But if getting beaten to within an inch of his life wasn't enough, what would be? Maybe he didn't even have an ability.

But she needed to try.

Vince had changed his tactics, trying to grab her rather than punching. This time when she dodged, she stepped back toward Ian, effectively retracing her earlier steps, creeping closer and closer to him. He was still on his knees recovering, looking exhausted and unsure whether he should intervene.

Ian was ten feet to her right when Erica made the mistake. The sticky floor impeded her left foot for a fraction of a second, just enough to cause her to stumble. Before she could recover, Vince leaped forward, grabbing her left arm and smashing his left fist into her face.

It was like being hit by a sledgehammer. Erica staggered and only remained on her feet because of Vince's unyielding grip.

"Unlucky," Vince said.

Erica looked directly at Ian, her face stark hopelessness. "Ian. I am going to die."

"You are," Vince said with a smile.

"Vince!" The shout emanated from deep within Ian's core. Vince turned his head to see Ian struggle to his feet, his face contorted with rage. Erica had known Ian for her whole life, but had never seen him like this. Never anything even close to this.

With a scream of impotent fury, Ian staggered forward, his wounds forgotten in the heat of his anger. There was no plan or reason in his charge. Only a need.

Vince stood there grinning as Ian came right up to him. He did nothing to defend himself, confident in his invulnerability.

Erica closed her eyes.

Ian poured all his wrath into the punch. As his fist shot forward, white dust, seemingly ripped right out of the air, coalesced into a crude glove around his hand and forearm. An instant later, Ian's fist became blinding white light and fire, as bright as the burning magnesium in chemistry class, brighter than the sun. Even partially shielded by Vince's form, the heat on Erica's skin was painful.

Ian screamed as his hand plunged into the side of Vince's chest. Steam exploded outward, but the fire continued to burn. If anything, it flared even more intensely. A second glove formed on Ian's left hand. That white fire entered Vince's stomach, adding its light and heat.

Vince stared down in disbelief, his mouth contorted in a silent scream as his torso evaporated and disappeared. Suddenly, he became flesh again, but with two gaping holes clear through his body.

Vince toppled over.

With a puff of gray, the gloves disintegrated. Beneath them, Ian's hands and forearms were blackened shreds of flesh and bone. The skin on his face was fiery and blistered while his eyes were empty, red orbs.

Ian continued to scream, looking down at the burned mess of his hands that he could smell but could not see.

The scream ended in a gurgle. He stumbled forward and collapsed. Erica was able catch him, though with his greater weight, she nearly fell. She eased him to the ground and rolled him onto his back.

Kneeling, she cradled his head in her hands. "Ian, can you hear me? Ian?"

He did not respond. His eyes stared blankly up at her.

Her plan had worked perfectly. She had created the threat Ian had needed to respond to. She'd drawn his ability out. She'd made him save her.

She had destroyed him.

Tears ran down Erica's cheeks. "I'm sorry. I didn't know. I swear, I didn't know."

She shifted one of her hands down to Ian's blistered neck to feel for a pulse. It was strong under her fingers and his chest still rose and fell. So he was alive, for now. But could anyone survive such wounds?

CHAPTER TWENTY-SEVEN

Suddenly, the exit door was flung open. Six soldiers, outfitted identically to the ones from the cube room, efficiently entered the room, their Javelins trained on Erica and Ian.

Erica only saw the weapons pointed at Ian. "No! He's had enough. He's going to die. There's no need for you to do anything more!" she screamed. She pulled him closer to her, attempting to use her body to shield his.

The soldier in the lead stepped forward and spoke with authority. "Step away from him now or we will be forced to fire on you."

Erica stared at him in disbelief. She had been kneeling without moving her legs for too long. "Are you an idiot? You stuck my feet to the floor. How do you expect me to step away?"

The soldier looked slightly embarrassed, but he remained stern. "Put your hands behind your head."

Erica glared at him. "Go to hell."

The soldier shouted, "If you don't do as I say, I will be forced to open fire on you."

"Do your worst. I'm not letting you take him."

The leader gestured to two of the soldiers. They stepped forward, sighting their weapons.

They paused. The lead soldier raised his hand to his ear and listened for several seconds. He motioned to the others to lower their Javelins.

"I will speak to you plainly," he said. "Ian's seriously injured. He has minutes to live. But we have the best medical technology anywhere. If we can get him to our hospital, we may be able to help him."

Erica raised her eyes to the soldier's face. She paused a few seconds, and then looked back down at Ian again, convinced it was just another one of their games.

The soldier continued, "We could shoot you and take him, but we want the same thing and we're wasting time. Trust me… and we may save his life. If you don't, he'll certainly die."

Erica thought about it for no more than two seconds. Some hope was better than none. Leaving Ian's head cradled on her knees, she put her hands behind her head. "Take him," she spat out.

The leader gestured to one of the other soldiers. Holstering his weapon, he strode forward and picked Ian up. He backed away from Erica and, once he was twenty feet away, turned around and exited through the same door he came in.

"That's great," the lead soldier said. "Now, I am here to inform you that your trial is over. We're going to take you to somewhere safe. You need to come with us."

Erica didn't see an alternative. At least she'd be out of here. She nodded.

One of the other soldiers came forward, detached some handcuffs from his belt, and secured her hands behind her back. He took a canteen from his belt, pouring it over her feet. The liquid burned her open wounds, but after a few seconds, she was free.

"Follow them," the soldier said.

"Look at my feet. I can barely walk."

"Deal with it."

Erica stood. Now that the adrenaline from the fight was subsiding, standing up felt like stepping onto hot coals. She tried not to let it show.

Two troopers led her out of the room while the other three followed. The next room was the expected mattress room, but, instead of leaving through the exit, they went into the bathroom.

One of the walls of the shower had been swung open to reveal an alcove. On the far wall was an open elevator door. They entered. A soldier pressed his palm against a panel and pushed a button near the top.

"What is this place? Why did you kidnap me?" Erica said, looking at the leader. When he didn't respond, she said, "Where are you taking me?" The soldier remained mute. Erica sighed.

They ascended fifteen floors. The elevator opened, and they exited into a long, white passage lined with numbered metal doors. Beside each door was a key pad, a glass pad with the outline of a hand, and foot-square miniature door about halfway up the wall.

They marched down the corridor, leaving red footprints on the pristine white floor. Erica was silent, but tears trickled down her face. She didn't know if it was from the pain of her feet or the loss of Ian.

After walking through an intersection, they reached their destination, room 1307. The soldier unclipped a key from his belt and, using the key, a palm print, and a code in succession, opened the door. Erica considered making a sarcastic comment about the necessity of having redundant locking mechanisms to keep a single teenager imprisoned, but she decided it was perhaps best for the soldiers not to think she was noting security features.

Despite her best efforts, as they marched her into the room, Erica couldn't hold back a fatalistic smile. It was a miniature replica of the sterile rooms below, with a mattress, a pile of folded clothes, and a curtain that she was certain would lead to a bathroom.

"Locked in here by myself, do I really need the privacy curtain?" she said. The soldiers stared at her, staying mute. Erica rolled her eyes. "It's not like I have any privacy anyway, right?"

"Turn and face the wall," the lead soldier said.

She sighed and did. Several of the soldiers trained their weapons on her while they removed the handcuffs, then they all inched back out of the room.

Before they closed the door, Erica considered attempting to escape, but saw that it was hopeless. She turned to the soldiers. "You said I'd be safe. So what now? I'm trapped in here forever to rot? And what about my feet?"

The leader looked at her, seemed to consider closing the door without replying, and then took pity on her. "It's not for me to decide."

"And what about Ian? You promised you'd help him. Will you tell me what happened?"

The soldier's mouth twitched in a slightly ambiguous smile. She didn't know if he intended it to be reassuring or if her naiveté simply amused him—that she still believed they'd be able to save Ian.

The door boomed shut.

Despite the throbbing pain from her swollen hand, bruised cheek, and bloody feet, Erica investigated the room, knowing that if she collapsed on the bed, she might not get up for hours.

It didn't take long. Her cell was as she expected, a room from below in miniature. Even the shower appeared to be made with the same familiar cream-colored, industrial tiles.

Apart from the room's size, there were three notable differences. First, there was only one exit. Second, the digital display, present in all the bedrooms below, was absent here. Finally, instead of a dumbwaiter, an enclosed box with a door on one side extended into the room from the outside corridor. A hamburger and fries were already waiting inside it.

And, Erica reflected while lying on the mattress after eating and doing her best to bandage her feet with some of the clothes, the other big difference was that she was alone. Separated from Ian.

Was it a mistake to let the soldiers take him without a fight? It seemed right at the time. But now that he was gone, and she was trapped here without him, she felt unsure. He had been so close to death. His hands and arms were all but gone, his face so horribly burnt that even if he somehow lived, he would be unrecognizable.

People couldn't survive injuries like that—she was certain. The soldiers must have been lying to her, saying whatever they needed to say to get her to follow their instructions. And, instead of dying in the arms of someone who loved him, Ian had died with strangers.

She should have held on, never given him up.

But how could she just let him die? However remote the possibility of him surviving, surely she needed to take that chance? Even if it cost them their last moments together?

Even if it cost them their last moments together.

No, that wasn't her mistake. Her mistake had been earlier when she decided to allow Vince to grab her. She should have found another way.

At the time, it seemed like a perfect plan, accomplishing everything she needed. Vince would be neutralized and Ian's powers revealed. Their captors would take them away.

But she should have anticipated the consequences even if her vision didn't extend that far. Five thousand degrees. That was the temperature of burning magnesium according to Mr. Ambrose. Of course Ian couldn't survive being that close to an inferno. She had provoked him, forced him to respond, and now he was dead.

It was her fault. She had failed Ian as she had failed Denise.

These visions gave her this power, the power to change the future. Yet, whenever someone truly needed her, when lives were on the line, she had fallen short. And her friends died because of it.

Erica's eyes widened as the vision of the door opening tore through her mind. She sat up before the door opened, wiping away her tears.

Erica's mother walked in, holding out her arms. "Darling, don't look so down. You're safe now." The door automatically closed behind her.

"Mom! You're here!" Erica gingerly got to her feet and buried her face in her mother's shoulder. They hugged for what seemed like an eternity, but was still not long enough.

"Congratulations, honey! You made it. You won't need to go through that ever again," Lois said. She had a massive smile on her face, looking proud.

Erica pulled back in confusion. "How do you know? How did you get here?"

Lois inspected Erica's bruised face, and then looked down at her feet. The blood had already soaked through her makeshift bandages. "Those look painful. I think maybe we should sit." Together, they sat on the mattress.

"What's going on, Mom? Why are you here? Why am I here?"

"It's complicated. And maybe hard to believe. I'm so glad I can finally tell you though. I've kept it a secret for years." She paused, organizing her thoughts. "You've probably figured out over the last few days that all of you are different. You possess special abilities."

Erica nodded.

"I am responsible for that."

Erica's eyes widened and her stomach dropped. "What? How?"

"After grad school, the government recruited me to be part of a project to explore the limits of genetic engineering. That project was more successful than anyone ever dreamed, and I was in the center of it. Many things resulted from that work. Girl glue, super wheat, and countless extraordinary creatures. But you are the pinnacle of our success. I created you."

"What? I'm... an experiment? A guinea pig?" Erica's head was spinning.

"No, not at all, honey. You're completely human, just like anyone else, except for a tiny 55,000 base pair sequence we spliced into your DNA when you were a zygote—a fertilized egg. You're not just a guinea pig. You're still my daughter." She squeezed Erica's hand.

Erica yanked her hand from her mother's grasp. "The others too?" She was made to be an experiment by her *own mother*?

"Yes, of course. All raised by families we trusted—families with the highest clearance. Then, when they're ready to realize their abilities, we bring them here."

"You should have told me. Warned me. You're my mother. You're supposed to take care of me!" Erica felt close to hyperventilating. She couldn't believe this. Her own parents had put her through this terrible ordeal?

"I'm sorry, honey, but it was necessary," Lois said, patting Erica on the knee. "It wouldn't have worked if you knew what was going on."

"But why? If we're not lab rats, why did you do this to us?" Erica swept her arm around. "Why did you put us in here?" Angry tears brimmed in her eyes and threatened to roll down her cheeks, but she held them back. She knew if she started crying, she might not stop, and she needed answers.

Lois sighed. "The problem is that, while we know our subjects will have extraordinary abilities manifesting after puberty, we can't yet predict what they will be able to do. So we built this place—the Gauntlet—to help people unearth their abilities in a safe environment."

Erica's jaw dropped, and she stared at her mother in disbelief. Her mother had been torturing them for days. She'd injured or killed all six of them. "Subjects? I'm your *daughter*! And what sort of twisted person calls this a safe environment? Denise and Vince are dead!"

Lois shook her head. "You're getting it backward. I meant safe for everyone else. You remember the gas station that exploded a few years back? Peter Lawson, Mandy, and the gas station attendants were killed? That was Peter discovering two things. First, that Mandy was pregnant. Second, that he could super heat metal in a fraction of a second.

"People aren't always immune to the effects of their own ability or the indirect consequences of using it. We need to be careful. Because Peter discovered his ability at a random time and place, he and three civilians died. They were senseless deaths because we didn't control the situation. And though that was a tragedy, it could have been much worse. Suppose someone happens to have the power to split atoms? Battlefield could be the next Hiroshima.

"So we designed the Gauntlet to draw out the abilities in a semi-controlled way. This facility is deep underground. Even a nuclear explosion nine hundred feet underground would barely impact the surface. We needed that depth to minimize worst-case scenario casualties.

"Two factors appear to impact when abilities appear. First, incidents increase dramatically during the longest days of the year. Second, extreme emotions seem to act as the trigger. So, when the manifestation risk skyrockets thirty days before the summer solstice, we insert the subjects into a Gauntlet designed to induce strong emotions. We make them hungry. We create punishing environments. We cause interpersonal friction. Anything we can think of to cause stress, to cause the emotions that trigger the abilities."

Erica looked down at her lap. She felt hollow. How could her mom be involved in something like this? How could she do this to her, to her friends, to countless innocent kids who had no idea what was happening to them? There was something very wrong here. "And the messages on the plates? Was there really a spy in our group?"

Lois shook her head. "No. That was more of the same. Those fake 'hints' increase conflict. It's the same reason we abduct one subject while they are awake—an inconsistent story will often lead to arguments. Paranoia is brilliant for bringing out some people's abilities. Boys are often triggered by physical conflict, though some seem to prefer being a white knight saving a damsel in distress." A faint ironic smile flickered across her face.

Erica sighed in numb disbelief. Her mother was acting as though everything she'd done to them was so scientific, like Erica should recognize the logic of her actions, calmly accepting the fact that her entire life was a lie. Was she mad? A few hours ago, she and Ian had almost died. Her mother being involved in the death and maiming of children wasn't something she could just ignore.

Lois contemplated her daughter's expression with a slight frown and pursed her lips. "It doesn't always work out perfectly," she said.

"All we can do is plan as well as we can and react quickly when things don't go as expected." At Erica's dubious expression, she continued, "Which is often, I'll admit. But it's the safest way to deal with the manifestation of these unpredictable abilities."

Despite her efforts to hold them back, tears streamed down Erica's face, though her voice was steady. "Well, it's not good enough. We wouldn't even have these abilities if it weren't for you messing with our DNA. We would just be normal kids!"

"You wouldn't exist at all," Lois said. "Which would be sad. I love you, Erica." She tried to put her arm around Erica's shoulders.

Erica removed it and then used her feet to push herself away from her mother. Even the slightest bit of pressure felt like someone was holding a blowtorch to her feet, but it was worth it. "How can you even say that after what you did to me? And the others? Denise is dead!" How could her mother act like everything was all right?

Lois sighed. "I'm sorry, honey. But Denise's death was inevitable. When people aren't immune to their abilities, there can be unfortunate outcomes. We call people like her a 'dead end'. Someone with an ability that would kill her. As far as we can tell, she absorbed other people's wounds. Anyone within five or six yards of her. They would be healed almost instantly, but Denise would suffer the same injury. She also seemed to heal faster than a normal person, but it didn't matter in the end. With such an ability, she'd inevitably die, sooner or later. The first time she drove by a traffic accident or visited a hospital. Dead end."

"And is Ian a dead end, too? Will he survive?" Erica brusquely said. She had been dying to ask, but dreading the answer. As long as she delayed, she could still pretend he lived. She closed her eyes as she waited, knowing the answer would hit her like an avalanche.

"It was close, but he'll pull through. And we can put him back together."

Erica's eyes opened wide. It seemed impossible. She raised her face and wiped her tears with the back of her hand. "He's going to live? He'll get prosthetic arms?"

"No, flesh and blood."

"What? How is that possible?"

"The government knows how important our work here is. We have an effectively unlimited budget and the best medical technology on the planet."

"But his arms. His hands! There was nothing left of them." She remembered with sickening clarity just what he looked like, and her heart dropped to her toes. How could he come back from that?

"Medical 3D printing has advanced considerably in the last few years. We can now print stem cells that become whatever organ is needed. It's very new—we only got it last week. I think you'll be impressed with the results."

"What about his skin? And eyes? They were red, almost bleeding. Can you fix them? Or will he be blind?" She was desperately clinging on to her mother's words, looking for a lifeline for Ian. Trusting anything her mother said was hard, but she prayed that, for Ian, it was true.

"Yes, we think so. We've dealt with burns before."

Erica was speechless. It didn't seem possible. Maybe her mother hadn't seen how badly he was injured. Still, he would live. That was enough.

Lois shook her head. "But honey, I don't want to get your hopes up too much. He still might be a dead end. We saved him this time, but that's because he used his ability within minutes of our medical facility. If it happened anywhere else, he would have died."

Erica swallowed deeply. Her mind spun. Ian lived, but was that even a good thing, if it was only to suffer the agony of being incinerated once again?

Seeing the shifting emotions splashed across Erica's face, Lois said, "But you never know. Spectrographic analysis showed that the fiery substance on Ian's hands was pure magnesium. In slow motion, we can see the atoms being torn from the cement floor.

"Now, obviously, he can't handle that level of heat without severe burns. But there's a good chance Ian's ability will be under his own control, at least with training. He might get burnt a few times and end up in our hospital again before he figures it out. But after he does, he could simply avoid ever using his ability. We have several people like that."

It wasn't hopeless then. Erica, her face haggard, looked at her mother. "When can I see him?"

Lois looked down at the watch on her arm and smiled. "How about now?"

CHAPTER TWENTY-EIGHT

"Ian's out of surgery already?" Erica said.

Lois nodded. "Yes, he's done. The technology works quickly. Ian was obviously our highest priority, but now that he's done, we should do something about your feet and other injuries." She stood up and walked to the door. It opened, and Lois grabbed a wheelchair hidden behind the wall. "I figured this might be more comfortable for you, honey."

Lois grabbed at Erica's arm to help her in, but Erica shook her off and climbed into it on her own, ignoring the fiery pain. After Lois pushed her out of the room, two menacing soldiers fell in behind them. Erica raised her eyebrow at her mom, a sneer trying to work its way onto her lips. Did her mom think she needed to be protected from her own daughter?

"Don't worry about them," Lois said. "As you'd imagine, occasionally people have some extreme reactions to the Gauntlet. Dangerous reactions. I wouldn't expect that from you, but it's protocol. Just pretend they're not there."

Erica's brow furrowed. She certainly wasn't going to pretend they weren't there. "Whatever." She remained silent as Lois pushed her back toward the elevator, her mind churning.

It was a miracle that Ian had survived, but now that the risk had passed, Erica was scared to visit him. Regardless of what her mother said about medical 3D printing, they wouldn't be able to save his arms. The fire seared away most of the flesh. She saw the bone.

Would he blame her for that? Would he hate her? Ian wasn't

stupid. If he hadn't figured out yet that she'd deliberately let herself be caught by Vince, he soon would. He'd realize that she had foreseen the fire that cost him his arms, but tricked him into doing it anyway. He should loathe her—never want to see her again.

The idea seemed unbearable.

But she had no choice, no other way. If she hadn't done something, Vince would have killed them both. Even if Ian didn't understand her decision, she had saved his life.

And for her, that was the bottom line. She couldn't let Ian die. Even if it cost him his arms. Even if he hated her for doing it.

Renee would probably hate her too when she found out.

Erica looked down. She didn't want to think about it anymore. "How are Renee and Cam?" she said as Lois hit a button on the elevator.

"They're doing fine. Cam has been handling it well. You saw the way the Javelin got embedded in his arm, right?"

Denying it seemed pointless. Erica nodded.

"Well, we did X-rays. The Javelin is still there and—while it's early—he has suffered no ill effects." Lois shook her head and scratched her chin. "Renee's transition has been harder, but she's adapting. She'll be fine. She's quite extraordinary."

The elevator door opened. A steel door with a red cross was directly across from the elevator. One of the soldiers pushed it open.

The room was large, easily as big as a classroom at school, and smelled antiseptic. Glass-doored cupboards filled with medical equipment ranging from tongue depressors to syringes lined the far wall. A long counter with a sink at one end ran the length of another wall. Near it were an operating table and a wheeled stool.

Erica looked to her left and gasped. Several chairs were against the wall with the door. A dark-haired doctor sat in one. She wore blue, and a stethoscope dangled around her neck. A man with dark hair sat in the other, talking with the doctor. Even from behind, Erica could tell that it was Ian.

Turning around, he looked at her. He leaped to his feet and walked to her chair, smiling. "Erica!"

Erica's jaw dropped. Ian's face was unmarked, his arms whole, as if he had not been burnt. "You... you're okay." She grasped his right hand in hers, running her hand along his smooth skin, hardly believing that it was whole again. She raised her hand to his neck and caressed his unscarred cheek. "You can see."

"Yes, I'm fine."

Tears ran down Erica's cheeks. "I thought you were dead. The burns."

He knelt beside her and gently wiped the tears away. "No, you're still stuck with me. I'm afraid if you want to get rid of me, you'll have to break up with me."

Was he serious? No, he was just maintaining the act, surely. Still, it didn't matter. Ian was alive and restored, and that was more than enough.

Erica pulled his head toward her and looked into his eyes, her face intense. "Never." She kissed him deeply.

Before Erica finished, Lois cleared her throat. "We should do something about those feet."

Erica ignored her. Ian didn't seem to mind.

Finally, Erica released Ian. Her cheeks were pink. She looked down. "I'm sorry. I thought you were gone. That I'd never see you again. Or that you'd hate me for what happened. Can you forgive me?"

He raised her chin to look at her face. "Erica, I trust you," he gently said.

Erica interlaced her hand with his and smiled. She swallowed, trying to hold back her emotions.

"Enough of this." Lois swung Erica's chair around. "You've only been apart for a couple hours. Stop acting like teenagers." She wheeled Erica up a slight ramp onto a short platform against the far wall, and then positioned the wheelchair against the wall.

"We are teenagers, no matter what weird stuff you did to our DNA," Erica pointedly said.

Lois sighed and walked to a button on the wall. "Anyway, after Ian, your feet should be trivial for the medical printer. It often takes a few seconds to warm up, evaluate the wounds, and analyze your genetic makeup. But after that, it should be almost instantaneous." She hit the button.

Red light bathed Erica. She looked up and saw that the lights in the ceiling had changed color. There was a low hum and regular thumps, like someone drumming on a metal door. Erica shifted uneasily and glanced at her mother.

Then, like socks being pulled up over her feet, Erica's soles were healed. The dull ache in her cheek and the throbbing in her hand—both of which had been only uncomfortable compared to her feet—faded at the same time. She jumped in surprise and stared at the back of her left hand. The swelling had completely subsided. Bending forward, she touched the sole of her foot. "Wow."

Her mother punched the button again, and the light faded. "Yes, it's very impressive. Running it costs a fortune, and that's nothing compared to the effort needed to get it in the first place. But it's worth it."

Erica stood up cautiously before bouncing up and down. Her feet didn't hurt at all. "I'll say." She walked over to beside Ian.

The doctor, who until now had been silently watching, stood up and put out her hand for Erica to shake. "I'm Dr. Rahal, the head physician here. I was just telling Ian that this medical printing technology is still experimental. We're the first deployment. It's been tested extensively with animals, but not as much on humans. So if you have any problems, let me know."

Erica's brow furrowed. "It hasn't been tested on people?"

Dr. Rahal shook her head. "No, there have been human tests, and we've done quite a few ourselves. But technology providers tend to talk about the benefits of their technology, not the problems. If something is going to surprise us, we want to know as soon as possible. We need to understand all its risks and limitations."

"I'm nervous using unproven technology." Erica shook her head, then looked at Ian and shrugged. "But I guess without it, Ian would have…"

"Yes," the doctor said. "That's the way I think about it too. In any case, if you have any health concerns, come by and talk to me."

Erica's brow furrowed. "You're speaking like I'll be staying here." She expected that, in light of the other missing students… but she was still curious about the explanation.

Lois nodded. "Yes, I'm afraid that you won't be able to go home for now. The Gauntlet can be traumatizing. It's our responsibility to take care of people when they get out. And when the people involved have abilities, well, that adds complications."

Lois stood up, opened the door, and gestured for Ian and Erica to follow. The soldiers, who had been stationed inside the door, fell in behind them. She pressed the button to call the elevator.

"How long until we can leave?" Ian said, his expression cold.

Lois pursed her lips. "We will decide that later." The elevator arrived, and they all entered. Lois pressed her hand to the panel, hit a number, and said, "We must consider many factors. You aren't the same people you were a couple of weeks ago. So you need to wait. But I can assure you, it won't be any longer than necessary and you'll be quite comfortable in the meantime."

Erica rolled her eyes. "Yeah, in a ten-by-ten antiseptic cell. I've seen it already, Mother."

Lois turned to her. "It's not that bad. And that's only temporary until you become acclimatized to life outside the Gauntlet—"

"You mean, until you're certain we're not dangerous," Ian hotly said.

Lois frowned. "Well, I wasn't going to put it that way, but—"

"I'm pretty sure I'm dangerous." Ian stared at Lois, his face like steel. "Very dangerous." Erica could see a muscle on the cheek of one of the soldiers standing behind Ian ripple. She put her hand on Ian's arm.

Lois's eyes narrowed and her voice was flat. "I'm not worried. I've already dealt with worse than you." Her tone brightened. "It may take you a while to figure out how to control your ability, and we can help with that. At minimum, we can keep you alive."

Ian looked at her for a few seconds, then nodded and turned away. "Yeah."

The elevator door opened. It appeared to be the level Erica had been on before.

"This floor is where we house the new arrivals. Erica, you're room 1307. Ian, you're 1308," Lois said. She walked down the hall with the others trailing. "You're free to go anywhere on this floor. However, only you can open the door to your room. Doors are coded to your palm print. Meals are served in the mess hall three times a day."

She rapped on door 1305. Without waiting for a response, she palmed the panel, opened the door, and walked in. Renee was there, rising from the bed, a book in her hands.

"Renee!" Ian pushed by Lois and wrapped his sister in a hug. "You're safe!"

"Yeah, I'm fine. You're the one I was worried about," Renee said. She turned to Erica, who was patiently waiting. "And you too." They hugged. "You both made it out."

Ian nodded. "We did."

Lois said, "I have an appointment now, but Renee can show you the ropes. I'll see you later."

"What?" Erica said. "You're just going to leave like that?"

Lois put her arms around her for a brief hug. However, Erica remained stiff in her mother's arms.

"Erica, I have important things to do and you don't need me."

"It's just that... I thought that..." Erica said.

Lois shook her head. "You'll do fine here, Erica. You're safe, and Renee can help you with anything you need. I'm busy and I'm already late. I'll be back tomorrow. Goodbye." She and the two soldiers left. Erica's shoulders drooped.

"Good riddance," Ian said. He turned from the door toward Erica and then paused. "What? Don't you think we're better off without her?"

Erica swallowed. Her mother had always been there whenever Erica needed her. The initial surge of white-hot anger at her mother's betrayal had subsided now that she knew Ian was alive. Saved, in fact, by Lois. Despite all her mother had done, Erica's heart yearned to forget everything that had happened. She wanted to collapse in her mother's arms, to be told that Lois would take care of everything, as she always had.

But how did thát make any sense at all when her mother had helped create the Gauntlet? Forcing Erica to run the Gauntlet was a cynical betrayal of their entire relationship. And, even if Lois had saved Ian, her Gauntlet had resulted in the deaths of Denise and Vince. Lois wasn't a mother. She was a monster. Erica shouldn't want Lois's comfort. So why did she?

Erica shook her head. It was so confusing. "Yes. It's just... strange."

Renee had been watching the exchange in silence. "Where's Vince?" Her expression was worried, like she knew the answer, but didn't want to hear it.

"Vince didn't make it. I killed him," Ian said. His voice quivered.

"What?" An emotion Erica couldn't identify flickered across Renee's face, and then her expression turned neutral. "How?"

They sat down on the bed, and Ian and Erica explained what had transpired in the Gauntlet after Renee's departure, although they still implied Erica's ability was luck. Throughout the discussion, Ian was unusually subdued.

"Sounds like Vince deserved it," Renee said.

Ian shook his head. "How can you say that? They imprisoned him just like the rest of us."

Renee rolled her eyes. "Whatever. He harassed and tortured me the whole time. He was worse than the trials."

Ian sighed. "He didn't deserve to die." He looked down. "It wasn't necessary. I shouldn't have killed him."

Behind Ian's back, Erica looked at Renee, shook her head, and shrugged. She agreed with Renee. During that final fight, in her visions, she saw Vince beat both her and Ian senseless in a multitude of ways. But Ian hadn't seen what she had.

Erica put her hand on Ian's shoulder. "It happened in the heat of battle, Ian. I don't know if we could have survived any other way."

Ian examined her face as if trying to divine whether she had seen all the possibilities or if she was just trying to comfort him. He sighed and looked at the floor. "Yeah."

Erica had never seen him so depressed. She didn't know how to help, how to make him feel better. She put her arm around his shoulder and looked at Renee. "How are you doing? My mom called you 'extraordinary'."

Renee shrugged and tilted her hand back and forth. "So-so. My memory isn't as good as it used to be. Lois tested me. I've been forgetting a bunch, and I have to really concentrate to memorize stuff. But I can do almost anything. They call it the Hundredth Monkey Effect."

"I don't get it. What does that mean?" Erica said.

"It's a science thing. A few decades back, these biologists saw this monkey on an island that learned to wash potatoes before eating them. The other monkeys watched and started cleaning their food too. But then, once a certain number of monkeys on that island learned to do it, suddenly the monkeys on all the other islands started doing it as well."

Erica looked at her skeptically. "Really?"

"Yeah. They theorized that there was a group consciousness. When the number of animals exceeded a critical mass, all the others would absorb the knowledge telepathically."

"It seems hard to believe," Erica said.

Renee's mouth twisted in a wry smile. "Yeah, well, you should be skeptical. In the end, they discovered that monkeys can swim.

Apparently, to the world's top scientists, swimming primates seemed less plausible than telepathy. But anyway, even if they can't do it, I can. If enough people know something, I know it too."

"What? Anything?" Erica said, blinking as her mind raced through the possibilities.

"In the last two days, I've juggled five balls, landed a triple axel, flown a helicopter, and assembled an M16. I know where the president is at all times and the weather in every city in the world. Yes, anything."

Erica shook her head. "But how does knowledge help you land a triple axel? Or juggle?"

Renee smiled. "Apparently, muscle memory is in the brain, not in the muscles. I have the muscle memories of the top athletes in every sport."

"No wonder you were able to climb up the walls in that room with the ramps."

"It all seemed so easy." Renee's face fell. "Until the end."

Erica rebuked herself for spoiling Renee's mood. "Yeah, but there's nothing you could have done," Erica lied. "Denise's death wasn't your fault."

"She's right, Ren," Ian said. He shook his head. "To me, it was inevitable that we'd lose someone. There were so many ways that something could go wrong."

Erica nodded and squeezed Ian's hand. "I think we were lucky to survive at all. At times, I was certain that none of us would escape."

"I never lost hope," Ian said. His mouth twisted. "But I'm also not certain we're out." He pointedly looked at the rest of the room. "We're still locked in a prison, just one with corridors rather than stairs."

Erica bit her lip and sighed. She had the same concerns.

The lights flashed twice. Renee pointed at the ceiling. "Five minutes until lights out. You should probably go to your rooms."

"Yeah," Ian said. He and Erica stood up.

Erica looked back as they reached the door. "See you tomorrow, Ren?"

"Of course. I'll show you around then."

The door shut behind them. The lock's click seemed to echo in the silent hallway.

Together, Erica and Ian walked slowly down the corridor, neither one of them speaking until they stopped in front of Erica's door.

"I guess I have my own room now," Ian said. He turned to face Erica.

"You do. But..." She looked at the floor.

Ian smiled. His right hand took her left while his other hand gently raised her chin. He looked into her eyes, tucked a stray lock of hair behind her ear, and tenderly kissed her.

Her face warm, Erica opened the door with her palm and, still holding Ian's hand, led him into her room.

If you enjoyed this novel, please consider leaving a review on Amazon.

ABOUT THE AUTHOR

R.B. Gibbons has a tech background, founding several companies and creating an artificial personality that failed a Turing test. He loves investing, to the extent that he invented his own automated stock-trading algorithm and, for several years, wrote freelance articles for investment website *The Motley Fool*.

He lives in Vancouver with his wife, two children, and too few dogs.

Blog & Mailing List: http://rbgibbons.com

www.ingramcontent.com/pod-product-compliance
Lightning Source LLC
Chambersburg PA
CBHW071857220626
47052CB00002B/153